D0429431

Golden & Grey

A Good Day for Haunting

Also by Louise Arnold

*Golden & Grey: An Unremarkable Boy
and a Rather Remarkable Ghost*

Golden & Grey: The Nightmares That Ghosts Have

Margaret K. McElderry Books

Golden & Grey

A Good Day for Haunting

LOUISE ARNOLD

Margaret K. McElderry Books
New York   London   Toronto   Sydney

Margaret K. McElderry Books
An imprint of Simon & Schuster
Children's Publishing Division
1230 Avenue of the Americas, New York, New York 10020

Copyright © 2007 by Louise Arnold
Originally published in Great Britain in 2007
by Hodder Children's Books
First U.S. edition, 2008

Book design by Ann Zeak
The text for this book is set in Bembo.
Manufactured in the United States of America
2 4 6 8 10 9 7 5 3 1
Library of Congress Cataloging-in-Publication Data
Arnold, Louise, 1979–
Golden & Grey : a good day for haunting / by Louise Arnold.—
1st ed.
p. cm.
Summary: When the television show *Exceedingly Haunted Homes of England* hears rumors of ghosts at Tom Golden's school, he and his "invisible friends" must track down some ghosts that have turned visible in order to restore the balance between the ghost and human worlds.
ISBN-13: 978-1-4169-0863-0 (hardcover : alk. paper)
ISBN-10: 1-4169-0863-3 (hardcover : alk. paper)
[1. Ghosts—Fiction. 2. Schools—Fiction. 3. England—Fiction.]
I. Title. II. Title: Golden and Grey.
III. Title: Good day for haunting.
PZ7.A73595Gl 2008
[Fic]—dc22
2007037992

Dedicated to Edward, James, Sophie, and Alex,
who I hope will never grow up having to be scared of the
ghost beneath the bed. Thanks also to Uncle Bill for
risking his ninety-eight-year-old toes to teach me
to waltz, and Auntie Nancy for helping me learn
the value of good tea and better company.

In loving memory of Auntie Em, and my godfather,
Peter—two of the most vibrant characters
you could ever hope to meet.

There is a secret world that exists alongside ours, a supernatural world, tucked discreetly out of sight.

In this world exist the mischievous Poltergeists, stealers of socks, rearrangers of furniture, players of practical jokes. There are the melancholy Sadness Summoners, ghosts that radiate misery. Faintly Reals are the most human of apparitions, able to become visible for short periods of time. Thespers are the dramatic spirits, often found marching across the ramparts at castles, dressed in period costume, reciting poetry or shouting battle cries. Stink ghosts, or Snorgles, live in toilets, sewers, and drains, dragging a foul stench wherever they go. The final ghosts that need introducing are Screamers, the most terrifying of all specters, ghosts draped in shadow, ghosts with long claws and a skeletal shape, ghosts who make a room darker and colder simply by walking into it.

There are more different types of ghosts than there are days in the year, but these are the more common ones, the ones you are likely to have bumped into on your travels, or even have living in your house, whether you realize it or not.

Most humans don't realize. Most humans don't even have the foggiest idea about the secret world wrapped all around them. Tom Golden is different, though. An otherwise average eleven-year-old boy, Tom has a secret of his own. Not only does Tom know about this supernatural world, he's best friends with a ghost—Grey Arthur, the first ever Invisible Friend.

This is their story. Or at least, one part of it.

Louise Arnold

When Things Go Wrong

YOU KNOW HOW SOME PEOPLE ARE UTTERLY PROFICIENT liars? People who can cheat at board games and still look the picture of innocence; people who can tell you that their parents are spies, or space explorers, or criminal masterminds and you believe every mind-boggling detail; people who can convince you that the word *derrière* is French for hungry, and have you spend an entire school trip to Paris telling bemused café owners that you are *bum*; people who never blush, who never look shifty, or stammer nervously, dry-mouthed, as they evade the truth? People who can lie as easily as they breathe, and you are never any the wiser?

Well, Grey Arthur isn't one of those people.

"Well, erm, it's not really that big a problem," he'd said awkwardly, eyes on the floor, tugging one of his wonky ears with his pale grey hand. Tom Golden looked at his fidgeting, evasive, twitchy ghost friend, and he slumped down on his bed with a sigh.

"This is so not good, is it?" Tom whined, before taking a deep breath and nodding. "Okay. Come on, break it to me. How big is not really that big?"

"Bigger than a small problem, I'll admit."

"Arthur."

"I mean, it's not like huge, not like Godzilla-size."

"*Arthur.*"

1

"I just don't want you to panic or freak out or anything. I just thought you should know, that's all. It's fine. Maybe."

"Arthur! How big a problem is this?"

Arthur looked up at Tom and bit his lip while he contemplated the scale. "Elephant?" he volunteered gingerly. "At worst. At best, more panda-size. Or a large dog. Or a small cow."

"You're going to have to start making some sense soon, Arthur."

"Okay," replied Arthur, beginning to pace. It was never a good sign when he began to pace. "You know how everyone is settling in as Invisible Friends, and we all agree that it's going very well, and everyone is happy, and that it was a good idea. Remember how we all agreed that it was a good idea? I mean, I specifically remember you saying that you thought it was a—"

"Arthur!" howled Tom. "This is killing me. Can you just get to the point?"

Arthur scowled, obviously not relishing having to say what he was about to say.

"Monty's human kind of worked out that he exists," he said, the words spilling out as quickly as possible before he could think better of it. Tom's eyes grew impossibly wide and his mouth dropped open. "Now, although it sounds bad, it's not as bad as it could be," Grey Arthur added hastily. "The good news is she doesn't entirely believe. She still thinks it's something to do with magnetic faults and geometric something or others, or latent psychic powers or whatever all that means."

Arthur grinned at Tom, that "Aren't humans odd?" grin that he used quite frequently, but when Tom remained looking serious, Arthur let the smile drop and licked his lips anxiously.

"Okay, fair enough, you're still not happy about it," continued Grey Arthur, before breaking off, an optimistic smile creeping back onto his ghostly face. "But I have something to tell you that will cheer you up. You know, every cloud has a silver lining, that kind of thing."

Tom wasn't quite sure what Arthur could tell him that would cheer him up after that bombshell, so instead of sharing Arthur's excitement, he waited uneasily to hear what was coming next. Grey Arthur's smile broadened as he indulged in a dramatic pause. He noticed Tom's frown deepening, so he sighed and went straight for the grand announcement.

"*She's called in* Exceedingly Haunted Homes *to investigate.*"

Arthur even punctuated the statement by waving his hands about, jazz style, while looking almost insanely cheerful.

It's possible Tom made a noise in response, but if he did, it was so high-pitched that only dogs and bats could hear it. If this was Grey Arthur's way of cheering him up, he hated to hear what he would do if he ever wanted to make him worried. Grey Arthur's jazz hands stopped waggling when he realized Tom wasn't sharing his enthusiasm, and he slowly placed them in the pockets of his waistcoat while he waited for Tom to say something.

It was quite a long wait.

Tom stared blankly at Arthur, his mouth moving silently, shaking his head.

"What's the matter, Tom? Why aren't you smiling? Or blinking? Why aren't you blinking, Tom? Tom? *Tom?* Do you want me to get you a cup of tea? Isn't that what we're meant to do in these situations? Or get someone to slap you? I mean, *I* can't, because of the whole ghost thing, but I could hit you *with* something, like a book, if that would help?" asked Arthur anxiously, when it became clear that Tom couldn't work out how to respond. Tom batted away that suggestion with a flick of the hand, and instead sat up straight, loosened his school tie, and looked at Grey Arthur, his forehead a mess of frown lines.

"You need to tell me," he said, his voice deliberately calm, "from the beginning, *exactly* what has happened."

In Good Spirits

TIME HAD HURTLED ON RELENTLESSLY FROM THE MOMENT Grey Arthur had established his very own Ghost School, and the colors of England dutifully changed to fit in.

4

Bright oranges, rich reds, and pale yellows seeped into the leaves on the trees, a final shout of defiance against the monochrome winter that lay ahead, and then chilling winds came that stripped everything back down to bare branches. The blue of the sky faded reluctantly to a washy grey. White frost decorated the grass, made clothes left on the line rigid with cold, and encased cars, triggering the merry morning ritual of hot water and deicer. Time crept on, dragging even lower temperatures with it. Hats and scarves appeared out of hiding, and shorts and skirts were consigned to the back of wardrobes throughout the land. It wasn't long before Christmas burst on to the scene in an explosion of tinsel, flashing lights, and jolly men wearing fake beards.

For every change that affected the weather, several more affected the lives that shivered and sheltered from it. A tidal wave of ghosts had been unleashed upon the land following the defeat of the Collector, and there wasn't a home in England that didn't feel the effect. Fresh hauntings sprang up across the land. The Laundry Run was undertaken by Poltergeists in previously unseen numbers, causing socks to be *The Number One Most Requested Item* on Christmas lists across the country. Castles were riddled with Screamers, Chain Rattlers, Headless ghosts, and Thespers, thrilling and terrifying unwitting tourists, tourists who came back again, and again, and again, desperate to soak up the spooky atmosphere. Sadness Summoners filled the empty seats in cinemas when weepy films were being shown, and not a soul left the building dry-eyed. It had been more years than any ghost could count since England had been this haunted, and the ghosts who had made all these changes possible worked hard to adjust to their new lives as Invisible Friends.

Mildred Rattledust moved in with Holly Mayer, Tike with Frank Longfield, and Monty, the legendary Montague Equador Scullion the Third, keen to put his own dramatic twist on the role, moved in with Mrs. Wilson, the latest in a long line of substitute teachers for Science. The Harrowing Screamer wasn't quite ready to be unleashed on his very own human yet, so he remained a guest of the Golden household, living in the shed. He didn't seem to mind though. "Harry," as Tike had taken to calling him, pottered around with the compost, the spiders, and the stored-away barbecue, and late at night you could see him doing very strange things in the garden indeed. Tom thought it best not to ask. Screamers aren't very forthcoming with answers.

So that was how it was. Tom's first ever haunted Christmas, full of laughter and turkey, crackers and party hats, advent calendars and visits from relatives who insisted on being kissed good-bye.

The festivities disappeared, and the new school term loomed ever closer on the horizon. With Christmas out of the way, strange things happen. Snow stops being beautiful and exciting, and starts being cold, seeping into your shoes, making your socks damp and your toes numb. The Norwegian spruce in the corner of the lounge stops being green and harboring presents, and starts looking sad, shedding pines and turning brown. December, the month of presents and time off school, turns into January, the time of having to go back to lessons and getting smacked in the face with a "snowball" that is mostly ice and dirt. The final thing to break the festive mood entirely, though, was the revelation that the old cricket field in Thorbleton was being turned into a theme park, and every morning at six a.m. trucks would rumble past the house. Mum and Dad, who only mere days ago had been eating mince pies and telling jokes about reindeer, now spent their time writing angry letters to newspapers and standing at the window, twitching the curtains and tutting.

The Season To Be Jolly was officially over.

The first day back at school was very much like every other first day back at school—a mixture of missed gossip, renewing dusty friendships, admiring new pencil cases, and bemoaning the end of the holidays. However, some time after the final bell had gone, things took an altogether different path. . . .

In Short Supply

As bleak winter days go, it was one of the bleakest. Ice etched ornate patterns on the outside of the

Science room windows, and the view of the sky outside was every bit as grey as the concrete school it hung above. White flecks of snow swirled on the wind and gathered in miniature drifts on the windowsill. Mrs. Wilson, hunched behind her desk, shivered, and the breath she blew on her hands to warm them was visible like smoke. Everyone else was long gone, back to their heated homes, their welcoming lounges, the beckoning soaps on telly, but she'd stayed on, weighed down by paperwork, marking, lesson plans, and a sense of foreboding at the massive task that lay ahead.

When she'd accepted the job as a substitute Science teacher here, nobody had warned her what it would be like. Nobody had mentioned the long string of substitute teachers that had gone before her, substitute teachers who had fled after one or, at most, two lessons. Nobody had mentioned tales of sulphuric acid being poured into bags, of fights in class that would rival those seen in Wild West saloons, of toxic potions mixed in the sinks, of Bunsen burners used as flamethrowers, or of entire classes with shorter attention spans than hyperactive kittens.

And certainly nobody had mentioned that as soon as it got cold enough for the heating to be really needed, that is the exact time, *without fail*, it breaks down.

Mrs. Wilson shivered again and wrapped her scarf once more around her neck for extra insulation. Still, she thought to herself, she was here now, and the last thing Thorbleton Secondary School needed was another teacher running away.

She'd tried her hardest to make the Science room feel like home, but it wasn't exactly the easiest thing to do. A CD player on the floor by her feet played soothing whale songs, and among the posters of periodic tables and advice on "What to Do if a Pupil Accidentally Ingests a Toxic Chemical," she had hung a picture of Stonehenge with the sun setting behind it, and a photo of a grumpy-looking cat sitting in a bubble bath. An incense stick that smelled of hippie shops and ladies who wear tie-dye dresses was burning on the desk (carefully placed away from anything that might explode if it met a naked flame). The wispy smoke almost drove away the smell of cleaning fluids, acids, and alkalines.

Almost.

Mrs. Wilson sipped slowly at her chamomile tea, hands wrapped tightly around the mug to steal its warmth, and tapped her feet to force some feeling back to her toes. Her nose was numb and it stood out, a beacon of red stranded between a woolly hat and a woolly scarf. She sniffed and carried on studying today's test papers.

It was meant to have been a simple quiz, just to give her an idea of where the class was up to, what they had learned so far. It made for difficult reading. Some of the highlights so far included:

Q) Name an acid.
A) The one in the big jar.

Q) If lemons are acidic, then milk is . . .
A) White.

Q) Batteries generate . . .
A) Chicken eggs.

She sighed—feeling a little bit overwhelmed, a little bit lost, and a lot cold—and placed her chamomile tea down as she struggled to adjust her scarf for the umpteenth time. She left the mug perilously close to the edge of the desk, distracted by what she was doing, and it hung there, teetering, threatening to spill on the CD player below.

Finally satisfied that she was as warm as she could be, given the circumstances, Mrs. Wilson reached out to reclaim her tea. Only, the cup wasn't where she had left it. It was nestled, safely out of harm's way, in the middle of the desk. She frowned, confused, and for the longest time she just stared at her tea, trying to work out if she was going slowly crazy. She ran through the process in her mind, remembering what hand she had used to place the cup down, picturing where she left it, and she laughed quietly at the absurdity of it all. She had to have been imagining it.

Scientific curiosity got the better of her though, and once again she moved the mug to the edge of the desk and concentrated on her scarf. She glanced up, and sure enough, the mug had been moved to the center of the desk. She shook her head and frowned again.

Montague Equador Scullion the Third, ex-Thesper, now Invisible Friend, looked on and nodded happily to himself. Ever since witnessing firsthand the trials and tribulations substitute teachers go through, he had decided that his calling was to adopt one himself. It struck him that in a school like Thorbleton, the teachers needed help every bit as much as some of the pupils. Still, this teacher seemed to need it even more than most. For the *third* time, she placed her mug on the edge of the desk, and for the *third* time, Montague moved it to somewhere safe.

"All in a day's haunting," he said to himself with a smile, while twisting his mustache into dramatic little points. He took a bow to an audience that wasn't there, a force of habit, and gave himself a polite round of applause. He was really getting used to this Invisible Friend lark.

Mrs. Wilson began rummaging in her multicolored, patchwork bag, and she brought out a well-thumbed copy of *Mysteries of This World*. The magazine was tatty and covered in tea rings, with some pages torn already from overexuberant reading. The front cover showed a rather plump man wearing a hat made from silver foil, with the caption ARE ALIENS MAKING YOU FAT? She threw the magazine open and began thumbing through, past out-of-focus pictures of graveyards, past quizzes that asked "Could You Be Psychic?", past an article about a dog from Aberdeen that had started barking a woof that sounds strangely like the word

Armageddon, or perhaps, *Army head on*, or maybe, con-
ceded the article, *I like bacon* . . . On and on Mrs. Wilson
went, thumbing through the pages at top speed. She
stopped abruptly, tapping a section in the adverts, nodding to herself. Grabbing the phone off her desk with
cold, clumsy fingers, she began to dial. Montague
watched, intrigued.

"Hello?" she said, her voice racing with excitement. "Is
this *Exceedingly Haunted Homes of England*? . . . Oh, good,
good. I have something that might interest you. . . ."

Montague looked on, a nervous grimace on his
ghostly face, and for once, he was lost for words.

Breaking the News

"SURELY HE MUST HAVE REALIZED SOMETHING WAS
wrong when he had to move the cup for the third
time?" howled Tom as he paced his bedroom.

"Oh, don't be too hard on him, Tom. He thought he
was being helpful," explained Arthur. "To be fair, we're
all quite new to being Invisible Friends, so mistakes
will happen."

Tom stopped pacing and leaned against the wall,
looking concerned. It was perhaps unfortunate that
he had chosen to rest right in front of his wall of
memories, where souvenirs, postcards, mementos, and

assorted nostalgia gathered, because his serious expression was a little undermined by the picture right next to his ear of him on the potty as a toddler.

"There's a bit of a difference between a mistake and calling in professional ghost hunters to film it all on national television, Arthur!" Tom complained. "Oh, this is a nightmare."

Grey Arthur frowned. "I know it's not ideal, but nobody expected their human to try and catch them out, Tom. He told me straightaway, and I told you, and now we just need to work out how to make sure it doesn't happen again, that's all. It's a problem, yes, as problems go it's a pretty big one, but hopefully we caught it in time."

"*Caught it in time?*" repeated Tom incredulously. He was so wound up that his hands began flapping wildly as he talked. "It doesn't sound at all like you caught it in time! How can you be so calm, Arthur? Aren't you at all worried about the TV crews? And the psychic? What if they spot you? What if they manage to get rid of you, you know, do some weird hocus-pocus that they do, and then you all vanish and I'm left on my own?"

Grey Arthur's mouth dropped open, a look of realization on his face. "Oh! So *that's* what you're worried about?"

"Of course that's what I'm worried about. What did you think?"

"Well, I thought it was because Monty might have to stop being an Invisible Friend since the whole idea was to help Mrs. Wilson, not to convince her she was being haunted. It means we might have to rethink the way we look after our humans." Grey Arthur ruffled his already ruffled grey hair, a bemused smile twitching on his lips. "But you're just worried over some make-believe psychic? Talk about worrying over nothing."

Tom shook his head. "What? No! It's not over nothing at all, Arthur. Monty won't have to stop being her friend, he'll just have to be a little more discreet, that's all. Obviously, it's not *ideal* but it's not the end of the world. What would be bad is you guys being chased all over the school by a group of ghost hunters. You know what happened with Dr. Brown. The last thing in the world we need is a repeat of that, or worse."

"Pfft!" said Arthur dismissively. "Nothing to worry about. It's a load of old codswallop. As long as Monty isn't moving cups around in front of them they won't have a clue he's there. It's fake, Tom—All *Begone, foul spirit* this and *sense of foreboding* that."

"Arthur," interrupted Tom. "That psychic guy isn't on the show anymore. They've got a new woman. How can you not know this? It's been in all the papers."

"Not *The Daily Tell-Tale*."

"Well, okay, all the papers apart from the ghost one. They've got this new psychic, and she's meant to be really good, Arthur. Like, scarily good. And now, thanks to Monty"—Tom threw his hands up in the air dramatically—"she's going to be coming to our school!"

"You're so gullible, Tom." Grey Arthur chuckled as he plonked himself down on the bed.

"I'm not gullible," protested Tom. "It's true! It was in the papers."

"You *are* gullible. It's not a bad thing, I'm just saying. You're the only human who can see ghosts. *Everyone* knows that. So, if they say this woman can see ghosts, they're lying. Or pretending. Or both." He looked at Tom thoughtfully. "I thought you'd be more excited about this, Tom. I actually think it's quite cool that *Exceedingly Haunted Homes* might be coming to school." Grey Arthur leaned over to one side on the bed, twisting so he could catch his reflection in the mirror on the wall, and began practicing his scary face (it was no surprise that he never made it as a Screamer, as his scary face was actually rather cute, like an angry kitten, or a fierce puppy, which was completely not the point). He snarled into the mirror, and then grinned at Tom. "I've always wanted to be on the telly." Tom watched as his ghostly friend continued enthusiastically "haunting" in the mirror, and groaned.

"No, no, no, Arthur. You can't. I don't care what you say, I still think it's too dangerous. Besides, you've already been on the telly once, remember?"

"That doesn't count. That was to help you out, and I didn't even look the right way. This will be my chance to do it properly. Our chance. All of us Invisible Friends on the telly together. Come on, you have to admit that would be pretty good fun to see."

"Arthur, listen, I don't want to argue with you and I'm not trying to ruin your fun, it's just something about this . . . It feels . . . dodgy . . . to me." Tom wished he could explain why, but there was just some odd, gnawing sensation at the back of his mind that wouldn't go away, like the feeling you get when you look down a dark alleyway you're contemplating taking a shortcut down, or the sensation you get when you stumble across an old improvised swing made from fraying rope. That little voice at the back of your head that quietly but firmly says NO. Tom looked at Arthur's disappointed face and sighed. "Look, if there was some way I could find out for sure that this woman definitely can't see ghosts, then I'd be more than happy for you all to go along, throw ectoplasm about, do whatever it is you want to do, but—"

Tom had a very good "but" lined up. It was convincing, mature, well-reasoned, and would have stopped Grey Arthur's whining dead in the water.

At least, it would have done if he had been given a chance to say it.

Which he wasn't.

There was a knock, and everything simply froze, eyes turning to the door, sentences stopping midflow. It wasn't Mum's knock, and it wasn't Dad's.

Mystery knock.

"Tom, I'm going to go and tell everyone the good news," whispered Grey Arthur, flashing him a very delighted thumbs-up. "We can sort out your plan to check out the psychic lady later. See you in a bit." And with that, he was gone.

The mystery knock came again.

Tom sighed and then leaped onto the bed, grabbed a book, and threw it open at a random page, trying very hard to look like a normal, average, book-reading boy who hadn't just been conversing with a ghost. A stubborn, excitable ghost who had refused to listen to what was being said, and just heard what he wanted to hear. Tom sighed again, just for effect, before turning his attention back to the mystery knock.

"Come in," he called.

Where Discussions Roam

A FAMILIAR FACE PEERED ROUND THE DOOR.

"Pete!" Tom gave up on his pretend reading and got to his feet. This was new—in fact, Tom thought it might be the first time he'd had a guest over at this house that wasn't either ghostly or an evil villain. Pete grinned and ducked through the door, closing it behind him.

"The sign said to keep out, so I figured I should probably knock first," he said. He tilted his head as he looked at Tom, smiling in a bemused way. "Did I catch you just talking to yourself?" Tom's greeting smile faltered, embarrassed that he'd been overheard after all. Pete didn't seem fazed though. He was already making himself at home, exploring Tom's room. He nodded approvingly at the Cold Fish poster on the back of the door.

"Yeah," Tom confessed. "I do that sometimes."

"Don't worry. I do too." Pete opened a jar of hair gel on Tom's shelf, sniffed it, and then placed it back where he'd found it.

"You do?"

"Yeah. I mean, not as full on crazy as you, but yeah. Mostly when I've lost something, or I'm late. That kind of thing. Nice sneakers, by the way." Pete nudged a pair of Tom's Christmas present shoes with his foot, and carried on inspecting the bedroom.

"Do you want a drink or anything?"

"No, you're all right. Your mum wouldn't let me upstairs until I'd had a hot chocolate and a mince pie. They made me sign a petition too. What's that all about?"

"Oh, *that*." Tom cringed. This was the first time Pete had called over, and Mum and Dad had already set about being as embarrassing as possible. Marvelous . . . "They've just gone a bit crazy lately. Some company or other is building a theme park, and the trucks take a shortcut down our road."

"And?" Pete prodded the white sock with gold lettering that was pinned to Tom's Wall of Memories, sniffed it as well, and then shrugged.

"Oh, I don't know. Something about Mum's flowers getting covered in dust, and the rumbling . . . structural . . . heavy . . . cracks?"

"Your parents are odd." Pete chuckled.

"Tell me about it. You're just lucky my dad didn't make you test-run a pair of socks. I once had to spend a whole evening jogging up and down the hallway, and then touching door handles to see if I got a shock." Tom rummaged in his sock drawer and brought out the prototype Anti-Static-Shock-Sock. It was looking a little worse for wear, a tad threadbare, and some of the wires protruding looked positively barbaric and likely to give you tetanus. Pete's mouth dropped, and he carefully took the sock from Tom, studying it.

"That's too cool . . . ," he muttered, as he turned it in his hands. "Your dad's, like, a mad genius."

"I suppose," agreed Tom, not sure whether to be proud or embarrassed. "So what's up? Why've you come over?"

"No reason. Was just nearby and remembered that you said you lived here, so I thought I'd call in and say hello. It's a nice day for a bike ride, anyway."

Tom peered through the curtains and could just about make out the faint glow of the streetlights, smothered by the falling sleet; the window rattled as cold, damp gusts of wind battered it. It was, quite positively, the worst day in existence to go wandering. Tom frowned as Pete sank down into Tom's rickety chair, finally finished with his grand tour of the bedroom.

"You're sure you're okay?"

"Course I am. Why wouldn't I be?" Pete smiled again, but this time the grin never reached anywhere near his eyes. You know how sometimes you look at someone and it's as if you've never properly looked at their face before? This was one of those times. Tom looked at Pete, and for the first time he saw how behind the mop of black hair, and the near constant broad grin, lurked a hint of something a little bit sad. Pete noticed Tom's expression and sighed. "Oh, I hate that look. It's nothing. Really. Dad was just arguing with Mum on the phone. It's cool, I'm used to it, but that doesn't mean I want to stick around and listen to it." Pete spotted Tom's mouth open slightly, that telltale intake of breath, that concerned frown, and he quickly added: "*Or* talk about it."

"But I didn't say anything!"

"You were going to though."

"Maybe . . . ," admitted Tom.

"Well, thanks, but honestly, it's cool. This has been going on for years now, so it's old news. I just need to get away sometimes, that's all. So come on, distract me."

"How?"

"Well, you can start by telling me what you were talking to yourself about." Pete went to lean back in the chair, but the amount of creaking noise it made convinced him not to. He pulled a jokey alarmed face, and sat bolt upright.

"Oh, nothing. Just, you know . . . ," Tom muttered. "Nothing."

"Shut up it's nothing." Pete laughed. "You're such a rubbish liar."

"No, really." Tom felt his cheeks burning already, which made Pete laugh harder.

"Oh, come on, Tom. It has to be interesting if it's making you go red."

"It's just a rumor anyway. It might not even happen."

"Won't matter if you tell me, then, will it?" replied Pete with a cheeky grin. There are some battles you're really not going to win, and looking at Pete, Tom realized this was one of them. What harm could it do to tell him, anyway? It's not like it could stay a secret if it was going to be on television.

"*Exceedingly Haunted Homes of England* might be coming to our school," he said, trying to make it sound as dull as possible.

He failed.

"No way!" yelled Pete. Tom winced, gesturing downstairs to where his parents were, and Pete silently mouthed "*Sorry.*" He carried on talking, just as enthusiastically, but at a lower volume. "That's awesome! Did you ever see that episode? You know, the one with the ghost yak?"

Tom rolled his eyes. "Not you, too! You don't actually watch that rubbish, do you?"

"Of course I do. That bloke that used to be on it was wicked. '*Why are you here, O spirit? BEGONE!*' Anyway, why do you think it's rubbish? I thought you believed in ghosts?"

Tom wasn't quite sure what to say to that. After the whole "running screaming out of the castle dungeon" thing that happened on the school trip, he'd gone to great lengths to tell everyone that he had been mistaken, and hadn't seen a ghost at all, that it had just been someone playing a trick on him. It hadn't occurred to Tom that he might not have been convincing.

"I don't believe that *he* can see ghosts," he replied carefully. Which wasn't really a lie. More of an evaded truth.

Pete shrugged. "I'm not that bothered either way. It's just a funny show. My dad watches it just so he can point out how fake it all is, but I just think it's a bit of a laugh."

"Well, anyway, it's not for certain that they'll be coming to school, so you probably shouldn't tell anyone."

"Sure." Pete's eyes were scanning the room when suddenly his expression lit up. "Oh, wow, you collect *Mr. Space Pirate* comics?" He'd spied the pile that Grey Arthur was slowly working his way through each night. "Do you mind if I have a look?"

"Go for it," Tom replied, grateful that the conversation had now steered on to safer ground. "I've even got the one with the first appearance of the Mighty Gravity Blob, if you're into that?"

"No way! I didn't think you could get hold of that copy in England?"

And that was pretty much how the evening continued. In this time they:

1. Played Shark Top Trumps (Pete won, aided by the fact that he started the game with a Great White).
2. Drank two pints of milk. *Each*.
3. Decided they should design their own comic together.
4. Drew a cartoon of Big Ben, dressed as a baby, being chased by a giant rhino that had lasers for eyes.
5. Discovered a shared hatred of olives ("They taste like your mouth after you've had the flu.").
6. Played "Uber Go-Kart Legends" on the computer (Pete won, aided by the fact that Tom was rubbish).
7. Made a list of theories about why Kate has no eyebrows, including the startling revelation that she could, in fact, be *50 percent boiled egg* . . .
8. Realized that, while Tom loved Jaffa Cakes, Pete thought they were made of cardboard and evilness.
9. And so on . . .

It was such a nice, pleasant, normal evening—two friends chatting, laughing, agreeing, disagreeing, everything that friends should do.

Which is why you'll probably be quite surprised to learn of all the chaos it caused.

Bringing Out the Crazy

TOM, GREY ARTHUR, AND THE HARROWING SCREAMER
(or Harry) wandered to school the following morning, each merrily lost in their own world (okay, maybe
it would be a slight stretch to describe the Screamer
as merrily lost, perhaps sinisterly lost, or merely indif-
ferently lost, but you get the idea). Grey Arthur was
daydreaming about becoming a ghostly space pirate,
Tom was chuckling, thinking about the picture of Big
Ben dressed as a baby, and the Harrowing Screamer
was imagining running his nails down chalkboards,
and then draping himself in a particularly splendid
shadow. If they had had any idea what lay ahead, perhaps they would have been less calm. Perhaps they
would have even turned around and headed back
home, hiding inside the Golden house until all the
insanity had subsided. But, blissfully unaware, they
ambled on, daydreaming, chuckling, and breathing
shadows respectively.

The snow crunched under Tom's feet, and Harry
scraped his claws through where it had gathered on
low walls and on top of cars, leaving tracks behind that
looked like a very mean, very unhappy cat had been
dragged to the vet's by its tail. Tom wandered along,
snug inside his coat, immersed in cartoonish thoughts,
when he was suddenly aware that he was walking

alone. He stopped, and turned round. Both Grey Arthur and the Harrowing Screamer were standing some distance behind him, heads tilted.

"What's up?" Tom called.

Grey Arthur frowned. "Do you hear that?"

Tom liberated his ears from the layers of scarf and listened. Threads of noise carried, the sounds of a playground, cars, the rumble of someone's music thumping from inside a house. He shrugged. His ears were already complaining about being exposed to the cold air. "Hear what?"

"The school," said Arthur, rather cryptically.

"What about the school?"

"It doesn't sound right. The volume's all wrong." Grey Arthur looked at the Harrowing Screamer, who made a low growl. Arthur nodded. "Something's happening."

"It sounds normal to me."

"To human ears, perhaps. Sometimes I wish you had ghost ears, Tom."

Tom looked at Grey Arthur's ears, ears that looked like someone had thrown them at his head from a distance and left them where they landed, and he smiled politely.

"I think I'll stick with what I've got, if that's okay with you. What are you hearing that's different?"

Grey Arthur closed his eyes and concentrated. "It's hard to pick out exactly, it's all so churned together, but there's louder excitement, more nerves, more . . ." Grey

Arthur opened his eyes wide, showed his teeth, and jangled his hands around. Tom wasn't entirely sure what that was meant to convey. "You know?"

Tom pretended he did. "It's probably nothing. Maybe Big Ben is early to school. Maybe there's a fight. Maybe a dog has run into the playground again."

"Maybe . . . ," Arthur agreed.

"We'll not find out standing here. Let's go see for ourselves." Grey Arthur and the Harrowing Screamer shared one final concerned look, and then jogged to catch up with Tom. There was something inherently amusing about watching a Screamer jog. His scrawny limbs seemed to jar, the old bones clicking too fast, sounding almost like the spokes on a rusty bike, his talon claws loping forward. Screamers were built to creep, to stalk, to slowly edge out of the shadows—definitely not to jog. Tom quickly wrapped his scarf back round his head to hide away his smile. They carried on walking toward the school, but the air of daydreams was gone, and all of them concentrated on the walk ahead.

They were still half a street away from the school when they saw Mildred waiting for them. She had her hands on her hips and looked even more serious than usual, which was no mean feat.

"What's up, Mildred?" called Arthur. "Is Holly not coming in to school today?"

"She is indoors, Arthur. Hiding in a broom cupboard."

"Hiding in a . . . ?" Arthur repeated, trailing off into confused silence. Tom tried not to be too conversational with his ghost friends in public, especially when he was so close to school, so he stopped and tapped his watch, pretending it was broken, all the while listening to what was being said. The Harrowing Screamer was never very chatty anyway, so he just hissed quietly at Tom's side: "Is this to do with the strange emotions coming from the school?"

"I will explain in due course," replied Mildred. "First there is something you must see."

Mildred grabbed hold of Grey Arthur by his elbow and began to hurry him forward. Arthur gave Tom a look, that eyebrows-raised, mouth-twisted look of "What's all this about?" Tom shrugged. Knowing Mildred, it could be anything from a poem she had written about black swans, to a new outfit she had made for her evil-looking toy monkey. The two events—Mildred's appearance and Grey Arthur's concerns—weren't necessarily connected. But, then again, ghosts don't really have time for coincidences. She marched ahead at a terrific pace, and Tom had to break into a near trot to keep up. She stopped outside the school gates, finally liberating Arthur's elbow.

"Observe," she said.

There were no poems about black swans, and no monkey costumes. Nor was there a fight, or a stray dog. Instead, in huge, dripping, yellow paint letters on the school walls were the words:

HAUNTED! KEEP OUT!

"Oh, dear," said Grey Arthur.

"Indeed," agreed Mildred. "And the situation deteriorates from here on in." She gestured for them to stand at the school entrance and look inside. Tom, Grey Arthur, and the Harrowing Screamer dutifully obliged.

It was madness.

Sheer, total, madness.

The caretaker was busy attacking a large painting of a ghost eating what appeared to be a small child, from off the main reception building. It was a losing battle. The paint determinedly clung to the walls, at the very best just smearing slightly. The caretaker was glaring at everyone that dared to look in his direction, muttering loudly about "the youth of today." Children stood around in huddles, talking animatedly, or whispering quietly, the whole school awash with gossip and rumors. Another painting on the side of the library window showed a ghostly apparition with red paint, which Tom supposed to be blood, dripping from its teeth.

"I told you something didn't sound right, Tom . . . ," Arthur muttered.

"My human is hiding in the broom cupboard, refusing to come out, in case a ghost will eat her," said Mildred. "I have tried explaining the human-free nature of a ghost's diet, but she remains unconvinced. Other children are refusing to enter the school. They say they are too scared to."

"How did this happen?" asked Tom, beyond caring about being seen as weird talking to himself in public.

Right now, that was positively normal, compared to everything else that was happening.

"Okay, I think I might actually have something to do with this . . . ," admitted an apologetic voice from behind Tom. Turning to see who it was, he came face to . . . *hood* with a familiar person. A gloved hand pushed the hood away from his face and waved cheerily at Tom. "Hey, there."

"Hey, Pete." Tom felt a sinking feeling as everything began to fall into place. Pete couldn't have looked guiltier if he was wearing a robber's outfit and was clutching a bag labelled SWAG.

"Okay, so I know you said not to say anything, but the thing is, I bumped into Sayid on the way home last night. You know Sayid, dark hair, quite tall, class F?"

"Yeah . . . ," replied Tom.

"Well, I bumped into him on the way home, and we got chatting, and it just . . . slipped out. . . ." Pete winced at Tom's pained expression. "I made him promise not to tell anyone, Tom. He swore."

"Right . . ."

"But, the thing is, Sayid's got five sisters . . . ," confessed Pete in a small voice.

Tom finally understood. There was no such thing as a secret in a house with five sisters. Poor Sayid never stood a chance. They probably smelled the withheld gossip on him the minute he wandered in the door.

"I'm really sorry, Tom," said Pete, looking exceedingly apologetic. "I just didn't think."

"Don't worry about it," Tom found himself saying. "It's fine."

"See, told you. You're a *rubbish* liar." Pete shuffled his feet awkwardly. "Still friends?"

"Still friends," agreed Tom. A fellow first year ran out of the school gates, nearly slipping on the ice, being chased by a group of older kids who were busy rattling their scarves as if they were chains. Grey Arthur held his head in his hands, mouth dropped wide open. After last year's Fire-in-a-Bin incident, Arthur thought he had seen it all. It would appear that was just a minor blip in the scheme of "How Mad a School Can Go."

Tike burst through a section of the school wall in front of them and skidded to a halt. It took a massive effort on Tom's behalf not to jump, and he tried to hide his flinch with a cough. The ex-Poltergeist looked equal parts disheveled and anxious. He nodded a brief hello at Tom, and dashed straight over to Mildred, Arthur, and the Harrowing Screamer.

"Okay, right," he gasped, licking his lips nervously, "say your human is trapped inside a bin and being rolled down the corridor by kids chanting 'Ghost Train, Ghost Train,' what d'you do?" He twitched up and down on the spot, desperately waiting for a response.

Grey Arthur turned to Tom. "We've got to go sort this out. You'll be okay?"

Tom bobbed his head in response, and Grey Arthur, Mildred, the Harrowing Screamer, and Tike ran off toward the school. Tom felt like turning back round, heading home, crawling into bed, and pretending this was all a dream. A cheese-induced dream. A fever dream. A hit-by-a-car-and-your-brain-is-a-little-woozy dream. Right now, he'd take any kind of dream over reality.

"You sure you're not mad at me?" Pete asked.

A larger child ran out of the school gates wearing a white sheet (just how on earth do you get a white sheet at such short notice?) and threw a sludgy snowball at Tom. It exploded on his chest in a mixture of cold and damp. Tom sighed and brushed the parts that hadn't melted on impact away.

"No, I'm not mad."

"Ready to head in?" Pete grinned at Tom, and despite everything, Tom couldn't help but grin back.

"As I'll ever be."

Mad as Several Hatters

THORBLETON SCHOOL WAS NOT USUALLY RENOWNED FOR its sanity. It was a place where legends were made, spawning retellings of outrageous acts that swept through playgrounds the length of the land. Children up north, down south, east, and west would gather in huddles on the field, swapping tall stories, and when someone would question the truth, when someone would say that *has* to be made-up, the additional statement "In Thorbleton" would be enough to quell any such disputes.

"Did you hear about the kid that stole all the goldfish and put them in the teachers' water cooler?" or "I heard that a kid brought fireworks to school and let them off in the middle of assembly" or "The football team was so angry at the decision that all eleven of the players tied the referee to the goalposts and left him there overnight."

"That's rubbish," someone would respond, and the teller would shake their head, lean in closer, and explain:

"No, it's true—*it happened in Thorbleton.*"

That would be it. That would be enough. In Thorbleton, such things occurred. Everybody knew that.

Even so, even against this backdrop of incredible, outrageous, and wild behavior, today was something completely beyond the pale. It would be a day that would go down in children's history, a day that grandparents would tell their grandchildren on cold winter days, when gathered round a fire.

The day when Thorbleton School completely lost the plot.

Tom and Pete waded into the chaos, and even Tom—Tom who had seen ghosts bowling their heads across his landing, Tom who had witnessed Screamers in the dark depths of dungeons, Tom who had traveled ley-lines and stood up against legends and smelled what the inside of a Snorgle museum smells like—was astounded.

Everyone had gone insane.

The school bell rang to order people to start making their way inside, and some children whooped and laughed, and charged forward, dragging less confident children in their wake, children who would look at the school entrance as if it was now Halloween manifest, imagining spiders' webs and gargoyles and dark shadowy corners where only yesterday they saw nothing but concrete and discarded chewing gum. Some children still milled around outside, apparently too afraid to enter. Some even cried, clutching mobile phones with freezing cold hands, phoning demands for parents to come and collect them. Beyond the spate of ghost-oriented graffiti, nothing about the school looked any different, but rumors can paint a picture ten times more vivid than reality. Thorbleton School was haunted, it had to be true, because the people from the telly were coming.

Of course, technically, the school *was* haunted, but really that's neither here nor there. It was haunted in a Ballpoint-Bill-eating-pens and a Snorgle-in-the-toilet kind of way, instead of phantasms appearing in mirrors, or headless horsemen hurtling down the corridors. Tom knew this, but what could he say? Hold an assembly to explain the true nature of the Ghost World?

Maybe put up some educational posters? No, all Tom could do was hold his head up high and trudge into the madness that would, for years to come, be known as "The Haunted Day at School."

An Oasis of Sanity

"OKAY, CLASS, CAN WE PLEASE GET ONE THING STRAIGHT?" Mr. Hammond rested against the whiteboard and wearily studied the classroom. It was only four minutes till home time, but today had felt like seventeen Mondays all strung together, at least for the teachers. For the pupils, the time had flown in a flurry of newly formed ghost stories, rumors, myths, legends, and bullying with a supernatural theme (locking people in dark cupboards, jumping out and screaming at people who were already looking like their nerves were frayed, and finally, just punching people while making ghost noises—for the less inventive bully). "There is no such thing as ghosts, this school isn't haunted, this is just a stupid rumor that has spiraled out of control. Okay?"

An unconvinced murmur came back as a response. He sighed. "Go on, go home. Yes, don't look at me like that, I'm letting you go early." In the blink of an eye, the classroom was empty. Mr. Hammond sank into his chair at his desk and after a moment's hesitation, placed his phone back on the hook. Immediately, it sprang into life. He made a low moan, briefly let his head slide into his hands, and then forced himself to answer.

"Mr. Hammond speaking. How may I help you?"

Outside the classroom, Tom, Grey Arthur, and the Harrowing Screamer lurked in the corridor. Grey Arthur looked so pale he was practically invisible, and the Harrowing Screamer looked drained. His swirling mist eyes seemed to swirl slower, his shadows seemed less dense, even his nails didn't look as sharp. Grey Arthur patted his head, like you would do to a furless dog (okay, you probably wouldn't touch a furless dog, but you get the idea), and the Screamer made a tired-sounding moan. It had been the most exhausting day. When Grey Arthur wasn't rescuing Tom from the clutches of Big Ben's punching-people-while-howling spree, he was helping Tike de-rubbish Frank, or assisting Mildred with keeping an eye on Holly, who was jumping at her own shadow, or trying to advise Monty in how best to console Mrs. Wilson in a subtle way that wouldn't get spotted. Thespers and subtle don't usually go hand in hand, and so that had been a long and slow process. The Harrowing Screamer, it had been decided, was probably not the most helpful person to have in a school full of already nervous children. It was tactfully put to him that he should guard smoker's alley and prevent children from running down there to bunk school or to choke their lungs. It's amazing the dissuasive power that a well-placed Screamer can have. Kids would walk toward the alley, and then suddenly veer back into the school. It was busy work. Arthur had collected him during last lesson, and Tom had looked out of his classroom window to see him escorting the visibly exhausted Screamer as he hobbled across the playground.

"Okay, so let's get this straight . . ." Tom cracked his knuckles, and then instantly regretted it, as it hurt. He shook his fingers to try and wiggle away the pain. "I'm going to go in there, speak to Mr. Hammond, find out what's going on with the TV people coming here, and then somehow try and make it so that I can come along and make sure that this new psychic lady can't really see ghosts, just so you guys can prance about on the telly?"

Grey Arthur and Harry nodded enthusiastically, and Tom couldn't help but smile, even as he sighed at the absurdity of it all. How on earth did he manage to get talked into this? Tom took a deep breath, nodded briskly at the two ghosts, and headed toward the door.

"How?" asked Arthur.

Tom stopped, and backtracked out of Mr. Hammond's line of sight. "How what?"

"How are you going to persuade him to let you come along to the filming?"

"Oh, I don't know. I'll improvise."

The Harrowing Screamer moaned softly.

"What? What does that mean?" Tom asked.

Arthur looked a bit awkward. "Well, it's just . . . you're not exactly great at improvising."

"It'll be fine! I'll work something out."

"Maybe . . . maybe you could say that you love TV cameras," volunteered Arthur.

Tom rolled his eyes. "That's rubbish."

"It's just a suggestion."

"Don't worry. I'll think of something." Tom nodded again, gearing himself up. "You two wait here. I shouldn't be long."

"Good luck," said Grey Arthur.

Tom edged forward and knocked gingerly at the classroom door. Mr. Hammond was still on the phone, but he gestured for Tom to come in.

"Of course I understand what you're saying, Mrs. Falton . . . ," he said, rubbing his beard. "Yes . . . Yes . . . I can assure you that I do take your concerns seriously . . . Yes . . . But it's perfectly safe, Mrs. Falton . . . *Indian burial ground?* What on earth do you mean, Indian burial ground? This school was built on an old landfill site, Mrs. Falton. Unless it's being haunted by the spirits of old shopping trolleys and tin cans, then I can't see . . . No, I'm not trying to be sarcastic, I was just trying to illustrate a point . . . Okay, so when will Ruth be coming back into school? . . . When it's no longer haunted? But it's not haunted now, Mrs. Falton. Mrs. Falton? Mrs. Falton? Hello?" Mr. Hammond stared at the phone in his hand in disbelief. "She's hung up. Can you believe this? Fifth phone call I've had like that today, and every other teacher has had to deal with the same. I hope you've not come here to tell me that you think this school is haunted too, Tom."

Tom glanced at the doorway and saw Grey Arthur and the Harrowing Screamer peering into the room. He frowned at them, and they retreated out of sight. "No, of course not, Mr. Hammond."

"Good." Mr. Hammond reclined back in his chair, massaging his temples. "Load of old nonsense. I left school last night and the only thing I really had to worry about is whether or not my car would start. Now it's ghosts. *Ghosts!* Absolutely ridiculous. How does a rumor spread so quickly?"

Sisters. That was, of course, the answer to Mr. Hammond's question. However, Tom played dumb, and just shrugged.

"No, I don't know either," agreed Mr. Hammond. "So, come on, then, how can I help you?"

"Is it true that *Exceedingly Haunted Homes* is coming to the school?"

Mr. Hammond sat back up straight and frowned. "Oh, not you as well, Tom. I thought you said you didn't think this school was haunted?"

"I don't!" Tom flustered. "It's not. One hundred percent not. No ghosts. None!"

Mr. Hammond raised an eyebrow. "So what's the interest, then?"

Tom felt color rushing to his cheeks, and the weight

of Mr. Hammond's scrutiny made his heart race. "I . . . well, thing is . . ."

Mr. Hammond waited.

"*I love TV cameras.*"

From outside in the corridor Tom heard a snort of ghostly laughter, which only made his cheeks burn hotter.

"You do?" Mr. Hammond asked. Tom nodded. "I had no idea, Tom."

"Oh yes. They're great. You know . . . zoom. And action. And, erm . . . cut. I find it all very interesting." Pete's voice echoed in Tom's head, reminding him how rubbish he was at lying, and it was all Tom could do to stop his teeth grinding together. He looked at Mr. Hammond hopefully. "So, I was wondering, if they *are* really coming to school, whether I could come along when they were filming, you know, to see how it's done."

"And why are you asking me?"

"Because you're the nicest teacher," replied Tom honestly.

Mr. Hammond snorted with laughter. "I am, am I? Well, thank you very much, Tom. I didn't know that." Mr. Hammond rubbed his beard again, smiling an amused smile. "The thing is, Tom, I'll be frank with you, because there doesn't seem much point keeping this secret, if such a thing can even exist in this school . . . The first any of us teachers had even heard about this was when we turned up to school today to see it strewn with graffiti and everyone acting ten types of crazy. *Exceedingly Haunted Homes* didn't even get in touch with us until lunchtime, so heaven knows how you kids found out about it before we did. . . ."

Tom stayed quiet, trying to look a picture of innocence.

"So, we turned them down. We didn't really want to encourage this idea that the school was haunted."

Tom felt so relieved, but he tried to hide it. At least now he didn't have to worry about psychics and exposés and Invisible Friends clamoring for their five minutes of fame. In the corridor, he heard Grey Arthur and the Harrowing Screamer moan in disappointment.

"*However . . .*," continued Mr. Hammond. Tom's heart sank a little. "Since it really looks as if this lunacy is not going to go away of its own accord, it was decided to allow them to come into the school, if only to dispel these stupid rumors. The hope is that they'll spend an unproductive evening sitting in the canteen, or in the unglamorous confines of the Science block urinals, discover it's a waste of time, and go home empty-handed. Then we can close the book on this funny little chapter of hysteria once and for all. So yes, Tom Golden, *Exceedingly Haunted Homes* is coming to Thorbleton."

"Yay!" cried Tom, trying to muster enthusiasm. Outside in the corridor, he could hear Arthur and Harry cheering. "That's . . . fantastic . . ."

"Yes, I had a hunch you'd say that."

"So, do you think it would be possible if I could

come in while they are filming? Like, you know, work experience?"

Mr. Hammond looked at Tom, not unkindly. "It's not going to be like you think it is, Tom. It'll be deathly dull. I've worked here for fifteen years now, and not even seen a whiff of anything supernatural happening here." The ghostly giggling in the hallway intensified. "If you're doing this hoping to witness some otherworldly phenomenon, you're going to be bitterly disappointed. If this school is haunted, then I'm Elvis Presley."

Even Tom nearly broke into giggles then. The mental image of Mr. Hammond, white sequined suit, sideburns aplenty, hip-wiggling in assembly, would be enough to send lesser kids crumbling into outright hysterics. Tom took a deep breath and managed to hold it in. Just.

"I know that, Mr. Hammond. It's just, I'm really very interested in being a cameraman when I grow up."

Mr. Hammond looked at Tom, and Tom wasn't sure if he looked suspicious or impressed by Tom's ambition. Hopefully, the latter. The pause before he answered felt like it went on forever. Finally, Mr. Hammond shrugged amiably.

"Well, I'll ask. No harm in asking. Maybe you can be a tea boy or something. Honestly, I just think this whole thing is a waste of time, but there's no telling Mrs. Wilson that, or the umpteen parents who have been taking their children out of school. The next thing you know we'll be burning incense sticks in lessons and doing yoga in the staffroom. Maybe change the school uniform to something tie-dyed." Mr. Hammond realized he was rambling when he saw the blank expression on Tom's face, and smiled. "Still, if they're happy to waste their time filming here, then let them. Maybe the council will see how run-down the place is, and will be embarrassed into giving us some extra funding. Wouldn't that be nice?"

"Lovely," agreed Tom, assuming that was the right response to make.

The phone rang, and Mr. Hammond groaned. "I'll let you know if I can sort something out, Tom. I shouldn't imagine it will be too big a problem." Tom recognized a cue to exit when he heard one.

They say good news travels fast, and this was no exception. Out in the corridor, Grey Arthur was already pretending to film the Harrowing Screamer through the "lens" of a toilet roll, while Harry hissed and posed. He was ankle deep in shadows, and loving every second.

Not for the first time in his life, or that year, or in fact that week, Tom began to wonder what on earth he had let himself in for.

Everything in Fast-Forward

"I DIDN'T KNOW YOU WANTED TO BE A CAMERAMAN, TOM."

By the time Tom got home, his parents were already

sitting at the dinner table, with a plate of food waiting for him. The ghosts had all stopped off at Mrs. Scruffles's house to discuss the latest events, and so (after having at least one cup of tea to be polite) Tom was left to wander home on his own. He'd gone the long route home, to avoid the Spitting Kids who were stockpiling snowballs on the corner. Tom had been hit by one of these snowballs before, and they consisted of one part snow to ten parts stone and gravel, and felt far from festive on impact. It was nearly an hour after school had finished by the time he dragged himself indoors. He sank down into the chair, exhausted, and was just about to eat when this conversation had started.

In the time between his leaving the school and making it home, Mum had received a phone call from Mr. Hammond, saying that Tom had been given permission to be the *Exceedingly Haunted Homes'* tea boy. It emerged that an old timberyard they were due to be filming at had burned down, so a break in the schedule had appeared, and the crew were arriving in Thorbleton this weekend. *This weekend.* It felt as if someone had accidentally left life playing in fast-forward, events accelerating at a giddy pace. It was only this time yesterday that a guilty-looking Arthur had floated into Tom's bedroom to break the news to him of Monty's little mistake, only this morning the school had gone insane, and already the camera crews were moving in, and Tom had managed to infiltrate the proceedings under the guise of "loving TV cameras." He chewed his food, biding his time, and pretended to have not heard what was said. This was all happening way, way too fast.

"Sorry, Mum, could you repeat that?"

"I said, I didn't know that you wanted to be a cameraman. Mr. Hammond phoned us with the good news, and I honestly didn't have a clue what he was talking about."

"Oh yeah, I've wanted to be a cameraman for ages," lied Tom. He moved his food around his plate with his fork, so he wouldn't have to make eye contact.

"Since when?" asked Dad. "I thought you wanted to be in a rock band."

"Since ages ago. Since last year."

"Last year was only a few weeks ago, Tom." Dad chuckled.

"Yeah, since then. I saw a thing about it online, and thought it would be cool."

Mum and Dad made assorted noises of understanding. It appeared that complete changes in life direction were perfectly feasible, as long as you said the Internet made you do it. Tom hoped that they'd forget about this by the time his birthday came round. He was harboring dreams of getting an electric guitar for his twelfth birthday (even though it was ages away) and Tom thought he might cry if he got a clapper board and a big fuzzy sound thing on a stick instead. The things he did for Grey Arthur . . .

"Well, whatever, I'm just not entirely sure this is a

brilliant idea . . . ," she said. She sighed and shook her head. "I do wish you hadn't sprung this on us, Tom."

Tom knew where this was heading. His heart picked up pace slightly.

"I think it'll be good for Tom, get behind the scenes, see how it all works. Can't beat a bit of hands-on experience," Dad said, blatantly missing Mum's point.

Mum rolled her eyes. "Well yes, that's all very well and good, but why does it have to be on a . . ." She hesitated, pouting. Dad looked blank, forcing her to continue. "Well, I'll say it, since nobody else seems to want to. On a *ghost* show?"

There it was. The dreaded G word.

Really, Tom couldn't blame her. He hadn't even considered what his parents might think about him going along to the filming. Ever since Tom's accident, and subsequent talks to thin air and a run-in with the criminal Dr. Brown, Mum had to sit on her hands to stop her wrapping her only child up in bubble wrap and refusing to let him out of her sight. Dad was a little bit more laid-back, and even seemed to entertain the notion that Tom could really see ghosts, but Mum? Mum thought it was a phase, or something triggered by being hit by a car, and she had decided to sweep the whole incident firmly under the carpet. A bit like when you wake in the middle of the night, convinced that something is in the room with you, and squeeze your eyes shut—if I don't see it, it isn't real. A bit hard to shut your eyes and ignore your son working with a TV crew dedicated to ghost hunting. Tom lined all the peas up on his plate into one long thin line, hoping that if he looked distracted enough the conversation would just stammer to a halt. It didn't. Mum made little huffing noises, waiting for a response. Luckily for Tom, Dad spoke up again.

"Well, it's not as if big film studios are lining up to record movies in Thorbleton, sweetheart . . . ," he said, pouring gravy over his food. Dad liked his food to float in gravy, if the option was open to him. "You shouldn't really let an opportunity like this pass you by. Besides, it could work out well for us, too—Tom could take the petition down with him. It certainly won't do any harm to get some people off the telly to sign it."

Now, Tom will think it was this statement from Dad that swayed Mum over, and maybe it played a part, but a bigger part was played by the reassuring squeeze Dad gave Mum's hand underneath the table, out of sight, the way he nodded at her, eyebrows raised, and the gentle smile he wore.

"Let him do this," he said, without saying a thing. And Mum, with a small sigh, and a good-tempered roll of her eyes, agreed.

So that was that. Next Saturday, Tom was joining the team of ghost hunters, undercover, on a secret mission to prove they were nothing more than a bunch of fakes, just so his Invisible Friends could prance around on television. Deep down, Tom hoped that it would never happen. Deep down, he hoped that the Invisible Friends would grow bored of their plans, or decide it wasn't a good idea after all, or maybe just forget all about it.

It wasn't to be.

The week sped past in a mania of haunted bullying at school, of frantic research into television cameras to aid Tom's cover story, and covert rehearsals, where the Invisible Friends would meet up and sneak off to a top-secret location to practice whatever it is they were practicing. And so quickly, far quicker than Tom would have liked, before he felt even vaguely ready, Saturday struck.

One Cold, Snowy Saturday . . .

SATURDAY STARTED JUST LIKE A SCHOOL DAY. THE ALARM beeped into life, and Tom groggily reached out and turned it on to snooze. Five minutes later, the alarm went off again, and Tom reached out and turned it off again. The traditional weekday routine.

"Come on, lazy bones, out of bed." Tom's mum strode into the room and pulled open the curtains, but the effect was a little wasted, as outside the sky was dark and bloated with clouds. Tom winced anyway, and rolled over, pretending to still be asleep. "No you don't. Come on, out of bed. You have a thirsty television crew waiting for their tea boy."

That little reminder woke Tom up pretty quickly. His stomach fluttered, and he sat bolt upright.

"I thought that would get you up. Breakfast is on the table. Now, I've baked some cookies for you to take along to go with the tea, I've picked you out a black outfit to wear . . ."

"Black outfit?" asked Tom, rubbing his eyes.

"Everyone in entertainment wears black, Tom."

"Why?" he asked, swinging his legs over the side of the bed.

Mum shrugged. "No idea. It's just the way it is. Anyway, cookies, black outfit . . . Oh, and your dad has made a special pair of socks for you to wear, ones that play the *Exceedingly Haunted Homes* theme tune when you walk."

Tom looked at his mum in horror.

"But if you get out of bed now, and remember to take the petition with you, I'll *forget* to give them to you."

Tom grinned gratefully at his mum. She sat down beside him on the bed.

"Now, you're sure this is a good idea? If you've changed your mind about going, there's no harm in that. Nobody will be angry."

"Mum . . . ," sighed Tom, and she ruffled his hair.

"Okay, okay, I just wanted to make sure. I'll meet you downstairs."

She smiled one last time and left his room, shutting the door behind her. Tom peered underneath his bed, looking for Grey Arthur, but he wasn't there. A little note was, though. Written in Grey Arthur's best handwriting on a scrap of paper torn from Tom's notebook, it said: IN GARDEN WITH THE HARROWING SCREAMER. REHEARSING. Tom chuckled as he screwed the note up and threw it in the general direction of his wastepaper basket. It was going to be a very interesting day. . . .

At breakfast, Tom found it increasingly difficult to concentrate on what his mum and dad were saying, as the sounds coming out of the garden shed were truly amazing. There were howls, and moans, shrieks, and screams . . . The shadows in there were so thick that Tom was unable to see what was going on, but he had an inkling that whatever it was, it was going to be pretty impressive. Tom's parents, oblivious to it all, were going through their tea advice, reemphasizing the need to use boiling water, and Tom would nod and agree, and occasionally shake his head solemnly at the prospect of using long-life milk.

"I think you're all set, then, Tom," Dad said finally. "You'd best get a move on. You don't want to be late."

"What time will you be back?" Mum asked, as she busied herself filling Tupperware boxes with cookies, and then loading them into a rucksack. She slipped the petition in there too.

"I don't know, Mum. They don't even do the proper filming till it gets dark."

"Then why do you need to go in so early?"

"To check sound levels and sort out lighting, I guess," Tom suggested. Mum and Dad exchanged impressed looks. Maybe all his research would pay off after all.

"Okay, well it snowed again last night, so wrap up warm. If you want picking up, just give us a call. If you finish your packed lunch and get hungry later, same again, and we'll drop something up. If you—"

"You'll be fine, won't you, Tom?" asked Dad with a grin.

"I'll be fine. I'll see you both later!" By the time he shut the front door, Grey Arthur and the Harrowing Screamer were already out front waiting for him. He smiled at them, and they smiled back. Well, Tom assumed Harry was smiling—he could certainly see a lot more teeth than usual.

"Let's get this show on the road," Tom said. Grey Arthur clapped his hands together gleefully, and the Screamer hissed excitedly.

And off they marched.

The Calm Before

THERE WAS SOMETHING ABOUT WINTER THAT MADE Thorbleton School seem even more depressing than usual. In spring, summer, and autumn, colors valiantly pitted themselves against the stern concrete grey—pink blossom swirling on the breeze, green fields riddled with daisies, trees decked out in red, orange, and golden shades—but in winter everything was harsh right angles, ugly buildings colored from an uglier palette, and gnarled trees with naked branches. Not even snow managed to make the view pretty, changing into discolored mush the second it landed on school property. Tom tugged his hat farther down, past his ears, then quickly plunged his hands back deep into his pockets. They dropped the Harrowing Screamer off at Mrs. Scruffles's, where he waited (not so patiently) with the other Invisible Friends for the all clear. Grey Arthur, however, stayed at Tom's side. He was still dressed in his familiar little outfit, ghostly shirt and waistcoat, and little ghostly trousers, except today he wore ghostly socks that matched, and today his ghostly shoes seemed polished. One other detail was new—despite being seemingly unaffected by the cold, he had decided to finish the look off with a hand-knitted woolly hat, striped red and white, with a small woollen bobble on top. Whether it was a real hat that Tike had "acquired" somewhere along the way for Arthur, or whether it was simply there because Grey Arthur wanted it to be, Tom didn't know. Either way, it was the kind of hat that garden gnomes wear, and it looked a tad daft, but Arthur seemed to like it.

"Where is everyone, Tom?" he asked, scanning the empty playground.

"It's Saturday. It's like a ghost school on Saturdays. The TV crew should all be parked round the back."

"And you really want me to just hide out here and wait for you?" Grey Arthur looked at Tom hopefully. Tom nodded, and Arthur pouted.

"Yes, I do. Look, we've been through this already. As soon as I know it's safe, I'll come out here, and then you can go fetch everyone else. Until then, you're meant to stay out of sight." Tom looked at his ghostly friend and sighed. "Though you're hardly camouflaged with that . . . *thing* . . . on your head."

"Oh, come on, Tom, I don't *need* to be camouflaged. I'm a ghost. Nobody can see me. I could be out here, playing the drums, wearing pink and green and doing my best Banshee impression, and still nobody would notice me. You're such a worrier."

"I can't help it," complained Tom, shuffling his feet through the snow. "Look, I'll try not to be too long. See you soon, Arthur."

"Have fun!" chirped Grey Arthur, by way of a goodbye. Tom snorted, that snort you do when you think "*not likely*," but he smiled a good-humored smile, and with a wave he began trotting off onto the school grounds, leaving Arthur to wait (not at all patiently) for Tom's return.

The school parking lot, usually brimming with the cars of teachers, now was populated with several large trailers latched onto white vans with the *Exceedingly Haunted* logo painted on the side. It all felt a little daunting, and Tom took a couple of trial runs at walking up to the only trailer that had lights on inside, before veering off at the last minute and walking away. He did this a few times, leaving curious circles of footprints in the snow, before a mixture of wanting to get in from the cold and wanting to get this over and done with kept him on track. He just needed to stick this out long enough to make sure that it was safe for the ghosts to do whatever on earth it was they'd been rehearsing to do, and then he could go. If he was lucky, it shouldn't take long. Just keep your head down, do what's asked, and hopefully this will all be over by teatime, he thought to himself.

Tom knocked gingerly at the door of the trailer, stamping his feet while he waited, to drive some sensation back to his toes and shake loose the snow. A tall, stocky man with a mop of ginger hair (the color that girls insist on calling strawberry blond, because for whatever reason they hate the word ginger) opened the door and beamed down at Tom. Contrary to what Tom's mum had said, he wasn't wearing black—he had on a rather brash shirt—and a utility belt loaded with all kinds of accessories was wrapped around his waist.

He peered down at Tom and grinned.

"Dogsbody?" he asked.

Tom looked around, confused. "Sorry?"

"Are you the dogsbody?"

"I'm the tea boy, if that helps?" asked Tom hopefully.

"Same thing. I'm Jeff. Cameraman extraordinaire. Well, don't just stand there, come on in before you freeze to death."

"Thanks." Tom nodded.

Tom stepped up into the trailer, and Jeff closed the door behind him. It was warm inside, a portable heater valiantly glowing in the corner, and Tom smiled gratefully as the coldness that clung to his skin began to slowly fade away.

"The bald guy in the corner is Mark, the soundman," said Jeff, as he ushered Tom inside.

"Will you stop introducing me like that?" Mark asked with an exasperated grin. He wasn't wearing black either—instead a faded grey T-shirt with the logo of a band Tom had never heard of hung over tatty jeans. Tom was beginning to feel a bit self-conscious, like he'd come along in fancy dress as a ninja. He'd have to set Mum straight when he got home. Mark had a bald head, a tidy brown beard, and thick, black rectangular glasses on. Jeff leaped into the chair next to Mark, and gestured to Tom to take the beanbag. Tom obliged. It's hard to look professional, or dignified, in a beanbag. It was so large it nearly swallowed him alive. He struggled to a vague sitting position, and took a second to look around the trailer.

The place was boy heaven. It was stacked with gadgets and gizmos, cameras, monitors, computers, games, and finally a threadbare armchair and a beanbag, the only nontechnical items in the space. Tom found himself grinning.

"Okay," said Jeff, "we might as well get right on down to it. I'm a milk, three sugars man myself. Just for the record. Mark's white, no sugars . . . Andrea, the presenter, she only drinks rubbish herbal teas. And Claudia," continued Jeff, "will probably stick to mineral water, so that's one less for you to remember."

"Claudia?" asked Tom.

"Claudia Sage, the new psychic. You must have heard all the rumors by now, about why we had to get rid of the old bloke?" Tom nodded, even though he hadn't. All he knew was that there was a new psychic, not her name, and certainly not why. "So embarrassing, really. I mean, it's one thing saying you can see ghosts when you can't, 'cause who can really dispute that? But hiring a local kid and covering him with flour . . . that's just degrading. Poor lad got snagged on the rope that was meant to suspend him from the ceiling, and Maxwell is trying to convince us that we've caught a live ghost on camera when this little chap starts crying that his trousers are ripping. I don't know how he thought he could get away with it, really." Tom was struggling to disguise his shock, trying to look like he'd heard it all before. It was a good job Arthur wasn't here—he'd be in hysterics right now, and Grey Arthur's laugh was highly contagious. "We had to let him go after that. Silly, really, 'cause the viewers loved him, but once you've suspended a floured kid from the ceiling there's really no turning back, is there?"

"No, there really isn't," said Tom solemnly. His mouth was twitching, and he could feel the laughter building up inside him, tickling in his throat. *Come on,*

Tom, he thought to himself, *hold it together, hold it together . . .*

Jeff, who was revealing himself to be a veritable goldmine of gossip, continued. "So, it's all changed now. The old presenter left at the same time, gone with Maxwell over to America, where they're setting up their own company. Fair play to them, I suppose. So, new psychic, and new presenter. You probably know her from the telly— Andrea Shine?"

Tom shook his head, and Mark shrugged, picking up where Jeff left off.

"You will when you see her. Used to present the lottery show, until that whole business with her crying on live television. Poor thing. Most out of character."

Tom felt a pang of guilt, which managed to successfully quell his urge to laugh. She'd been the lady on the telly when Dr. Brown had been trying to rig the lottery, the lady that Woeful William had reduced to tears in order to buy some time. Tom had never even thought about what would have happened to her afterward. He changed the subject, not wanting to dwell on the memories that were being dredged up.

"What's Claudia like?" Tom asked. "Is she here? Can I meet her?"

Jeff and Mark grimaced and shared a look. It was subtle, a quick flutter across their mouths, a tiny glance at each other, but Tom spotted it. "She's not here yet— we don't know when she's going to turn up until pretty much the moment she appears, and then it's straight on to filming, no hanging about. You can get away with that when you're the big name, apparently. She's pretty good at her job, though. A bit serious, mind, but I guess you would be serious if you could see ghosts, wouldn't you?"

"Oh yes," agreed Tom, as sincerely as he possibly could. "It's no laughing matter." Sensing there was more to tell, he gently pushed for more details. "What's she like to work with?"

Jeff laughed softly and theatrically looked left and right to make sure they weren't being overheard. "What's she like to work with?" He leaned in and whispered conspiratorially. "Well, let's put it this way. All those rumors you've no doubt read? They're all true. She won't even turn up to work unless she knows there are five bottles of mineral water (still, not sparkling, all at room temperature), a box of Turkish delight, seven figs—don't even ask me why—and a bowl of potpourri waiting for her in her trailer. You should probably know this, because it's best not to get on the wrong side of her: We're instructed not to talk to her, not to touch her, not even to look directly at her. . . . We're meant to look at the floor when she passes, like she's royalty. I mean, come on, you're a TV psychic, you're not the queen. . . ."

Mark took over from Jeff, warming to the subject. "She arranges all her own lighting for the set so it'll catch her in the most flattering way. . . . Also, it has to be said, the woman has absolutely no sense of humor.

Last week, we got pranked. They got us good and proper. You've heard of *Just for Giggles* before?"

"The show where they play tricks on people?" asked Tom.

"That's the one," agreed Mark. "Well, they set us up. I mean, it was really well done, we were running about like headless chickens, fell for it hook, line, and sinker." Mark and Jeff chuckled at the memory. "Only afterward, from what we've been told, when they revealed to Claudia that it was all a joke, she went ballistic. Ordered the video footage of it destroyed, refused to let it air, went seriously off on one about it. We never even got to see the crew; she sent them packing, tails between their legs. She's been grumpy as anything since then. Talk about a sense of humor bypass."

Jeff shrugged nonchalantly. "It happens sometimes. People let the whole celebrity thing really go to their head. What's she like? She's a real . . ." Jeff faltered, looking at Tom and remembering how young he was. Mark interrupted, choosing the next word carefully.

"*Professional.*"

"Still," added Mark amicably. "Shouldn't complain, really. It's certainly been a lot more interesting since she came onboard."

"Really?" asked Tom.

"Oh yeah. Much," agreed Mark. "Truth be told, it all used to be something or nothing. Stood around in the dark, poor Jeff having to base whole episodes around some dust floating past the lens, me waiting for hours, carefully recording the sound of creaking pipes. With Claudia, it's a whole different kettle of fish. Real dramatic. Well, I don't want to give too much away, you'll see for yourself later on. I will say this though—if there is something spooky going on at your school, don't worry, she'll find out about it."

Which was precisely what Tom *was* worried about.

Mark looked at his watch, groaned, and got up out of the chair and gestured for Jeff to do the same. "No rest for the wicked," he said with a wink. "We'd best go set everything up. The school's out of bounds till later on, it's all wires and gear everywhere, so you'll just have to kick your heels around here for the time being. Kettle's in the corner somewhere, if you want to get brewing."

Not for the first time, and definitely not for the last time, Tom quietly hoped that the Invisible Friends appreciated this. It was going to be a long, *long* day.

Showtime

THEY SAY A WATCHED KETTLE NEVER BOILS. DURING THE long, monotonous, tea-making day, Tom discovered this wasn't true. A watched kettle does indeed boil, it just makes you very bored while you wait for it to happen. Tom wasn't sure how he imagined a day as a tea boy to be, but he'd certainly expected TV work to be a bit more glamorous. Paparazzi, perhaps, Rolls-Royces, maybe, larger than life people with American accents talking on mobile phones and barking commands . . . The reality was much more mundane. Tom made tea, poured tea, distributed tea, and then repeated the whole process again, and again, and again. Morning turned to afternoon, and afternoon to evening, and what feeble amount of sun had shone that day soon vanished into a winter night. Tom was making his (seventeenth? eighteenth?) round of tea when Jeff barged into the trailer.

"Claudia's here, and so is Andrea. We're all set to start filming. What I'm going to do is sneak you into the back of the room, so you can see how it's done. You all set?"

Suddenly Tom felt a million miles from ready. He looked anxiously at Jeff.

"Oh, don't fret," Jeff said. "There's nothing to be worried about. You just stand at the back and try to make yourself as small as possible. Just remember to be quiet, because the mikes pick up the smallest noise, and you'll be fine. Oh, and be careful where you put your feet because there's lots of wires everywhere. And remember to steer clear of Claudia, she hates distractions on set. Oh and . . ." Jeff saw the worried look on Tom's face deepen, and he stopped. "Just . . . enjoy it."

Jeff led Tom out into the dark parking lot. It was one of the clear, cold, winter nights where the air feels crisp and the sky positively shimmers with stars. Tom would usually have stopped to look up, to think how beautiful it is, how small it makes you feel, but instead he just put his head down and concentrated on following Jeff. There was a back entrance into the school, an entrance Tom had never used before because it was for teachers only, and Jeff quietly pushed it open and gestured for Tom to follow.

Normally, Thorbleton School isn't creepy. Ugly, yes, noisy, definitely, threatening, sometimes, depending on where Kate or Big Ben were lurking, but *creepy* was never a word Tom would use to describe it. Not until now. There is something a little chilling about a place you are so used to seeing crowded with people during the day, as an abandoned building at night. The sound of your feet squeaking on the floor echoes loudly, the shape of the corridors seem different in half-light, the absence of children's chatter making the area take on a whole different character. It was almost as if Tom wasn't in Thorbleton School anymore, but wandering around its more sinister alter ego. He felt goose bumps rise on his arms, and his breathing race a little faster. This is stupid, he thought to himself as they walked along. If there was anything supernatural here, I'd be able to see it. Even so, the feeling didn't fade. Tom guessed sometimes things just felt creepy for creepy's sake.

Jeff twisted and turned through the school corridors and finally stopped outside a room in the Science corridor. He stooped down and whispered to Tom.

"Here we go. When we go inside, just stay at the back by the door. It'll be quite dark in there, because we film in half-light—more atmospheric. Just stay quiet, and observe. If we need anything, then someone will get you to go run for it, but mostly you're just there to see how it's done. Okay?"

Tom nodded. Jeff grinned at him.

"Welcome to the glamorous life of showbiz, Tom."

Jeff opened the door and ushered Tom inside. He planted him by the back door and went over to stand by Mark, swiftly hoisting a large camera up onto his shoulder. He turned, giving a quick thumbs-up at Tom, and then turned to face the room. He hadn't lied when he said it would be dark in there. Two free-standing lights had been erected among the desks, but the amount of light they cast was feeble at best. Strange, stretched shadows clung to the walls, and it took a while for Tom to realize that Andrea and Claudia were already in the room.

Andrea he recognized immediately—the bouncy blonde hair, the sugary sweet smile . . . She was pacing at the back of the room, tapping a small microphone taped to her smart-looking blouse, and running through her lines. The other woman, though . . . Tom couldn't peel his eyes away from her.

You could describe Claudia Sage as intimidating, if you liked your understatements to be on the large side. She was standing, stock-still, in the corner of the class-room, seemingly lost in concentration. She towered head and shoulders above Andrea, her shocking white hair pinned tightly in an old-fashioned twist. Tom had been told that her hair had turned white as a young child, the first time she had seen a ghost. Seeing her now, if this was true, Tom wouldn't have been surprised if the ghost was more scared than she was. Everything about her was flawlessly stern, and endlessly serious. She was dressed in a black lacy blouse, which looked like something a Victorian schoolmistress would wear in one of those period dramas Mum insisted on watching at Christmas. It buttoned high on her neck, perfectly accentuating her haughty stance. She wore a long grey skirt, ankle length, and beneath it peeked out shiny black heeled boots that ended in a sharp point. She looked as if she had never slouched in her whole entire life, marching boldly into life with a back as straight as an ironing board. Large rings, set with shiny black stones, adorned long, tapered fingers. Her eyebrows arched in effortless contempt, and her lips fell naturally into an unimpressed pout. She noticed Tom staring at her, and when she turned her gaze on to him, he immediately looked at the floor, trying to make himself as invisible as possible.

"If everyone's quite ready, we should start filming," Claudia said, her voice cutting through the room.

Andrea took her place at Claudia's side. They made an odd pairing—you could not have two people look more like polar opposites (not even Mildred and Holly came close). Tom watched with bated breath as filming commenced.

"Good evening, Ghost Hunters!" chirped Andrea. "You're joining us tonight in Thorbleton School, in what promises to be one of our most unusual locations to date. Rumors are rife of paranormal activity taking place within this school—spectral entities stalking the corridors, objects moving by themselves, unexplained shadowy figures loitering in the broom cupboards . . . As usual, we're here with world-renowned psychic, and expert on the paranormal, Claudia Sage." At the mention of her name, Claudia turned on her smile. It was a faintly terrifying smile, much like the one Tom imagined the wolf to have in *Little Red Riding Hood*. Perfect, shiny white teeth, in a flawless made-for-TV smile. "We're starting off in the Science room, and will be later exploring the rest of the grounds. Claudia, what are your first impressions of this school?"

Claudia let her smile drop and sniffed the air, head tilting ever so slightly. She paused dramatically, and Andrea looked at her, wide-eyed, waiting.

"There is definitely something here," Claudia said. She twisted the rings on her fingers, brow furrowed in concentration. "It's close, too. Very close."

Andrea paled slightly and shuffled closer to Claudia, glancing anxiously around. Tom, in contrast, began to relax. There were no ghosts in the room at all. No ghosts in the school. They were all at Mrs. Scruffles's house, drinking tea and rehearsing. A slow smile spread on Tom's lips.

"Is it . . . a nice ghost?" asked Andrea nervously.

Claudia gave her a look that said she thought the question was stupid, but didn't respond. Instead she tilted her head further, listening.

"Come out, spirit," called Claudia. Well, it actually sounded more like a demand. "Reveal yourself!"

Tom wasn't expecting what happened next.

Nobody had thought to warn Ballpoint Bill.

The bleary-looking Poltergeist wandered out through the closed cupboard door, pudgy arms stretching, and then he froze, arms in midair, and stared in amazement at the camera crew before him. A half-chewed ink cartridge hung from his open mouth. Even underneath the smears of different inks that stained his body, a faint flush of shock colored his cheeks red. He began slowly stepping backward, like a cartoon character who had just walked into a bank robbery.

"Stay!" barked Claudia, turning to face Bill. Andrea nearly jumped out of her skin, and began to hyperventilate, eyes desperately scanning the room. Ballpoint Bill froze on the spot, looking alarmed. "What do you want, little spirit?"

Bill looked around, desperately hoping to see someone standing behind him. When he realized he was alone, he pointed to himself nervously. "Who? Me?"

Tom couldn't believe what he was seeing. This shouldn't be possible.

"Yes, spirit. What do you want here?" Claudia asked.

Andrea was scanning the room wildly, trying to work out where this ghost was. She pulled in her arms tight to her chest, swallowing dryly. Tom would have found it comical that anyone could be afraid of Ballpoint Bill, if he wasn't so busy being shocked that Claudia could see him.

"I, erm . . ." The multicolored Poltergeist glanced around, looking equal parts nervous and guilty. "I just came to get some pens. . . ."

Claudia turned to face Andrea, who was by now nearly beside herself with terror.

"There is the ghost of a young boy here, a ghost drawn to this location by the presence of other children," Claudia explained.

"No, not children, pens," corrected Bill.

Claudia stumbled, trying to ignore him. "By the presence of other children, by the memories of a life gone by, by . . ."

"Pencils, too. But sometimes the wood gives me mouth splinters."

Claudia rolled her eyes and glared at Ballpoint Bill to be quiet.

Bill shifted awkwardly, not enjoying the attention. "Can I go now?" he asked in a small voice.

"Yes, spirit," intoned Claudia. "Go! Go into the light!"

"What?" Bill spun around, frantically looking for a light source. He noticed the two spotlights set up by the TV crew, and frowned. "Which one? I just meant back into the cupboard. I don't like you staring at me," he complained feebly.

"He's gone," Claudia said triumphantly. Andrea clapped manically, visibly relieved.

"No, I haven't," disagreed Bill, his poor little face creased with confusion. He finally spotted Tom at the back of the room and, glad to see a familiar face, shrugged at him, as if to say, "*What was all that about?*" Tom frantically gestured for Ballpoint Bill not to look at him. Bill, now even more confused than ever, stared miserably at the floor.

"It's so draining," sighed Claudia. "Sending them on."

"But I'm still here!" shouted a frustrated Bill. When Claudia ignored him, he huffed and stormed back into the cupboard, muttering about how odd humans are. Tom stood in uneasy silence at the back of the room, still not entirely sure what had just occurred.

Claudia had seen Ballpoint Bill. There was no denying that. She'd lied about what he'd said, and she'd lied about him leaving, but there was no refuting the fact that she *had* seen him. Tom and, in fact, the whole of the Ghost World were convinced that he was the only human that could see ghosts, and yet here, clearly, was another.

"And, cut!" called Claudia. Jeff lowered the camera from his shoulder, and Mark laid down the boom. Andrea was still looking around a little anxiously, worried that more ghosts were in the room. "I need a break after that. I'll be in my trailer."

And with that, Claudia swept out of the room.

It even surprised Tom when he found himself following her.

And Then There Were Two

CLAUDIA WALKED AT SUCH A BRISK PACE THAT IT WAS impossible for Tom to keep up. Instead, he let her stride ahead, out of sight, and took the time to think.

That shouldn't have been possible.

Tom had stopped the Invisible Friends from coming along today because he wanted to make sure, because that had felt like the sensible thing to do, but deep down he'd never really believed that Claudia could be a psychic. A strange feeling coursed through Tom, and for a while he struggled to place it. It wasn't worry, it wasn't even shock . . . Tom was annoyed. It surprised him to realize it. Tom was annoyed because now he wasn't the only human who could see ghosts. No matter how he tried to nudge that feeling aside, or try to replace it with other emotions (relief that he was no longer a freak, happy that he could have someone else to compare notes with), the feeling of annoyance outweighed everything else.

Tom slowly came to the conclusion that he had grown to quite like being special. Unique. One of a kind. One of a pair just didn't have the same ring to it.

Another thought hit him, and dragged with it a hint of sadness. If Claudia could see ghosts too, then maybe he wasn't even one of a pair. Maybe there were lots of other people out there that could too. That thought actually made Tom grind to a halt and sigh.

It was one thing to be normal, another to be special, but to be in the murky middle ground of neither didn't appeal at all.

Just as Tom was getting braced to sulk about his latest revelation, more thoughts came cascading his way. Now that Mr. Hammond's plan to prove the school wasn't haunted had so spectacularly backfired, what would happen next? Some children would probably never return, too scared to set foot inside. Instead of calming the situation, *Exceedingly Haunted Homes* might actually have escalated it. Tom envisioned the long, daunting years he had left at Thorbleton, a never-ending gauntlet of ghost-inspired bullying, hysteria, and people howling "OooOoooOOOoo!" Tom had had nightmares more pleasant than that thought.

Then Tom suddenly remembered Grey Arthur. Poor Grey Arthur, sitting out on the grounds of the school, patiently waiting to perform his haunting with the other Invisible Friends. He'd have to tell Arthur to abandon his plans now. He pictured his little ghostly face dropping, his smile fading, and it made Tom feel even worse. He was in no hurry to break the bad news to him.

First he had to talk to Claudia.

Maybe there was still a way to put a few things right.

All Is Revealed

Tom knew which trailer was Claudia's. It was the one at the far end of the parking lot, the one that was twice as big and at least twice as shiny as the others. He hesitated outside it, shivering in the cold night air, contemplating the right thing to do. When no answers presented themselves, he decided just to barge on in. If he knocked and waited, he might lose his nerve and run away.

Even after listening to Jeff and Mark's stories of Claudia's demands, he was still faintly surprised by what he saw. The trailer was decorated like a fortune-teller's paradise—fat, white, waxy candles burned in various locations around the space, filling the trailer with flickering light. Lavish rugs covered the metal floor, and Tom's soggy cold feet sank down into them as he set foot inside. A large crystal ball took pride of place on a low table in the middle of the trailer, and inside offered a distorted reflection of its surroundings. On the table too, just as described, sat a silver platter boasting seven figs, nestled next to a bowl of potpourri. Ancient, leather-bound books, with gold-etched mysterious names on the spine, were scattered about the floor. Obviously Mrs. Scruffles and Claudia used the same library.

She was standing at the far end of the trailer, arms crossed, glaring at Tom.

"You're not meant to be in here. I specifically said no

visitors. Go and wait outside—I'll sign an autograph for you later." She turned her back on him and resumed reading her book, shaking her head with each new word that she read. After a while she paused and raised her head from the page slightly, still not bothering to face him. "You're still here."

"My name's Tom Golden. I need to talk to you," Tom said, wringing his hands nervously.

"I don't recall asking your name. Send me a message through the website like everyone else does."

"*You can see ghosts.*" Tom didn't know that was what he was going to say until he'd already said it. Claudia turned to face Tom. He didn't think it was possible for anybody to look more irritated than she did at that second.

"I'm a psychic. That's what we do. Now, if you're quite done, I'm meant to be relaxing, which isn't exactly easy to do with an intruder in my trailer."

"Did you get hit by a car?" Tom asked. His voice was wavering slightly as he spoke, but he hoped she didn't notice.

"Do I look like I was hit by a car?" she asked, one eyebrow arched.

"No . . . ," agreed Tom. "But you might have gotten better. I was hit by a car once, and you wouldn't really know to look at me." He was babbling, he knew it, and yet somehow couldn't stop.

"That's fascinating. Can't you go and annoy someone else with your life story?" She tapped her pointy shoe impatiently on the floor. Thanks to the thick rugs, it made a soft *thump* rather than an annoyed clicking. The effect was the same though.

"How long have you been able to see ghosts?" Tom asked.

Claudia rolled her eyes. "Since always. It's a gift. Why are you still here?"

"Because you can't say this place is haunted. You mustn't!" Tom blurted. Claudia changed from looking annoyed to outraged. Tom grimaced. Maybe he should have spent a little while longer working up to saying that. She wasn't giving him much opportunity though. . . .

"How *dare* you come in here and start giving me orders? Who do you think you are?" She stormed forward, ushering Tom toward the door. "Out. *Now!*" she barked. Tom stumbled back a few steps, searching for the right thing to say to soothe Claudia's temper. In the face of such an imposing woman, though, his mind just went blank. Desperately, he reached out to grab hold of her arm, to stop her opening the door to throw him out.

Tom's hand passed straight through.

For a second, he didn't understand. Tom stared dumbly at his empty hand, and then back at Claudia. Claudia looked back at him, her expression unreadable. She seemed to be waiting, to see how Tom would react. Tom looked at her, then at his hand, then back at her again, slow wheels turning.

"You're a ghost!" he gasped, as everything finally fell into place. All the clues had been there all along: the fact that she wouldn't let anyone light her from behind; the fact that people had to avoid eye contact with her just in case they caught a glimpse of her in a see-through moment; the fact that Jeff, Mark, and everyone else were ordered to never touch her; the fact that she would just turn up out of the blue; the fact that she could actually see Ballpoint Bill. Tom felt like an idiot for not working it out sooner. Claudia sighed and stepped back from Tom, retreating to the far end of the trailer once more.

"Tom Golden . . . Tom Golden . . . ," she said, mulling over his name. "I knew I'd heard that somewhere before. He-Who-Can-See-Ghosts." She stared at him, eyes scanning him from head to toe. Tom shifted awkwardly, not enjoying the scrutiny. He was waiting for her to be impressed, but that moment never came. Claudia shrugged, a small gesture, the tiniest rise and fall of her shoulders. "I always thought you'd be taller."

"I haven't finished growing yet," replied Tom defensively.

She peered down at him with an amused smile. "If you say so . . ." Claudia Sage closed the book that she had been reading through and leaned back against the wall of her trailer. If she was at all put out at having her secret ghostly identity discovered, it didn't show. "If you could hurry up and say whatever it is you came here to say, I'd be grateful. I'm a busy woman."

"So, you're a Faintly Real, right?" Tom asked. "Am I right?"

"If you're going to get technical, I'm part Faintly Real, part Thesper. First of my kind, as far as I know."

"Like a hybrid," said Tom, trying to show he understood. Claudia looked at him blankly. "You know, like a tigon. Or a liger? Or wolphin?"

"I'm sure this is a fascinating little tangent you're trying to take me down, but can you just skip to the end? I've got a lot on my mind at the moment, and frankly I don't have the time for your babbling. What is it that was so important you had to burst in here?"

Feeling a little chastised, Tom got back on track. "You can't say that my school is haunted."

"Oh yes, you mentioned that before. Why ever not? It blatantly is. There's that tubby little pen-obsessed Poltergeist, a Snorgle in the toilets, not to mention some odd little grey ghost in a ridiculous hat sloping around the school grounds making snowmen."

"Snowghosts," corrected Tom. "And his name is Arthur."

Claudia dismissed his interruption with a wave of her ring-clad hand.

"You can't blame me for pointing out the obvious. Your school is haunted."

"That's not the point! You have to pretend it isn't."

Claudia picked up a fig and began lazily taking it to pieces. "There'd better be a very convincing argument lurking around the corner, Tom. This is show business. I can't just change everything on the whim of one short little human."

Appealing to someone's better nature is difficult when you aren't even sure they have one. Under Claudia's rather intimidating gaze, Tom set about pleading his case.

He mentioned the ghost graffiti that appeared overnight, the children too terrified to set foot inside, the supernatural twist that bullying had taken on. He talked of the Invisible Friends' hopes of appearing on the telly, unnoticed, the rehearsals they had done. Once he started, he just couldn't stop. New concerns formed as rapidly as he could speak them. Concerns of ghost-seeking strangers descending on the school, worries that Montague's teacher might get the sack if things really went wrong since it was her phone call that had started all this in the first place, fears that the Invisible Friends might have to abandon their humans if everyone started becoming hyperaware of every unusual event that took place. Claudia listened, but her expression gave nothing away. She chewed her figs, and when they ran out, began chewing her way through the potpourri. Tom carried on talking, nerves getting the better of him, and it all churned into one big sentence, no pauses for breath, no full stops, no commas, just a single long torrent of speech. Finally, he ground to a halt, having said everything on his mind, and a few more things he plucked out of thin air. His mouth was dry.

"You actually want me to go back in there and get them to throw away everything we've just filmed and start again, don't you?" she said, glaring at Tom. "I'd have to pretend that I made a mistake, that the school isn't haunted after all, which would make me look a fool. And I hate looking like a fool."

Tom nodded. "I know."

"It's a lot to ask."

"I know. It's just that after defeating the Collector, the last thing we need is another disaster."

Claudia's expression changed when he said that. It was a minuscule alteration, a slight lifting of the eyebrows, a small twitch of the lips, but something had definitely changed.

"You owe me, Tom Golden."

"I know." Tom stopped, realizing what she'd just said. "Wait, was that a yes?"

"Go fetch your Invisible Friends. If we're going to film the most boring episode in the history of *Exceedingly Haunted Homes*, I might as well have some tap-dancing ghosts in the background." She returned to her book, picking up where she had left off. "It will entertain me, if no one else."

"Thank you!" yelled Tom. He was already halfway out of the door, grinning wildly. "Thank you!" He skidded on the snow, nearly falling flat, but even that didn't manage to slow him down.

It was time to find Grey Arthur.

The Inner Thesper

IT DIDN'T TAKE TOM LONG TO FIND GREY ARTHUR. All he needed to do was follow the trail of snowghosts that were dotted across the field. It did, however, take much longer to explain everything that had taken place. Tom spoke at such a hurtling pace that Grey Arthur struggled to keep up.

". . . only, she spotted Ballpoint Bill! And Bill was all shocked, and didn't know what to do, and neither did I, because she isn't supposed to be able to see ghosts, except obviously she can, and she was all, like, go into the light, and Bill didn't have a clue what she was talking about, and then she stopped the filming, so I followed her out, and I confronted her."

Grey Arthur shook his head, struggling to take it all in. "Another human that can see ghosts? That's huge news, Tom," he breathed. Tom grinned triumphantly at him, dying to break the news.

"That's the thing, Arthur . . ." Tom paused to increase the suspense. "Turns out, *she's not a human*." He waited for Grey Arthur to realize what that meant. His face creased in confusion briefly, and then a flash of fear took its place.

"She's a . . . *robot*?"

It took another five minutes to persuade Grey Arthur that Claudia wasn't a robot at all, but a Faintly Real Thesper. Or a Thesperly Faintly Real. Even then, Arthur didn't seem convinced.

"And you're sure she's a ghost?"

"One hundred percent. My hand passed straight through her, Arthur. Besides, she admitted it." Grey Arthur shook his head, still finding it all very hard to understand. Tom smiled at him. "Anyway, no time to stay and chatter. Go fetch the others and do whatever it is you're planning to do."

"What about you? Aren't you sticking around to watch?"

Tom shook his head. "I'm exhausted, Arthur. And I've seen enough TV cameras to last me a lifetime. I'll see it how it's meant to be seen, on the telly. Besides, I have to make a very important phone call to Pete and make sure he tells Sayid that the school isn't haunted."

Grey Arthur grinned at Tom, and as quick as that he was off and running out of the gate toward Mrs. Scruffles's house. Tom stretched tiredly and began the slow walk home, happy to finally be able to get out of black clothes, happy to be home in the warm where people made him tea, and not the other way round, happy to be out of the way of Claudia's glare, and happy that despite so many things going wrong, everything had turned out right in the end.

Skip Foward Six Days . . .

"COME ON!" CRIED TIKE. "YOU HAVE TO DO SOMETHING."

They were sitting in a huddle in the bedroom of number eleven, Aubergine Road, all waiting for *The Decision* to be made. Tike was in the throes of some very profound fidgeting. He'd do everything from finger tapping, hair ruffling, through to making his knuckles create exceedingly disturbing clicking/crunching noises that set Tom's teeth on edge. Tike, it had to be said, wasn't great at being patient. Montague was downstairs, apparently trying to find a newspaper, although Tom suspected it was as much to do with the need to escape Tike's hyperactivity as it was to do with research. Mildred sat, cross-legged, mismatched eyes fixed on Tom, head slightly tilted, though her perfect fringe stayed against her forehead, ignoring all the laws of physics. Grey Arthur tried to busy himself by going through all the *Mr. Space Pirate* comics and sorting out the ones he had read from the ones he hadn't. The Harrowing Screamer, who was crouched in the dim recesses of Tom's cupboard, let out a motivational wail, which was somewhat muffled by all the coats and sweaters that were crowding him.

"Just . . . hang on!" mumbled Tom, biting his lip. It would be much easier to think if he didn't have everyone hassling him. As distractions go, ghosts rank fairly highly—at least on a par with elephants and explosions . . . "I'm trying to work it out!"

"It's all right," Grey Arthur said in his very best "I'm trying not to rush you" voice. He casually slung another comic on the "Read" pile, and picked up a new one to look through. "Take as long as you need."

"Bah, don't say that! We'll be here all blimmin' night. Ignore him, Tom, and get a move on. This is important." Tike was literally rocking back and forth now, and every time Tom made the mistake of making eye contact with him he would burst out in a flurry of encouraging hand gestures. Tom stared at the ceiling.

"It is getting quite late, Thomas," agreed Mildred. "Between the moment you began contemplating this issue and now, the sun has set. Perhaps a little haste would be advisable."

"That's putting it mildly . . . ," Tike muttered.

Tom sighed, defeated. "Fine! I'll buy it. There you go. Marylebone Station. Bought. Okay? Happy?"

It had been a fairly sedate week for the Invisible Friends and Tom—well, by ghostly standards, at any rate. Tom's phone call to Pete, telling him how the *Exceedingly Haunted Homes* filming had been the most boring, nonhaunted affair in the universe, had filtered through to Sayid, and then to his many sisters, and by extension, everyone else within a twenty-mile radius. Come Monday, the whole haunted school madness had all but vanished, and the conventional school drama of homework, and playground fights, stolen lunches, and passing notes had fallen back into place. Mrs. Wilson put the moving cup saga down to nothing more supernatural than the extreme cold making her brain go a bit funny, and that was that. Just one more strange footnote in Thorbleton School's checkered past. The episode of *Exceedingly Haunted Homes* wasn't due to air for a while yet, and while Tom sometimes twitched to find out what the Invisible Friends had done with their five minutes of fame, mostly he was content to wait. Friday rolled around, and as a nice way to end the week, it was decided that everyone should meet round Tom's and play games.

Playing Monopoly with a bunch of ghosts isn't the easiest of activities. The Harrowing Screamer tended to shred anything paper he touched, Mildred insisted on reading the rules at least three times before making a decision, Tike preferred to steal money rather than earn it, Arthur lacked the mean streak necessary to demand rent, and Montague had taken on the role of a property developer a little too seriously and was currently dressed in a pinstriped suit, rummaging around in the kitchen to try and find a copy of the *Financial Times*. Still, for all its faults, Monopoly was by far the most successful game they had played together. Snap is awfully difficult to judge when ghostly hands can simply pass through each other, making every game a draw. Hide-and-Seek turned out to be equally problematic, as the Invisible Friends could hide in very hard to locate places, like *inside the walls*, and Wink Murder had to be halted after Montague once took forty-five minutes to act out his death scene.

So, Monopoly it was.

Tike snatched the dice away from Tom, and (after much mystical shaking of the dice, blowing on the dice, jiggling of the dice, and talking to the dice) he threw them across the board. Two fat sixes rolled to the surface, and Tike leaped to his feet with a roar, punched the air, and did his victory dance (this basically involved wagging his clenched fists back and forth next to his ears while his feet jiggled on the spot). Poltergeists, while being terrible losers, were even worse winners. "Tike! Champion of the Dice! Ruler of the Monopoly! You can keep your Marley . . . boney . . . Station, I'm going—"

"Straight to jail," interrupted Mildred, deadpan. Tike's face crumbled, his victory dance halted mid-shake.

"What? No way. You got it wrong. You missed a square out. I rolled . . . thirteen . . ."

"You're such a liar!" Grey Arthur laughed. "You can't roll thirteen."

"Well, yeah, obviously you can, because I did, so . . . Oi, Mildred, what d'you think you're doing?"

"Putting your little metal boot in the jail section, in accordance with the rules." Mildred pushed Tike's token to the far corner of the board, as the little Poltergeist sunk to the floor, looking thoroughly miserable. Tom was trying very hard not to laugh at Tike's misfortune, but following on from the Victory Dance, it was difficult to resist smirking.

"*We have a problem.*"

Nobody had even noticed Montague's entrance into the room. He hovered by the doorway, waiting for everyone's full attention.

He didn't get it.

"Too right we have a problem!" agreed Tom. "Tike's cheating."

"I'm not cheating."

"You just moved yourself out of jail. You can't do that."

"I can."

"You can't!"

"Yeah, I can. I'm a ghost, remember? I just floated through the walls, and now I'm outside."

"You're not a ghost in Monopoly. You're a . . . boot."

"A *ghostly* boot."

"Tike, get back in jail."

"You're just jealous 'cause you can't walk through walls," muttered Tike, as he pushed his boot back into place.

"I am not."

"Yeah you are, and 'cause we won't tell you what we did for the telly. You'll just have to wait and see. Honestly, you humans, no patience."

"That's rich coming from you!" Tom chuckled.

"I said, we have a problem," Montague repeated, louder than before.

"What's the matter, Monty?" asked Arthur, without turning to face him. "Couldn't you find the newspaper? Mildred, it's your go. Roll the dice."

Monty nearly howled with frustration. "It's nothing to do with that. Will someone *please* listen to what I'm trying to say?"

"We are listening. Carry on, we can hear you," replied Tom, a little distracted. "Old Kent Road, Mildred. Do you want to buy it?"

Before Mildred could read the rules again and come up with a response, the sound of trumpets playing blared like a melodic and dramatic foghorn, accompanied by flashing lights and blue smoke. Tom coughed, not because it hurt his lungs, but because it just seemed that blue smoke should make you cough. Tike took the opportunity of a smoke screen to steal everyone's money, down to the very last note. The Harrowing Screamer threw back his head and howled, his voice jarring awfully with the brass noise.

And as soon as that, it was over. The music faded, the lights dimmed, and only faint wisps of blue hung in the air, resisting Tom's best attempts to bat them away with his school sweater sleeve.

"*Now that I have your attention . . .* ," bellowed Montague.

"Was that necessary?" Tom asked. "I thought we agreed you weren't going to do that anymore."

"Trust me, Tom. It was necessary." He drew himself up to full height, took a deep breath, and put on his very best I-Am-a-Bearer-of-Bad-Tidings face. He was rather proud of that face—it had just the right mix of earnest worry and dramatic tension. He'd won rave reviews before, on that expression alone. It seemed to be working, too. The Monopoly game was forgotten, and everyone was staring at Monty, waiting to hear what he had to say. "Tom, you need to go downstairs. Now."

Out of the Blue

Tom was halfway down the stairs, with Grey Arthur in pursuit, when Dad started coming up the stairs to greet him.

"That's good timing, Tom. I was just coming to get you. Didn't you hear the doorbell?" Dad had a strange expression on his face, a cross between serious and bewildered. It wasn't a good expression. It made Tom feel a little anxious. "You have a visitor."

Tom paused, and looked quizzically at his dad.

"I do?"

"You do."

Tom waited for more details, and when none were forthcoming, he laughed nervously.

"Do I get a clue?" he asked.

"Nope. Just hurry on down and say hello."

It was unusual for Dad to be this vague, and Tom was starting to feel suspicious. *Please don't let it be another psychiatrist, please don't let it be another psychiatrist, please don't let it be . . .*

Grey Arthur picked up on Tom's anxiety, and he darted past Tom's dad to get a quick peek. There was a long pause before Grey Arthur reemerged, looking a little shocked. "You're not going to believe this, Tom. . . ."

Tom, not entirely reassured, followed his dad into the kitchen.

Mum was standing by the sink, frantically trying to smooth out her postwork hair with one hand, and with the other desperately cleaning the kitchen worktop. A washing-up towel had been hastily thrown over the dirty bowls and plates stacked by the sink, as if the floral patterning would somehow camouflage them from sight, and the room smelled almost unbearably of air freshener. The Good China (the set Mum had inherited from her great-grandma) was set out on the table, and the kettle was boiling. Dad shuffled in the door, sucking in his belly, and cleared this morning's newspapers off the table.

Claudia Sage stood, a picture of haughtiness, in the middle of the Golden kitchen. She was so tall that her white hair, swept up into the most perfect of French twists, nearly reached the ceiling (and its associated cobwebs and kitchen grime, and all the things you don't really notice until a famous person stands in your house). She peered at her surroundings, obviously ill at ease in such a domestic setting, and put on her famous made-for-television smile. It was a smile that looked like it had been painted on, and then hair-sprayed in place. "What a charming little place you have here, Mrs. Golden. Very quaint." She leaned over by the window, pushing the curtain aside to study the garden beyond. "Of course, you do know that your shed is haunted, don't you?"

"Hahaha!" cried Tom, with possibly the most forced laugh in the history of the universe. "Haha! Psychic humor! That's very funny." Tom's mum and dad looked as if they really didn't get the joke. Claudia turned to face Tom, and her television smile broadened.

"I'll just . . . erm . . . go send everyone home, Tom," said Arthur, sensing that now was probably not the best time to stick at Tom's side. "If you need me, I'll be at Mrs. Scruffles', playing with the cats." He waved good-bye to Claudia, who acknowledged him with a brief nod of her immaculately groomed head, and then he dashed out of the house.

"Thomas! So good of you to join us." Claudia pulled out a chair from the table and sat down. "Do take a seat."

Tom found himself instantly obeying, even though it was his house. Dad sat down as well. Claudia just had that kind of effect on people. Mum had (with an exaggerated sigh) given up on scrubbing the work surfaces clean, dramatically throwing the sponge into the sink in surrender, and was busy making tea instead. She glared over at Tom, and he shrugged apologetically. Mum may well have wanted more warning about a celebrity coming over to their house, but Tom was just as surprised as she was.

"I was just in the area, and I thought I'd call over and see how my favorite tea boy was doing." As she spoke, she brushed crumbs from the tabletop with a well-manicured hand. Dad blushed slightly. Mum cringed. Tom's mind whirred, trying to make sense of what was going on.

"Erm. I'm fine, thanks. Well, it's a bit too cold at school at the moment, I thought my fingers might drop off in History today, and, actually, it's quite funny really, Mr. Hammond tried—"

"That's nice," she interrupted. "Always good to catch up." Tom took the hint and abandoned his story. So much for pleasantries. He decided instead to just sit back and see where all this was heading.

"I was just about to tell your parents how you have a glittering show business career ahead of you."

Tom nodded, playing along. "Oh yes?"

"Oh yes." She smiled graciously, perfect white teeth appearing from behind perfect red lips. "*The world is crying out for another good psychic.*"

Time froze, and everything stopped, suspended in that moment, caught in a painful tableau. Tom winced, everything in his body clenched, from teeth to toes. He looked at his mother's expression, her mouth gaping open, her eyebrows crashing together, raised so high that they seemed to disappear into her fuzzy postwork hair, and then at Dad, who was grimacing, and turning to see how Mum was taking it. In front of Tom hovered Claudia's perfect smile, full of perfect teeth, oblivious to the carnage her statement had caused.

"You mean cameraman," corrected Tom pointedly.

"I'm pretty sure I don't."

"*I'm pretty sure you do.*" He was nodding now, his head bobbing up and down, his eyes big. Hoping that

Claudia would catch on. She laughed dismissively, swatting the notion away with a flick of her hand, the same way you'd swat a mosquito.

"Oh no, Tom, you'd be a terrible cameraman. Far too weak. You wouldn't even be able to lift the camera, and that's not even to mention your height. Far too short, unless you filmed everything at hip height, which is far from a flattering angle."

There's never been an awkward silence quite like it. Claudia finally realized that Tom had been frantically trying to stop her, but the revelation came too late. It couldn't be unsaid. Dad watched Mum anxiously, Mum stared at Claudia, openmouthed, Claudia looked at Tom, and Tom kept his eyes fixed on the table, taking slow, measured breaths, feeling his cheeks burning red-hot.

Claudia sensed now would be a good time to make an exit. She got up, straightened out her skirt, and turned her smile back on for the benefit of Tom's parents.

"It's been a pleasure to meet you both. Thank you for your hospitality. Sorry I can't stay long enough for tea, but I really have to go now." Tom's parents were still sunk in the sticky pit of not knowing what to say, so they just nodded dumbly. "I was wondering if I could just borrow Tom for a while? I got a little lost on my way here and was hoping he could walk me back to the school."

Mum didn't disagree, so Tom took that as a yes, and slowly dragged himself to his feet. It's funny how bad atmospheres make you feel at least nineteen stone heavier, and it was such a struggle, shuffling out of the room, walking to the door, escorting Claudia outside. She called good-bye to Tom's parents one more time, complimented them on their begonias, and insisted, "It was lovely to meet you—we must do it again sometime." Tom dearly hoped that wouldn't happen. It was like having a tornado hit town, throw caravans around, tear roofs off houses, chuck trees as if they were javelins, spin cattle about like balls in a bingo machine, and then have it thank you for letting it stay, signing the guest book on the way out.

"I won't be too long," Tom called, as he wrapped himself up inside his warm winter coat and tugged his woolly hat down past his ears. He waited for a response, and when there was none, he gently pulled the door shut after him.

Cut to the Chase

"WELL, THAT WAS AWKWARD," SAID CLAUDIA AS SHE strode down the road. Tom struggled to keep pace, avoid slipping on the ice, and glare at her at the same time. "How was I to know you hadn't told your parents?"

"By, oh, I don't know, *asking*?" he growled. It's amazing

how an average day can so quickly descend into a full-blown horrid one. Tom stomped angrily as he walked, and the ice made his feet shoot in opposite directions. He didn't quite fall, but had to do some weird dance-like balancing to stay upright, which didn't improve his grumpiness at all.

"It just seemed obvious to me that they would know. It's hardly the easiest thing to hide. Why haven't you told them?"

"Well, it's complicated," he replied. Claudia stopped walking and turned to face Tom.

"How is it complicated? *'Mum, Dad, I can see ghosts.'* There you go. What's so complex in that?"

Tom shook his head. "It's a long story."

"I once spent a year living with a whole company of Thespers. You have no idea how long stories can get. Tell me."

"Fine. If you must know, Mum and Dad overheard me talking to Grey Arthur once, and they called in a psychiatrist called Dr. Brown, because they thought I was a bit loopy."

"That's not that long a story."

"And then he kidnapped me."

"Right . . ."

"But I got rescued."

"Evidently." She waited for more details to follow, but none did. "As long stories go, it's still pretty short. So what, now you just pretend you can't see ghosts?"

"Yeah . . . I suppose."

"And they have no idea?"

"No. Well . . . a little?"

"Goodness me, getting sense out of you is like getting blood out of a stone. Either they know or they don't know. It can't go both ways."

"Well . . . Dad knows. And I think he mostly believes me, with a smidge of still not sure. Mum . . . Mum's not that happy about it. I think she just wants a normal son who will be a fireman or a policeman or sell cars or something, and not talk to things nobody else can see. She certainly doesn't want me to grow up to be a flipping TV psychic. Me and Mum, we just don't really talk about it. Dad reckons she hopes it's just One of Those Phases. I'll grow out of it and be all ordinary."

"*Ordinary.*" Claudia repeated the word with obvious disdain. "No parent should ever wish their child to be ordinary. It stunts growth." She looked down at Tom and put on her famous smile. "If you want, I could have a word with her. Try to explain just how different you are. Lay down a few home-truths. We ghosts aren't really meant to interfere, but I suppose this does constitute an unusual situation."

"No. That's quite all right. I think you've said plenty already."

Claudia's smile vanished, and she shrugged. "Suit yourself. I think I'd be rather good at it, though, should you change your mind. I've been watching a lot of TV talk shows. Research. I've been thinking of branching out." She held her pale, delicate hand in front of Tom's face, and gestured in a show biz fashion. "*Claudia Sage Presents Sage Advice.* This week's topic: 'My Parents Don't Know I Can See Ghosts Because I'm Too Cowardly To Tell Them.' What do you think?"

"I think you didn't just come here to find ways to shock my parents, did you?"

"No. You're right. I didn't. Although it was an entertaining little diversion." Claudia pulled herself to her full height, looking every inch the media star. "I need your advice. You and your funny little team of helpful ghosts."

"Invisible Friends."

"Whatever." She looked up and down the road. "Is there anywhere we can talk? Standing on a street corner and talking is so . . . vulgar. Besides, your lips are turning blue, and it's terribly off-putting. I'm assuming that your house is now out of bounds."

"Got that right." Tom sighed deeply and twitched his nose, just to make sure he could still feel it. He could. Just about. "Come on, follow me."

They walked along for a little while in contemplative silence. Tom was going to have to wade through some rather heavy-duty conversations when he got home, and he wasn't looking forward to it. Perhaps even more worryingly, though, he still had no idea why Claudia had decided to turn up in his house, unannounced. What kind of advice could he give her? His specialist subjects were the band Cold Fish,

James Carefree films, books on wizards, half the Morse code (he'd learned up to M, or "dash dash" at Cubs, and then gave up), and *Mr. Space Pirate* comics, and somehow, just somehow, he very much doubted that Claudia had any interest in these things at all. Perhaps he was just there to make up the numbers. Or perhaps she had just decided this was Make a Child Miserable Week.

They stopped outside Mrs. Scruffles's house, and Tom gestured toward the rusty gate.

"After you."

Claudia stared at the mass of weeds, thorns, and debris in horror.

"You expect me to go in there?"

"Erm . . . If you want our help, then yeah."

She rolled her eyes theatrically. "Thank goodness I'm not Real. I think I'd be torn to ribbons before I reached the other end. Not to mention grimy as an urchin."

Despite not being Real, she still hoisted her ghostly skirt above her ghostly knees, and took small, dainty, disgusted steps, like a ballet dancer unleashed in a field full of cow manure.

Tom, who as a human *did* have to navigate through the scratchy bushes, discarded rubbish and sludgy, muddy snow to get to the door, bit his tongue and said nothing. Trust Arthur to make an exit and leave him to have to make small talk with the most stuffy and irritating Faintly Real in existence.

To the Crux of the Matter

"She said *what*?" spluttered Grey Arthur.

Arthur stared at Tom, ghostly mouth wide open. He was holding Agatha Tibbles in his dusty, grey arms, and Carrot Cake was perched on the back of his chair, leaving Arthur very much steeped in cat. It has to be said, it's hard to look serious when steeped in cat. He shook his head, as if he couldn't believe what his lopsided ears were hearing. Tom nodded wearily.

Mrs. Scruffles, ever the hostess, had already laid the table with a feast of cakes and nibbles, and she set her new teapot (huge, white, with red polka dots) down in the middle of it all. Claudia poured herself a cup, completely unfazed by Tom's moody expression. Arthur kept looking at Claudia, who was polishing a teaspoon with her sleeve and admiring her reflection in it, then back at the thoroughly miserable Tom, then back at Claudia again. Tom began, rather sullenly, adding excessive amounts of sugar cubes to his tea. Perhaps if all his teeth fell out, then Mum and Dad would be so distracted they'd forget all about ghosts and concentrate on dentists instead.

Bert, a fat, white cat with ginger ears, a cat who was, with the best will in the world, a rather dim creature, approached Claudia's feet, purring loudly. He tipped his weight and waggled his bum, ready to leap onto

Claudia's lap, but she took one look at him and Bert rather wisely decided that the floor was as good a place as any to sit. His purring abruptly stopped. Tom didn't blame him. He realized Arthur was still waiting for a response, and so he sipped his tea (so sweet it made his eye twitch) and sighed, for good measure.

"She told Mum and Dad that I had a great future ahead of me as a TV psychic."

Arthur's hands shot to his face in a cross between amusement and horror. "Oh no, Tom. What did they say?"

"That's the worst part. Nothing. They didn't say a word." Tom did his best impression of Claudia's clipped tones. "*Oh yes, Mr. and Mrs. Golden, your son is a crazed ghost-watching madman, just like you always feared. Oh, I do like your curtains!*"

"I sound *nothing* like that!" snorted Claudia. "Besides, I did you a favor. Now you don't have to pretend anymore."

"Oh yeah. Thanks a bunch."

"Come on, Tom, there's no need to be like that." Mrs. Scruffles pushed a French fancy his way. "It sounds like it was a genuine mistake. Besides, it probably didn't tell them anything they didn't already know, or at least suspect."

"That's not the point," Tom muttered. "We were quite happy pretending everything was normal. Now that it's all pushed out in the open, we might actually have to talk about it."

"Oh, stop feeling sorry for yourself," Claudia said as she stirred her tea. She held the spoon in a very odd way, her little finger aloft in the air like an antenna. "It's hardly going to matter in a few days anyway."

"Why? What's happening in a few days?" asked Arthur.

Claudia turned to face Mrs. Scruffles. "Do you have anywhere I can play this?" she asked, pulling a DVD from out of her bag.

Tom laughed. "Mrs. Scruffles doesn't have a TV, let alone a—"

"Third cupboard on the right, above the sink," replied Mrs. Scruffles. Claudia got up, and after weaving her way through the moving carpet of cats, pulled open the cupboard door. Sure enough, sharing the space with a jar of pickled eggs, six tins of cocoa powder, and a selection of different floral cake cases, was a television and a DVD player. Tom shook his head in disbelief.

"You do know it's a bit weird to keep your TV in a cupboard above the sink, don't you?" he asked, as tactfully as possible.

Mrs. Scruffles smiled. "It may be weird, but when I kept it in the lounge . . . Well, let's just say Puddles earned his name. And let me tell you, the smell of . . . *that* . . . gently heating on a warm television . . . It's certainly not like a bowl of potpourri. So, it stays in the cupboard now, safely out of harm's way. Besides, sometimes I like to watch gardening shows while I bake."

"If you've quite finished talking?" snapped Claudia, from by the television. Tom and Mrs. Scruffles both pulled the "Whoops, I've been told off" face at each other, and then sat up straight and looked as obedient and attentive as possible. Grey Arthur was busy building a mini igloo out of sugar cubes, and only stopped when Claudia coughed. Twice. Loudly. "We'd had reports of a haunting taking place in an old abandoned monastery, up near Liverpool. The locals had apparently been catching sight of several different ghosts in the area: a weeping woman, a large black dog, a monk whose face was concealed . . . same old, same old, all the traditional favorites. Honestly, you do have to wish people would be a bit more original when dreaming up these ghost stories. Anyway, we were sent to investigate." She paused, maybe for dramatic effect, maybe to make sure she had everyone's attention (Grey Arthur's hand had begun creeping back toward the sugar igloo, but, realizing he had been spotted, he gave up). "This is what happened."

She pressed play and stepped back to join Tom, Grey Arthur, and Mrs. Scruffles.

Claudia stood in the center of the screen, adjusting her hair and straightening her blouse. Andrea, ever-smiling, stood at her side. They appeared to be in an abbey, a huge, gloomy space, draped with shadows and gothic shapes carved into stone. The filming was done in the dark, and everything the camera captured had an eerie green tint to it. Claudia tapped a small microphone on her chest and coughed impatiently.

"Testing . . . testing . . . I swear, Mark, if you mess up the sound again and have me sounding like a deranged Dalek on this take I'll . . . Oh, are we filming? We are?" Claudia's trademark smile fell effortlessly into place, and Andrea began her speech.

"Greetings from Bournedean Monastery, a location that has recently become a hotbed of paranormal activity. Locals have described several apparitions manifesting here, from the weeping lady said to be mourning the loss of her soldier husband, to a canine apparition said to herald bad news, to finally, the mysterious monk figure widely believed to haunt these corridors. As ever, we have Claudia Sage, world-famous psychic, here with us tonight."

Claudia nodded, as if she approved of her description, and took over the introduction. The camera zoomed in close, so just her stern face filled the screen. "*Exceedingly Haunted Homes* will be filming here throughout the night, armed with the latest supernatural-detecting equipment, hoping to capture a ghost on camera."

"Heh . . ." Grey Arthur chuckled. "That's funny. Because, you're a ghost."

"I know why it's funny," replied Claudia. "Keep watching."

The Claudia on the television dropped her smile like you'd drop a hot coal, and glared off camera. Her eyebrows rose quizzically, then quickly twisted into a frown. "Where's Andrea gone? Andrea? Hello? . . . HELLO? If you're going to run off in the middle of filming, you could at least have the courtesy to let me know." She stared haughtily to the right and began marching in that direction, Jeff the cameraman and soundman Mark obediently following, always keeping her in shot—they zoomed out from her face and managed to capture the full length and breadth of her annoyance as she stormed away. Her hands were on her hips now, and she strode forward purposefully through the murkiness of the abbey. "Hello? Will someone please speak to me? Can we stop filming yet? Don't you dare ignore me. Hello? Where is that useless presenter hiding?"

That's when it all went weird. Weird with a capital W, underlined a few times for good measure. That "useless presenter" was hiding on the floor underneath her "useless presenter's" coat. Claudia was very lucky that she didn't accidentally walk through it while being filmed, stopping just short in the nick of time.

"What on earth are you playing at?" she demanded.

"Hiding," came the muffled response.

"I can see that. Why?"

The answer to that question came striding into shot, seven feet tall, decked in tarnished armor. A sword was held in his gauntlet-clad hands, a long sword, chipped and vicious-looking, a sword that was being swung through the air as if it weighed nothing at all. The visor on the suit of armor was down, obscuring the face, and he stalked slowly toward Claudia, the sword sweeping ahead of him, his feet never actually touching the ground, always hovering a good couple of centimeters above it. The scene suddenly spun down to the floor, and then up to the ceiling, as both Mark and Jeff, bound together by cables, decided to flee in opposite directions, before the connecting wires jerked them to a halt. The view then plummeted as the camera was dropped, leaving everything filmed at a wonky angle—the corner of Andrea's shaking mound of coat just in sight, and a snippet of Claudia's ankle. There was the sound of not particularly manly screeching becoming ever more distant (which could have been Jeff, or Mark, or both, as they made their exit), of Andrea slowly shuffling away underneath her protective layer of duffel, and of a very annoyed Claudia demanding to know who this ghost was, and what on earth it was playing at. Above it all could be heard the grating, relentless creaking of armor, and the swishing noise of the sword. The film stopped abruptly then, and Claudia switched the television off before turning to face Mrs. Scruffles, Tom, and Grey Arthur, her expression deadly serious.

"Well?" she demanded. "What do you think?"

What did they think? Tom and Grey Arthur looked at each other, and immediately raced to the same conclusion.

"That was *awesome!*" cried Tom. "How cool was that knight?"

"He was all . . ." Grey Arthur grabbed a teaspoon and mimicked the way the knight had swung his sword. Tom laughed and clutched hold of a spoon as well, and together they had a miniature, seated, play fight, complete with totally unnecessary *swish*, *waaah*, and *kerchink* noises. Arthur had a rather suave fencing style, jabbing the air with his cutlery and holding the other blurry grey hand aloft, while Tom went for the full-blooded barbarian approach.

Claudia didn't look impressed.

"Tom . . . Arthur . . . ," Mrs. Scruffles said quietly. "I think you're missing the point."

Grey Arthur and Tom begrudgingly called a truce, laying down their spoon-swords, struggling hard to suppress smiles. That became a whole lot easier, though, when they saw how deadly serious Mrs. Scruffles looked. It drained all the humor out of the room.

"I don't get it. What's the problem? Is he an *evil* knight or something?" Tom asked.

Claudia looked as if she might actually howl with exasperation. She paused, mentally counting to five, and shook her head in despair.

"Well, this is just perfect," she muttered darkly. "I suppose this serves me right for seeking the help of two spoon-fighting imbeciles." Claudia snatched the DVD out of the player and thrust it into her bag.

"Now, Claudia, there's no need to be so rude," Mrs. Scruffles replied, without even looking up. She was staring fixedly at the center of the table, deep in thought. "It's a lot to take in."

"What's a lot to take in?" demanded Tom. He hated this "*We're Ghosts so we don't need to explain what on earth is going on*" thing. It really irritated him. He turned to Arthur, to get some support, and his stomach tugged slightly when he realized that Arthur was now wearing the same awful expression as Claudia and Mrs. Scruffles. "What is it? Come on, Arthur, tell me!"

Grey Arthur looked at Mrs. Scruffles and Claudia, for a second lost in that quiet, terrible shared understanding, and then he slowly looked back at Tom.

"They saw him," Grey Arthur said. "That's what this is all about. The other humans. They saw the ghost."

The Dividing Line

"BUT THAT'S MEANT TO BE IMPOSSIBLE." TOM SHOOK HIS head, not quite sure of what to make of it all. "Isn't that meant to be impossible?"

"Which is precisely why I'm here." Claudia paced back and forth, dispelling cats in her wake. "I thought you might know what to do."

"Us? Why us?" Grey Arthur asked.

"Well, you managed to sort out the Collector, didn't you?" she responded, as if it was glaringly obvious.

"That was a bit of a one-off," admitted Tom. "We're hardly Ghostbusters."

"You're the closest we've got." Her voice softened, losing a little of its piercing edge. "I didn't know what else to do. Ever since this happened I've been researching and researching, and then when you turned up, Tom, I just . . . well, a problem shared . . . you know how it goes."

"So, you knew?" asked Tom. "When we met at the school, you already knew this had happened. That's why you agreed to help us? Why didn't you say something at the time?"

"I thought it might be something I could fix, which it has become painfully obvious that it is not. Anyway, the fewer ghosts know about this, the better. I'm sure you understand."

Tom didn't. But he pretended that he did.

"This isn't right. . . ." Mrs. Scruffles tucked a wisp of grey hair behind her ear and tapped her fingers lightly on the table as she thought. "And they've never shown the slightest hint of being able to see ghosts before?"

"Never. This is a new development."

"So, whatever happened, must have happened that night," Mrs. Scruffles said, thinking out loud. Claudia nodded.

"Maybe it's a spell? Or, erm, they all got hit by a car, like Tom did, on the way in to work?" suggested Grey Arthur.

Mrs. Scruffles smiled at him, but shook her head.

"Humans don't do spells anymore. And humans don't tend to get run over in groups of three," she said gently. "But it was a good idea. Keep thinking."

"Maybe it's just that location? Like, it's a magical . . . ghost-viewing . . . place," suggested Tom.

"No, that's not it. When we were setting up, a Poltergeist popped in to see what we were doing, kept unplugging all the wires, and nobody spotted a thing. She was dressed in pink and green too. Made my eyes hurt just to look at her. If it was the location, they'd have been able to see her with their eyes closed." Claudia chewed her lip and shook her head. "The only thing I can think is . . . the reason I've come to you . . . is maybe we're looking at this wrong. Maybe it's not the humans that have changed, and maybe it's not the location, either. What if it's the ghost?"

"It can't be," Mrs. Scruffles said. "That doesn't even bear thinking about."

"Why not?" asked Tom.

"Because," she said, "it would change everything. From head to toe. Ghost World, Real World. Everything."

"It's just one ghost. . . ." Tom shrugged. "I don't get why you're all so worked up about it. How much damage can he do?"

Claudia glared at Grey Arthur. "Have you even bothered to explain anything to Tom about ghosts?"

"He knows plenty!" responded Arthur defensively. "He knows about ley-lines, and about how we can't touch humans, and the Laundry Run, and—"

"And nothing about ghost history," Claudia said, finishing Arthur's sentence. She raised an eyebrow at him, and Arthur just sank into his seat and began picking apart a doily. Claudia turned her attention back to Tom. "You know why humans stopped being able to see ghosts, don't you?"

"Erm . . . Oh yeah, wait, I do . . ." Tom had the answer buried in his memory somewhere, hidden under a layer of Maths homework and Cold Fish lyrics. He bit his tongue and rummaged through the dusty compartments of his brain. It was hard enough having to remember human history, without having to remember the distinctly different ghost history on top. "Because . . . humans started loving science, only they couldn't work out ghosts by using science, so they ignored them, and then got so good at ignoring them that they didn't even have to try anymore." Tom smiled proudly at Arthur, who gave him the thumbs-up. Mrs. Scruffles nodded approvingly.

"Right, so you do understand," Claudia said. "There's no medical reason that humans can't see ghosts. It's all to do with that grey . . . squishiness . . . you carry around in your bony skulls." Tom self-consciously touched his forehead, not comfortable with the way Claudia was staring at where his brain was safely tucked away. "Let me see if I can explain this in a simple way . . . Jeff, the cameraman you met. He lives in a pokey little house, with a garden that backs on to the train tracks. Terrible racket, those trains cause, rumbling up and down every half an hour, sounding their horns. He complained all the time when he moved in there. Now, he doesn't even notice it. He's so used to it, he doesn't even realize that it's happening. His ears still work, not that you'd know it by the awful music he listens to, it's just his brain ignoring it. It's the same with humans and ghosts. Little soft pudgy new humans . . ."

"Babies," corrected Arthur.

"*Babies* . . . can see ghosts. Humans think their offspring laugh, cry, stare for no good reason whatsoever, but really it's because they can see what's in front of their snotty little noses. Babies learn quickly, though, and they see that all the people ignore the spooks that surround them, so they start ignoring them too. And, just like the train tracks, they get so used to it that they just stop realizing the ghosts are there anymore. All this, before you're even old enough to realize that you're doing it. Marvelously odd contraption, the human brain. So, now do you understand why a ghost that humans can't ignore would be such a terrible thing?"

Tom nodded slowly. Then shook his head. Then did a hybrid of nodding and shaking. "Kind of," he admitted. "But if this knight could make you see ghosts, then how come Jeff and Mark and Andrea didn't see Ballpoint Bill?"

"I told them the knight was a prank," replied Claudia. "That it was some stupid television show playing a trick on them, and the whole thing was done with wires, and just pretended that the tape had been destroyed so they couldn't see it again for themselves."

"And they believed that?" asked Tom incredulously. "After seeing him float across the floor?"

"Obviously they did. Arthur, you saw them the other day. Tike was practically doing handstands on set, and then making vulgar noises . . ."

"Armpit farts," said Arthur helpfully. Claudia's nose wrinkled in disgust.

". . . right in front of their faces, and they didn't even bat an eyelid. It would appear that if you can act quickly enough to snuff out any belief they have, then they can quite happily go back to being happy little deluded humans in a ghost-free world." Claudia saw Tom's face twisting into that familiar look of confusion, and softened her tone slightly. Just slightly. From annoying to merely grating. "The human brain has all kinds of weird defense mechanisms in place to stop it being stretched too much in odd directions. People would rather believe that they were tricked by a skinny comedian hiding inside a knight fancy dress costume, than to trust their memories and realize they saw a ghost, realize that this world isn't as straightforward as they thought it was. The problem arises when people don't let those niggles of doubt set in, when they believe one hundred percent wholeheartedly, that's when the floodgates open. We have to find this knight character and stop him before he can haunt anyone else." She looked at Tom and noticed his eyes had all but glazed over. "Arthur, your turn . . . ," she sighed, a hint of despair in her voice. Grey Arthur crackled his knuckles.

"This knight is so powerful humans can't ignore him. Once they see him, if that makes them totally believe in ghosts (if they don't pretend they imagined it or whatever), then they'll start to realize that the world is just chockablock with the supernatural. They'll be able to see it all, Tom. Just like you."

Just like you . . . Tom had been upset when he thought that Claudia might just be one more human who could see ghosts. He'd been upset when he thought it might make him less special, but somehow the thought of everyone being able to see ghosts actually formed a mild comfort to him. Tom pictured the knight ghost running through a crowded street, and everyone who saw him suddenly saw the Ghost World all around them too—the Snorgles in the drains, the Screamers in the shadows, the Poltergeists crawling out of laundry baskets . . . The word would spread, more and more people would start to believe, to see, and eventually the whole country would be exposed to the secret world they've walked through all their lives. Tom visualized the shared smile on their faces, the shaking of their heads, the way they would see this previously hidden world and cry, "Finally, it all makes sense. . . ." Tom imagined his parents, apologetic, sweeping Tom up in their arms, begging his forgiveness for ever thinking something was wrong; the kids at school, sorry for ever calling him Freak Boy. He imagined . . .

Claudia looked at Tom dreamily smiling, and she scowled. She clicked her fingers in front of his face, trying to drag his attention back. It worked. Tom looked at her quizzically.

"Whatever was going on inside your head while you were wearing that dopey expression, I can tell you right now, you're wrong. This is absolutely nothing to smile about," she barked. Tom looked at Grey Arthur and Mrs. Scruffles, and something inside his chest shifted uncomfortably when he saw the glumness mirrored there.

"Why isn't it?" he asked in a small voice. "I don't get why you are all acting so strangely."

Claudia took a deep breath, an inverse sigh, the way you do when you need to impart some ugly truth. "Individually," she said in a careful, measured tone, "some of you humans may be pleasant, in small numbers you may be bearable, but as a herd you are a blight. You think we'd just be accepted with open arms? You think the world would roll out the red carpet? The scientists would probe us and study us and try to work out all the whys. What army wouldn't want, or wouldn't live in fear of, soldiers who couldn't be hurt, and couldn't be killed? The law and the politicians would be terrified of us, spirits that can walk through walls, Poltergeists who steal, Faintly Reals impersonating humans . . . You humans would scream at us, and you would point at us, and you would tear our world apart just so that you could understand and control us. . . ."

"That's not true," said Tom in a small, hurt voice.

"It is. And deep down, you know it is." She grabbed her bag and got to her feet, all the while staring at Tom, and he couldn't work out if it was with pity or anger. "Look at how they treat you at your school. Just because they sense that you are different. Think of that, on a global scale, think of how, if they call a small, brown-eyed, brown-haired boy like you a Freak, just imagine how they will react to a Snorgle, a Screamer . . . to Grey Arthur. They're not ready to see us, Tom. They might not ever be."

"Where are you going?" asked Mrs. Scruffles.

"I can't stay around here all day. I've done what I came here to do, I need to get back to the studio, in case anyone phones up to report seeing a knight ghost. I'll let you know the second I hear something that could be of use." She dragged a manicured hand across her hair, and readjusted her bag strap on her shoulder. "Failing that, I'm booking a flight to somewhere incredibly remote. I have absolutely no intention of being surrounded by humans when this breaks loose."

And with that she was gone, marching out of the front door, sending the cats scattering as she went.

Grey Arthur shook his head. "I know Tom said he owed her a favor, but still . . . You can't just walk in, drop a bombshell like that, and then just wander off and leave us to deal with it. Can you?"

"Well, obviously you can," replied a disheartened Tom, "because she just did."

"Don't be too hard on her, boys," Mrs. Scruffles said softly. "She's doing what she can. That's all you can ask of anyone."

Tom looked at Mrs. Scruffles and chewed his lip. "Do you agree with her? With Claudia? About how it would be if humans could see ghosts?"

Mrs. Scruffles smiled thoughtfully, her fingers tracing around the rim of her teacup as she spoke. "Sometimes I think it would be nice. To sit at the window table in a café, the sun flowing in, and to have a waitress always spot you there. To be invited to barbecues with the neighbors. To get stopped in the street by the people with questionnaires—"

"Oh no, you don't want that," interrupted Tom. "Mum hates that. She pretends she's French when they speak to her."

Mrs. Scruffles laughed, and it was nice to hear the sound, a brief moment of lightness in a very serious talk. "Well, okay, maybe not that, then. But I won't lie to you, Tom. It does get lonely sometimes, wandering through a world where nobody notices you. I can catch a glimpse every now and then, maybe a brief conversation, a shared smile, but it's all so fleeting. I used to be able to manifest for hours at a time, and maybe I'm just getting old, or perhaps the world is a little bit more demanding these days, but . . . It *is* disheartening. Sometimes I'd love nothing more than for humans to believe once again. But, at the end of the day, I know it's just a pipe dream. There's a world of difference between how we would like these things to be and how deep down we know they would turn out. I'm not silly enough to confuse the two. Claudia's right, no matter how much I wish she wasn't. Humans aren't ready to be reintroduced to the Ghost World."

"Well, I suppose we should gather all the Invisible Friends and work out what to do with our rampaging knight ghost, then," said Grey Arthur, breaking the heavy silence that had once again descended upon Mrs. Scruffles's lounge, a silence peppered with small sighs and frequent meows. "No point sitting around, twiddling our thumbs, when we've got the Ghost World to save. Again."

The Longest Walk

TOM, FIRMLY COCOONED ONCE AGAIN IN HIS LAYERS OF winter clothing, dragged his feet on the way home, and would find occasion to stop and stare at anything. Literally, anything. The thick ice on puddles, lost gloves, abandoned Christmas trees with naked branches, the way the salt and grit piled up at the edges of the road, the trail of wooden sticks, a carrot and coal bricks that indicated the Spitting Kids had killed a snowman . . . When Tom paused to consider the beauty and interest of an abandoned handkerchief,

Grey Arthur, sensing what was weighing on Tom's mind, spoke up.

"Maybe they won't mention it," he said, trying to push as much optimism into that sentence as possible. Tom looked at him, raised an eyebrow, and then stared back at the handkerchief. It was paisley-patterned, and the cold had frozen it into shape, like a cartoon ghost made from a sheet.

"I bet you they will." Tom sniffed, the cold air making his nose run. "Why do we have to go back now anyway?"

"Because I've got to collect Harry and then go fetch the others back."

"Yeah, but you could do that on your own. No need for me to come back at all."

"Apart from the fact you live there? Oh, come on, Tom, you've got to see your parents sooner or later. They'll start to worry if you stay out for too long."

"Stop being so sensible. I don't want a sensible friend right now. I want a friend who will panic with me."

"Oh. Okay, then." Grey Arthur paused, and then looked at Tom, wearing his absolutely best deadly-serious expression. "Maybe your mother will be running around the house, with . . . bagels . . . in her hair . . . screaming about how her son can see ghosts."

"*Bagels?*" Tom repeated, an amused (if slightly confused) grin visible from beneath the woolly hat and above the scarf. "Why on earth would she have bagels in her hair?"

"Because she has gone mad from the shock?"

Tom shook his head, trying hard to hang on to being worried and panicked, but Grey Arthur's lopsided grin combined with an image in his head of his mum with bread products in her hair made it impossible. He laughed, admitting defeat, and started walking again, with Grey Arthur at his side.

"Come on, might as well get this over and done with," Tom said, increasing his pace. "You go straight to the shed and then gather up everyone else, and I'll go see what Mum and Dad have to say. I'll meet you back at Mrs. Scruffles's."

"You sure you don't want me to stick around for a bit first?" Arthur asked. "For moral support?"

"Think this might be easier without a ghost in the room, but thanks anyway."

Tom looked up, and with a start realized that he was already outside the front door. He'd been on autopilot, his feet automatically knowing where to go without any intervention from his distracted mind. Even more surprisingly, the door was open, and there, braving the bracing air, stood Mum. She had her arms wrapped around her chest for warmth, and her cheeks looked pinched with cold. Leaving a door open in winter was one of Mum's pet hates, causing her to bellow the famous line "*You're Letting All the Warm Air Out,*" but yet here she was. Tom knew why.

She was waiting for him.

"Come inside," she said. "We need to talk."

We need to talk. That dreaded phrase that heralds conversations you really don't want to have. The same phrase Dad used before telling him they might lose the house. The one Mum used after Tom's goldfish died because he'd been too lazy to clean the water. The one they had both used when they had told Tom they were moving to Thorbleton.

Still, it could be worse.

At least she didn't have bagels in her hair.

Saying the Things Left Unsaid

Mum walked into the lounge, and Tom dutifully followed. He'd dumped all his outdoor winter clothes on the floor in the hallway, and Mum hadn't even barked at him to hang them up. Not a good sign. She sat down in her armchair, and Tom sat on the settee, perched on the edge, bolt upright, unable to relax. Mum looked exactly the same. For a while they just studied each other's tense expressions, the floor, the ceiling, and the contents of the coffee table. Tom realized she was dreading this chat every bit as much as he was.

"Where's Dad?" Tom asked, deciding to kick-start the conversation.

"Hiding in the garage. You know how he hates this kind of thing."

"What kind of thing?"

"You know what I mean, Tom. *The Big Talk* kind of thing. He says it gives him heartburn."

"We don't have to do this, Mum. Really, there's nothing to talk about anyway." Mum sighed, and stopped what she was doing. She looked at him, and Tom couldn't work out if she was sad or angry, or something in between.

"Tom, if you still think you can see . . . ," she hesitated, not wanting to say the word. In the end she had to look away when she said it. "*Ghosts* . . ." She looked back at him, took a deep breath, and started again. "If you still think you can see ghosts, then we need to talk about it. We need to sort this out."

"What's to sort out?"

"It's not normal, Tom! An eleven-year-old boy should not be imagining that he is talking to ghosts."

"I'm not, Mum." He'd meant it as in, not *imagining* it, but Mum took it as a blanket denial. She shook her head and just continued.

"And this Claudia woman, she shouldn't be encouraging you. She should know better. Filling your head full of all this nonsense again." She looked at the hurt expression on Tom's face, and she faltered. "I just . . . want what's best for you, Tom. I'm not saying this because I want to control you, or because I'm a horrible mother, I'm saying this because I want you to have a happy, normal life."

"But I am happy, Mum," Tom replied. Mum bit her

lip, noting the absence of the word "normal," and took a couple more deep breaths, run-ups at sentences, before she finally responded.

"I just don't understand why all this has started up again, Tom. You're an intelligent boy. You have to know deep down that ghosts don't exist. Is it for attention? Are your dad and I working too many hours? Because I can cut back, if that's what this is about. Just say the word." She paused, waiting for a response that didn't come. "Are you ill? This could all be just down to a temperature. Once, your dad got so feverish when he had the flu he thought he saw wasps all over his bed. Come here, let me feel your forehead."

Tom shook his head and drew away from Mum's outstretched hand. "I'm not ill, Mum. You know I'm not."

"Do you want to move back home? Is that it? Is this because you're missing your old friends?"

"You don't get it."

"Then *explain* it to me, Tom!"

"What's the point? You won't believe me anyway."

"Try me."

Tom inhaled deeply, and held on to it.

Here goes nothing . . .

"I'm not doing this for attention, or to punish you, or because I want to move back home. It's not something I get a choice in, Mum. After the car accident, I don't know, it just happened. I can see ghosts."

"Ghosts don't exist!"

"Oh, for crying out loud, Mum, you work with a ghost!" Tom hadn't meant to say that. He was quite surprised when he heard the words snap out of him, and immediately he wished he could drag them back. Too late now.

Mum laughed, not the kind of laugh you make when jokes amuse, but the short, sharp, bark of a laugh you make when you are presented with something almost offensively ludicrous, like homework written on a napkin, or a pie in a restaurant with a bite already taken from it. "I do not work with a ghost. I think I'd know if I worked with a ghost."

"Janet."

"*Janet's a ghost,*" repeated Mum, her voice heavy with disbelief. "Since when do ghosts serve tea, tell jokes, and enjoy a good natter, Tom?"

"Since, I don't know, *always.* Well, some of them."

"Do you have any idea how ridiculous you sound?"

Tom made a soft howl of exasperation. "Mum, think about it! Have you ever touched her? Shaken hands? Anything? No?"

"So, you're saying Janet is a ghost because she isn't very touchy-feely?"

"You're not listening."

"Yes, I am, Tom. I just don't like what I'm hearing. I don't get why all this has started up again."

"It never went away, Mum. You just ignored it."

Tom's mum sighed, obviously not happy with the way this conversation had gone. Tom assumed he was meant to have leaped in the air at some stage and declared, "That's it, I won't see ghosts anymore, I'm cured!" and then they would have had dinner and Tom would have led a normal life and grown up to become a farmer, or a fireman, or ideally, a rock star.

"Well, I'd best get going . . . ," Tom said.

"You've only just got back."

"I know. I just popped in . . . to get some things. I'll be back later, Mum."

Mum nodded, not wanting to argue anymore. Tom got up, and just as he did, Mum launched from her seat and grabbed him into a huge hug. She smoothed down his hair and kissed him on the top of the head. Tom wasn't quite sure what was going on. Eventually, she pulled away, but still held him by the shoulders, looking him in the face. She smiled, a thin-lipped smile that was more about making friends again than being happy, and let him go.

Tom nodded, and wandered out into the hallway, genuinely unsure whether that talk had gone better or worse than he'd expected. A hard knot of emotion nestled in Tom's chest, pressing against his ribs, a heavy bundle of upset, annoyance, bleakness, and *alone*, the mix you get when someone you care about feels disappointed by you. The parting hug had smoothed away the sharp edges of it, but hadn't made it vanish.

All this did rather leave Tom in quite a quandary. Stop this knight, and spare the Ghost World from the scrutiny of all humans. Leave him to it, and Mum might finally believe Tom that ghosts existed, and this horrible feeling that burrowed inside his chest might vanish for good. The conclusion Tom came to couldn't help but make him smile, not because it was particularly funny, but because it reminded him of how all this began.

"*Life isn't fair.*"

Ghosts of the Round Table

MRS. SCRUFFLES'S KITCHEN WAS A LOT LESS SEDATE WHEN Tom returned. Calling together all the Invisible Friends into one smallish room will do that.

"Okay . . . three questions." Tom finally felt like he was making some headway. He sat down at the table, and everyone stopped what they were doing and paid attention. "First: How come he's so strong that he can make humans see him in the first place? Not even Sorrow Jane or the Red Rascal get noticed."

Mrs. Scruffles shrugged. "That's the golden question. It's something that's not been possible for countless centuries."

"So that would mean he's something new?" asked Tom.

"Or something very, very old . . . ," mused Monty, shutting the book he was thumbing through.

"*Stonehenge*," Mrs. Scruffles said. Immediately, Tom's mind was thrown back to those imposing stone doorways, the light of ley-lines bristling between them, the closed doors at the center, the dark shapes beyond, and his heart flickered out of beat. By the look on all the Invisible Friends' faces, they felt exactly the same. This was not a good train of thought. "There was an earthquake there, a month or so ago. The stones were quickly put back in place, and so we thought that we had gotten away with it, but maybe that was just wishful thinking."

"Got away with what? What is kept in there?" asked Tom anxiously. Instead of answering, Mrs. Scruffles got up from the table and reached up on a shelf for a large and weighty book. It was titled *Ye Olde Ghost History of Times Bygone*, which wasn't exactly a catchy name, and it was nestled rather absurdly between a book on *Clothes for Cats* and a recipe guide for Victorian sponge cakes.

"Never thought I'd get much use for this," muttered Mrs. Scruffles as she placed it down on the table. "I just got it to press flowers in, really."

The book fell open halfway and revealed a withered flower, complete with stalk, leaves, and roots still caked with powdery dirt. Tom was pretty sure that wasn't quite how you were meant to press flowers. Mrs. Scruffles skipped through the pages, searching.

"Okay, now where are we?" she asked herself. "Sadness Summoners, Screamers, Stinklebert the

Malodorous, aha!" She tapped a finger on the page. "Stonehenge. It's all a bit wordy, so I'll just skim through and tell you what you need to know. Could have done with a decent editor, this book. Thirty-five pages dedicated to the different shades of color Snorgles come in. If that's not excessive, I don't know what is." She caught Tom's impatient look and began tracing a ghostly finger down the page, lips moving quietly as she did so.

"Right." Mrs. Scruffles looked up from the page and pushed a wisp of grey hair behind her ear. "It's all a bit vague—a lot about Stonehenge remains a mystery."

"Ghosts and mystery. Now there's a surprise," moaned Tom. Grey Arthur chuckled.

"Well, Tom, that's the trouble with Druids. They spent all their time drinking heaven knows what, dancing around fires, and doing odd scraps of magic, and not a great amount of time on the paperwork. From what I can gather, and bear in mind this is based on stories that have been passed down through so many generations that the truth might have gotten twisted beyond all recognition but, popular opinion is this: Stonehenge was built around the ley-lines as a thank you to the ghosts, a tribute for assistance they gave, a way of keeping the ghosts happy, that kind of thing."

"I know this already," replied Tom.

"A little bit of patience goes a long way, Tom. Let me finish. Where was I? Oh yes. *However*, two entrances were later blocked by the Druids with mystical stone, creating a fragment of sealed ley-line between them."

"The two doors every ghost knows to steer clear of, but Tom wandered up and rubbed his grubby hands over, you mean?" asked Arthur, grinning cheekily at Tom.

"Tom!" cried Mrs. Scruffles, shocked.

"What?" protested Tom. "It's not like there was a sign!"

Mrs. Scruffles shook her head, and Tom found his cheeks getting hot. It was hardly his fault. It wasn't as if he'd been handed a list of Ghostly Dos and Don'ts when all this had started. He was glad when Mrs. Scruffles stopped looking at him in horror and continued describing what she had read.

"This book seems to think the doors were sealed intentionally, to keep a ghost inside," revealed Mrs. Scruffles. Tom nodded, understanding.

"Like a prison?" asked Tike.

"Exactly." Mrs. Scruffles nodded.

"Do we know what the crime was?" asked Montague, in between sips of tea. "It must have been something quite impressive, to make them go to those extremes."

"Well, here is what the book says . . . 'The Terrible Theo's guilts were threefold: thievery, impersonation of royalty, and manifestation of fear in both Real and Unreal. For these crimes, the doorway was sealed, protecting all from the lawlessness within. For it was decided that that which cannot be controlled, must be contained.'"

"The Terrible Theo? What an odd name," murmured Tike, as he knocked down Grey Arthur's completed sugar cube bridge with a teaspoon. Grey Arthur moaned and began rebuilding it.

"Heh, says *Tike*." Tom chuckled.

"What? Tike is a great name for a Poltergeist. What's that they call it? Apt. It's apt."

"Very," complained Arthur, pushing his elbows out to defend his creation this time round.

"Is there no mention as to why this ghost should be visible to humans, Mrs. Scruffles?" asked Mildred, dragging the conversation back on track.

"Mildred, when this ghost was locked away, all humans could still see ghosts, so there is no reason why it should. However, no ghost has ever remained trapped within the magic of the ley-line for so long before. Ley-lines are old, wild magic, and nobody really understands them properly. The only thing I can possibly imagine is that it has somehow had an effect. Infused them, if you will. Made them magically more potent."

"Well, that makes it the stupidest jail ever," replied Tom. Tike snorted with laughter.

"I think the point was that they were never meant to get out again, Tom . . . ," explained Montague.

"Mrs. Scruffles, do you think *it* getting out was Tom's fault?" piped up Tike.

"Tike!" protested Tom, looking awkwardly around the table.

Mrs. Scruffles smiled gently. "I don't think it's productive to point the finger of blame. . . . Hundreds of humans must have touched those stones over the years, Tike."

"Yeah, but none like Tom."

Tom buried his face in his hands.

"We'll just call it a coincidence, Tike," Mrs. Scruffles said diplomatically.

"Right," said Tike, winking theatrically back at her. "*A coincidence.*"

"Anyway, on to my second question: How do we fix it?" Tom asked, keen not to dwell on the issue of allocating blame.

"Honestly? I don't know if we can, Tom." It wasn't the answer Tom had been hoping for. "The Druids didn't exactly share their magical knowledge, and I doubt there's anyone Real or Unreal today that would know how to re-create the prison, and that's without even thinking about how we would get the Terrible Theo back inside in the first place before we seal him in. I'll phone around, and I'll read up on the subject, but first things first, we still need to find him. Heaven knows where he could be by now, and every minute he's out there could mean another human bumping into him."

"They won't all necessarily start believing in ghosts though, not enough to see us," clarified Monty. Mrs. Scruffles nodded, but she still didn't look too reassured.

"That's true, but eventually someone will. Maybe only one person in a hundred will not write it off as a dream, a prank, a stray actor, a mirage, a trick of the light, but if he stays out there long enough, it will inevitably happen. The longer he is loose, the more people could end up like you, Tom."

"So how do we find him?" Tom asked.

"That's the problem. A ghost looks like a ghost to us. Do you have any idea how many spooks mimic knights? There must be over a hundred Thespers in London alone who dress that way. We can ask everyone to keep an eye out, but I'm afraid the only real way we'll be able to track this escapee down is by closely watching the human world."

"*Sword-Wielding Knight Maniac Storms Oxford Circus,* that kind of thing?" asked Tike, gesturing with his hands to display a newspaper headline.

"Hopefully not, but something like that would really point us in the right direction, I suppose. . . ." She rubbed her eyes, looking tired. "It's not ideal, but I think our best bet right now is just to play the waiting game."

As plans go, it was a little lackluster, but they really didn't have much choice. Tom, Grey Arthur, and the Harrowing Screamer retired back to Aubergine Road, Montague to Mrs. Wilson's semidetached house on the outskirts of town, Mildred to Holly's cupboard, and Tike to Frank's laundry basket, and they waited, and watched, and resumed their normal routine, constantly on the watch for that one clue, that ripple in the human pond that would lead them to the Terrible Theo.

Later on, nobody would be quite sure whether it was good luck, or bad, when they didn't have to wait very long at all.

Luck of Undetermined Nature

TOM WANDERED INTO SCHOOL ON HIS OWN THE NEXT morning—Grey Arthur had stopped off at Mrs. Scruffles's to see if she had been able to make any progress tracking down the mysterious knight ghost. The Harrowing Screamer had accompanied him, though Tom suspected it was more to do with visiting the cats than trying to solve problems. For a scary-looking ghost, he certainly had a soft spot for kittens.

It always felt strange, entering the school on his own, like that feeling when you pack for holiday and remain convinced that you've accidentally left all your pants at home. At least all the ghost business had died down and school had gone back to its normal, savage self, which was almost pleasant compared to its super-natural turn. Even so, Tom was still relieved when he spotted Mildred on her lonesome as well, standing by the reception entrance, and he trotted over to say hello.

"No Holly today?" he asked.

"She's inside, discussing the merits of her new pink fluffy pencil case with some other children," explained

Mildred. "I thought it best to leave her to it. Pink is not my specialist subject."

Tom chuckled, trying to picture Mildred getting excited about something so girly. "Fair enough," he replied. "How's it going, though? You enjoying being an Invisible Friend?"

Mildred paused, contemplating the question. "It is certainly rewarding, and highly educational. I have managed to fill three notebooks already on the subject of lunchtime seating arrangement politics alone." Mildred stared up at Tom and tried to smile. She was getting better at it, no denying that, but there was still a hint of discomfort and sternness that infiltrated those dusty lips. "I can lend you the notes, if you wish to read them."

Tom grinned. "Cheers for the offer, Mildred, but I think I'm okay. Don't sit next to Big Ben, don't eat cheese and onion crisps if you want to have a close chat, and don't let your mum cut your sandwiches into little hearts. That's pretty much it for me."

Mildred rummaged in her satchel and brought out her notebook, carefully adding Tom's advice. "No . . . bread . . . hearts . . . ," she muttered aloud as she wrote. "Thank you, Thomas."

"Glad to help," he replied. He looked up and groaned. "Incoming . . . ," he whispered.

Kate Getty, she of the absent eyebrows, wearer of the orange foundation, was marching toward the gate with her entourage of preening girls in tow. Marianne and

Isabelle trotted after her, wobbly on heels that Tom was convinced had to be against the school dress code, and they were calling for her to stop.

"Slow down, Kate!"

"Talk to us, Kate!"

"Tell us what happened!"

Kate spun around, not a meter away from where Tom and Mildred were standing, and faced her friends.

"I told you I don't want to talk about it!" she snapped.

"Yeah, but you always say that, just so we have to work harder for the gossip," replied Marianne.

"And you can't phone me at three o'clock in the morning and then not tell me why I've got a missed call, Kate!" cried Isabelle.

"Was it Ben? It was Big Ben, wasn't it? Has he dumped you?" asked Marianne.

"*What?*" screeched Kate. "We were never going out. Did he say we were going out?"

(You'd have thought Tom would have learned his lesson by now and have realized that this was an ideal time to make a discreet exit, but there is something transfixing about three girls, speaking at the speed of light, with the promise of gossip on the horizon.)

"Kind of," said Isabelle.

"Hinted," said Marianne.

"I'm so going to get my brother to beat him up. He's such a liar. It's nothing to do with him." Kate sighed. "I just got a bit scared last night, is all."

"Parents arguing again?" asked Isabelle.

"How about you shut up and let me tell you, instead of spouting off about my parents?" growled Kate. "It's nothing to do with my parents. If you must know . . . I saw a ghost last night."

"You're such a liar," said Isabelle.

"That's old now, Kate. The haunted school thing is so last week. You can't scare us," said Marianne.

"I'm not trying to scare you. You asked, and I'm telling. I saw a ghost."

"Okay, let me guess. Hiding in the PE room, waiting for girls to wander into the shower . . . ," said Marianne, putting on a scary-storyteller voice. Kate reached over and slapped her round the back of the head.

"Don't make fun of me! Don't you dare," she snarled.

"Sorry . . . ," muttered Marianne, rubbing the back of her head.

"It was in my bedroom *actually*, a woman ghost, huge nasty ratty dreadlocks. I woke up with her peering over me. I pretended to be asleep, eyes all closed, you know, but I definitely saw her."

"Then what?" asked Marianne.

"She went to grab hold of my throat," said Kate dramatically.

Tom will think over this moment again, and again, and each time he will cringe and want to kick himself. Sometimes he wished there was a longer distance between his mouth and his brain, so he would have time to stop his thoughts just flying out past his lips, as it was becoming something of a bad habit. However, having a head of normal-size proportions, he found himself saying out loud:

"*Ghosts can't touch humans.*"

Kate spun to face him. "You what, Freak Boy? Was I talking to you?"

If there was a way to grab things you have just said and Wite-Out them from existence, Tom would have done it. As there wasn't, he found himself shrinking under Kate's glare.

"No . . . you weren't . . . I just . . . heard you say . . . And, I didn't mean . . ."

"What makes you such an expert anyway, Freak Boy?"

"No, no . . ." He laughed feebly, hoping it would defuse the situation. It didn't. "Not an expert at all. Just . . . was . . ."

"Sticking your nose in where it doesn't belong. If you'd have let me finish, FREAK BOY, I was saying . . . She went to grab hold of my throat, but instead she just snatched my necklace off from round my neck. Then she dove into my cupboard, right, get this, *through the closed door*, and was gone. You got some smart comment to say now, Freak Boy?"

"Maybe you just dreamed it?" Tom said.

Kate stepped right up into Tom's face, her nose practically pressing against his. Mildred drew protectively closer to Tom, anxiously watching the situation unfold.

"If I dreamed it, then where is my necklace?" Tom managed to drag his eyes away from hers and looked down at her neck. Sure enough, the necklace that Kate had been wearing every day since Christmas was gone. Tom looked back up at her, swallowing dryly. Kate leaned in even closer and whispered in his ear, "If you ever talk to me like that in front of my friends again, I will make your life a living hell, do you hear me?" Tom nodded. "And you can tell that odd-eyed, goth weirdo friend of yours to stop staring at me too, if she doesn't want a slap." She prodded Tom in the chest, and then marched off, with Isabelle and Marianne in pursuit.

"That's not good," said Mildred. Tom nodded, rubbing the point where Kate had prodded him. It was one of those pains that carried on at the same intensity for ages, and he grimaced, waiting for it to fade.

"Oh, don't worry about her. I'm beginning to think her bark is worse than her bite. Besides, she'd have a hard job if she did try to slap you." Tom patted his chest and grinned. "Didn't even hurt," he lied.

"No, I don't mean that, Thomas," Mildred said. "I wasn't even trying to appear human."

"But that's great news, Mildred. See, it's getting easier." Tom looked at his watch and gasped. "I've got to go. I'll be late for registration."

Mildred scowled and shook her head. "No, Thomas, wait," she said, even more seriously than usual. "It's not good news. You're misunderstanding me. I wasn't trying in the slightest. She shouldn't have been able to see me."

"Oh . . . *Oh!*" Tom finally understood. "Oh, that's not good at all."

"I believe I said that already."

Tom paused, letting it all sink in.

"She wasn't lying about seeing a ghost, was she?"

"No, Thomas. I don't believe she was."

Tom stared at Mildred, his eyes growing wide.

"We need to get all the ghosts out of the school," he said. "*NOW.*"

To Absent Friends

IT WAS A BEAST OF A DAY. TOM NEVER REALIZED JUST how much he relied on Arthur's company until he wasn't there. Tom's conversation with Kate was now the stuff of playground legends, and his Freak Boy status had rocketed accordingly. Kids would make ghost noises when he passed, pass notes about him in the classroom, and ridicule him whenever they got in earshot. Tom didn't quite understand how it was Kate who had seen the ghost, yet he was the one getting ridiculed for being a "ghost expert." It didn't strike him as particularly fair. He stared at his watch constantly, counting the seconds, the minutes, the hours, longing for the end-of-school bell to ring.

It wasn't just Tom, though, who struggled through an Invisible Friendless day.

Mrs. Wilson hurried past Tom in the corridor, her forehead lined with a frown, and as he turned to watch her go he saw that her white Science jacket was streaked with blue and black splashes of ink, victim to pupils flicking their fountain pens at her as she passed. A kid, someone Tom didn't recognize, saw her coming, saw her arms filled with paperwork, and with a mischievous grin carefully placed his school bag down in her path. It all happened so quickly. She caught it with her foot, sprawled to the ground, elbows hitting the floor, and all her work was strewn throughout the corridor. The children who had seen this happen all laughed—all except for Tom. Mrs. Wilson, not knowing she had fallen victim to a rather cruel prank, even apologized to the boy whose bag she had fallen over, as she gathered up her work. Tom sighed. Monty would never have let her trip.

Holly was wandering the corridors on her own, looking lost, with a note on her back claiming I CUT MY OWN FRINGE (Tom assumed this was an insult, but he wasn't 100 percent sure). Then there was Frank Longfield, poor Frank Longfield, last seen being chased through the English department block by Big Ben, running as if his life depended on it, his pants riding high above his trouser waistband, a sure sign of an aborted wedgie.

An Invisible Friendless day was undeniably a long and painful day.

The bell finally rang, and Tom traipsed down to his locker to collect his PE gear before heading home. There was a crowd of kids gathered by it, giggling, and when they saw Tom coming they quickly left.

As Tom got closer, he realized why.

I SEE DEAD PEOPLE had been written on the door in thick black pen. Tom sighed for about the billionth time that day, feeling utterly wretched, and leaned his head against the locker door, not even having the energy to open it. He stared sullenly at his feet.

"They're not even dead people . . . ," he muttered to himself. "If I'm going to get teased, they could at least get it right."

"Pssst . . . Tom . . ."

Tom stood up straight and looked around. He nearly jumped out of his skin when he spotted Grey Arthur's face peeping out through the locker next to his. His body was tucked safely out of sight, and only his grey blurry head poked into view.

"You're not meant to be here," he hissed at Arthur.

"I was extra careful. Kate didn't spot me. I just had to run in to let you know we're all hiding out at your house. Meet us there after school."

"Will do," agreed Tom. "Why not Mrs. Scruffles's house, though?"

"She's popped on the ley-line to London, to see Lost and Found Freddie. She's going to see if he can help us track this Terrible Theo ghost down." Grey Arthur looked at Tom and suddenly frowned. "Not been a good day?" he asked.

"How'd you guess?" asked Tom miserably.

"Mostly from your forehead," admitted Arthur. Tom didn't understand at first—it needed a little while to process. Then he took a sharp intake of breath, and his hand shot to his forehead.

"No? No?" he begged.

Arthur nodded apologetically.

"Afraid so. Guess the ink hadn't dried yet on your locker."

Tom made a noise, part whimper, part growl, and fled in the direction of the nearest toilets, hand firmly clamped over the offending mirror text on his forehead.

"See you soon!" called Grey Arthur cheerfully after him.

Intervention and Ventilation

LUCKILY FOR TOM, HE HAD A WOOLLY HAT TO WEAR ON the way home. Unluckily for Tom, you can't really get away with wearing one around the house. He ducked in through the front door, removed the hat, and carefully pushed his hair down to cover his forehead. He licked his hand (which yes, is disgusting, but needs must sometimes) and slicked the hair in place.

Mum wandered into the hallway and raised an eyebrow at him.

"Why have you done that with your fringe?" she asked.

"I don't have a fringe, Mum. Boys don't have fringes."

"Ohhh, I see. Don't they?" Mum seemed amused by this fact. "Okay, in that case, what have you done with the hair that grows at the front of your head?"

"Slicked it down."

"I can see that, Tom. I guess I was really wondering why."

Tom sighed and lifted up his hair to reveal the writing beneath. EP DA was clearly visible, in thick black mirror letters.

"How'd that happen?" she asked, shocked.

"I rested my head on wet ink."

"That wasn't very clever, was it?" She studied the writing, a Mum-will-fix-it glint in her eye. "And it won't come off?" she asked.

"It won't come off."

"Not even with soap and water?"

Adults think anyone under the age of thirty is utterly deranged. It's true. *Not even with soap and water?* What did she think he'd used? A mango and a brick?

"Not even with soap and water. It's permanent marker, Mum."

"Oh, dear. Well, I have some foundation in my

makeup box, if you want me to cover it up for you?"

"*Mum!*" whined Tom. You know the kind I mean—the one that says "No, I Don't Want to Wear Shorts to School, Even If It Is the Hottest Day of the Year," the one that you make when your mum offers to drop you off right at the playground when you are running late for school, the one where you invite new friends over and your parents get out the photos of you, two years old, naked as the day you were born, and clutching on to a teddy bear. That was the "Mum" whine Tom made.

"Fine!" she said with a friendly smile. "I was only trying to help." She smoothed his fringe—sorry, front-head-hair—back down into place, grimacing slightly when she realized it was damp. "By the way, I opened the window in your room. It just smelled a bit ripe in there. Needed airing. You can close it when you go up if you're too cold." Mum hesitated for a moment, and Tom thought she was going to say more, but she just nodded at him and wandered back to check on the oven. Tom raced up the stairs to see what the ghosts were getting up to in his absence.

Two's Company, Eight's a Crowd

TOM'S MUM HADN'T BEEN LYING WHEN SHE SAID IT smelled ripe in his room, and it didn't take a genius to work out why. The Snorgle from the boys' toilet at school was fast asleep on top of Tom's most aromatic of sneakers, snoring contentedly. It didn't look like a particularly comfortable spot to take a nap, but it didn't seem to bother the little ghost. He was clutching one of Tom's socks like a comfort blanket, stubby little fingers hugging it close. It would have been an almost endearing sight, if it hadn't been for the awful stench that accompanied it. Tom decided there and then that the window was staying open—if need be, he'd wear all the clothes he owned to stay warm, but there was no way that bracing fresh air was being taken away.

Montague, Mildred, Tike, the Harrowing Screamer, Grey Arthur, and Ballpoint Bill had also taken refuge in the room. Grey Arthur was trying to play the host, with mixed results. Mildred was going through Tom's history project, correcting the spelling mistakes, while Tike was trying to force the Harrowing Screamer into a woolly hat and scarf. The Screamer was protesting bitterly, and Tike was chasing him round the room, demanding he stay still. Montague was trying to appear relaxed, casually draped in Tom's chair, book in hand, but even he couldn't pull off such a look in this chaos. His eyebrows twitched every time Tike and Harry came crashing past. Grey Arthur sat with Bill, chatting. He had even, rather thoughtfully, constructed a snack for his inky Poltergeist friend. Tom assumed it was his very own twist on a sandwich—a piece of A4 paper carefully folded in half, with a crunchy ink cartridge filling. Bill was chewing noisily when Tom entered, blue ink spilling from his lips and dribbling down his chin.

"Wow," breathed Tom, as he gently shut the door behind him. It wasn't quite as bad as when all the ghosts had hidden here from the Collector, but it definitely came a close second.

"Hey, Tom!" called Tike, finally giving up on dressing Harry. He dropped the hat and scarf and slumped down on the bed. "Still got writing on your head?"

Tom glanced at Arthur, who shrugged apologetically. Tom nodded sadly.

"Never mind, eh? Worse things happen at sea." Tike grinned.

Tom didn't quite know what he meant, but it filled his head with images of marauding pirates brandishing marker pens and scrawling on unsuspecting fishermen. He sat down on the edge of his bed (a location chosen as much for its distance from the sleeping Snorgle as its comfort) and stretched, trying to shake loose all the tension the school day had forced into him

"So, anyone have an idea what to do about Kate?" he asked. An assortment of blank faces told Tom the answer was no. Tom loosened his tie, creating enough space to pull it off over his head, and then flung it toward the laundry basket. "Well, in that case, maybe we should just leave her that way. Maybe we should send Harry over to chase her around the school corridors."

"That's not very nice, Tom . . . ," said Montague. He

didn't say it sternly, he said it very gently, which oddly made his admonishment feel even worse.

"But neither is she! She's horrible. And mean. And spiteful. And . . . *orange*," Tom complained. "She's every bit as bad as Big Ben, only she doesn't punch people as much. I don't see why I should be wasting my time working out how to make things better for her. I think we should leave her as she is. See how she likes being Freak Girl."

"Tom," replied Montague, a concerned look on his ghostly face, "I know that she is really beastly to you, but this whole thing, it's about more than just bullying. She might be an atrocious person, but without an Invisible Friend to help her through this, she could be really, really terrified. Not funny scared, but crying, screaming scared, and not even she deserves that. Also, you are surrounded by nice, friendly ghosts because you are a nice, friendly person. Not all ghosts are like that. To go to the other extreme, what would happen if Kate somehow manages to cope with her new ability, manages to befriend some less-than-kind ghosts—just imagine the type of bully she could turn into."

"How come it's the ghosts being sensible?" moaned Tom to Grey Arthur.

"I guess we just take it in turns," replied Arthur with a kind smile. "I know you wouldn't do it, anyway, that you're just venting, but Monty is right to point out what could go wrong."

"The situation is worse than you think," interrupted Mildred. Mildred only ever spoke in tones of seriousness, ranging from moderately humorless to the gravest of news. The way she spoke now lurked somewhere at the far end of the scale, and it made Tom sit up straight.

"How can it possibly be worse?" he asked.

"I spoke with Holly after school." Mildred pushed her black hair behind her pale ears, and those unblinking mismatched eyes stared intently at Tom. "She informed me that she believes that Kate may be telling the truth, and that ghosts do exist."

Panic fluttered inside Tom. This was getting out of hand. "What did she say, exactly?" he demanded.

Mildred looked up at the ceiling, recalling the conversation. "She said that Julie from class G is an evil skank beast, she disclosed that she fancies Jeff from the boy band Jumping Jays, that her mother is a cow because she is angered by a larger-than-average phone bill, but it wasn't her fault, because she had to phone Sue to discover which celebrity had been voted off of—"

"About the ghosts, Mildred. What did she say about the ghosts?"

"I see. She didn't really say much more than that, Thomas. As soon as she mentioned it, she noticed she had a hair with a split end and squealed until she found a pair of scissors. I can only stay visible for so long, and by the time she had examined every single strand of hair on her head for imperfections I was exhausted. She couldn't see me when she returned, Thomas, so it is safe to say she doesn't entirely believe."

"Yet," added Tike.

"Yet," agreed Mildred.

"Marvelous. If anyone could bully or shout you into believing something, it's Kate Getty." Tom felt like crawling under the duvet cover and waking up when this was all over. Having to be responsible the whole time was exhausting. "When is Mrs. Scruffles getting back? Do you know if she's had any luck with Lost and Found Freddie?"

"She's not due back until later on tonight. We didn't even get a chance to explain the Kate situation to her, Tom. She just left a note pinned to the front door saying where she'd gone," explained Monty. "We won't know anything until the morning now."

"Okay, then. What happens if we don't do anything?" asked Tom.

"The longer Kate carries on believing, the harder it will be for her to stop. Also, there is a risk that she will run into more ghosts, a risk she will convince people that ghosts exist, a risk—"

"Okay, okay . . . ," Tom said, thinking. "So it's up to us to change her mind."

Tike snorted with laughter. "Right. What're we gonna do, Tom? *Haunt her* into not believing?" Ballpoint Bill and Grey Arthur chuckled at the suggestion.

Tom didn't, though.

Instead, he grinned wildly.

"Arthur, your human is looking crazy . . . ," complained Tike, his laughter fading as he saw the manic glint in Tom's eyes. "Make him stop."

"What is it, Tom? What are you thinking?" asked Grey Arthur quizzically.

Tom leaned forward, the grin he wore growing by the second.

"I'm thinking that I've got a plan."

The Worries That Come Before Sleep

LATER ON, WITH THE SNORGLE AND BALLPOINT BILL sharing the shed with the Harrowing Screamer, and Mildred, Tike, and Montague long gone, Tom and Arthur settled down for the night. Grey Arthur was, as usual, curled up underneath the bed, sharing the space with comics and shoes and a rather tatty doll. Tom lay under the covers, head on the pillow, staring up at the ceiling. It was late already, and he should be sleepy, but instead concerns whirred and churned and raced around his head, constantly keeping tiredness at bay. It wasn't just about the plan, although that was nestled in there in his stack of worried thoughts. He thought about Kate, about his parents, about his mum's talk she had given him the day before, about what would happen if they couldn't find a way to stop the the Terrible Theo, about what a world where everyone could see ghosts would be like. He'd try to flush the thoughts away by daydreaming about summer, about rock bands, about books that he had read, but always they would creep back in and push all else aside. He turned on the bedside lamp.

"Arthur? Are you still awake?" he whispered.

From beneath the bed, Arthur's voice piped up: "Yeah. Are you?"

Tom grinned. "Yeah. Can't sleep."

"Me neither," admitted Arthur. "What's on your mind?"

"Lots of things," sighed Tom.

"Name one."

Tom rolled onto his side and propped himself up on an elbow. "Don't you think it's weird that Claudia and the TV crew saw a ghost dressed as a knight, but Kate saw a woman with dreadlocks?"

"Not really. She probably dressed up like that to play a prank. Poltergeists have an odd sense of humor."

"You think she's a Poltergeist?"

"She stole Kate's necklace, didn't she? It's only Poltergeists that do things like that."

"I suppose. Maybe she's a mix of Thesper and Poltergeist. Maybe she's a hybrid. Like Claudia."

"Like a wolphin," agreed Arthur. (Tom and Arthur had both watched the same documentary about hybrid animals.)

"Or a liger," agreed Tom with a smile. He rolled back down and stared up at the ceiling again. "What about you? What's keeping you awake?"

"Nerves, I guess. Do you think the plan is going to work?"

"Honestly? I don't know. I hope so."

"I hope so too, Tom."

They both lay back in silence for a while, thinking. It was Arthur who spoke again first.

"Tom . . . If it doesn't work . . . and if we can't find a way to stop this Theo, or put her back . . . What do you think will happen to me?"

Tom rolled across and peered over the side of the bed down at Arthur.

"What do you mean?" he asked.

"You know . . . if all the humans start seeing ghosts. I mean, I look pretty ghosty, don't I? There's no way that I could just blend in. I can't even get my ears on straight," he said sadly.

"Your ears look fine, Arthur. You don't need straight ears."

"And . . . I'm *grey*, Tom."

"I know you're grey. Why are you telling me you're grey?"

"Because I don't want people to be scared of me. I'm a really nice ghost, and I think it would be horrible having people scream when they see me."

Tom smiled at his friend. "Nobody would scream at you. You look too friendly to scream at."

"You screamed at me."

"No I didn't. Did I?"

"Kind of. More of a weird warbling noise. And then you threw a cactus at me."

"I did?" Tom's recollection of the moment he first properly met Grey Arthur was a little fuzzy. It had all been such a shock. "I'm sorry, Arthur. I didn't mean to."

"I know you didn't, Tom. But that's the point. The more I think about it, the more I worry about how other humans would respond, and then I get a horrid feeling in my stomach."

"Well, it's not going to come to that. The plan will work, Lost and Found Freddie will track down the Terrible Theo, and then we'll . . ." Tom wasn't entirely sure what they'd do then. "Then we'll think of something."

"I suppose," agreed Arthur, halfheartedly. Tom smiled at him, then rolled back onto the bed. They both lay there in silence for a while.

"Do you think the tests would hurt?" asked Arthur. Tom frowned, and peered back over the side of the bed.

"Tests? What kind of tests?"

"Sciencey ones. Claudia seemed to think they'd want to do tests on us, if they knew we existed. Do you think they'd hurt?"

"Arthur, nobody is going to do tests on you."

"How do you know?" asked Arthur in a quiet voice.

"Because . . . ," Tom said. "Because if everyone could see ghosts, then my mum and dad could see them too, and my mum and dad would never let a thing like that happen to my best friend."

"What if they couldn't stop them?"

Tom laughed. "Trust me. They'd find a way. It'd be a brave sciencey-test-man that tried to take on my mum."

Grey Arthur nodded. "Okay. Thank you, Tom. Good night."

"Good night, Arthur."

Tom rolled back onto the bed, and was just about to turn off the light when he realized Arthur was talking again.

"Does it make you sad?" he asked. "That your parents can't see ghosts."

Tom thought about the question, and then sighed. "I guess. I mean, I know Mum finds it all a bit odd, but she's trying to be nice about it—but I thought Dad actually believed. But he can't, can he? Not really. If he did, then he'd see you."

There was a long, heavy silence before Arthur spoke again. He chose his words carefully, spoke gently, hoping to make his friend feel better.

"I don't know, Tom. I think the difference is he believes you. I think maybe he even believes in me. I don't think I ever told you, but after the Dr. Brown thing, after I left a note for him to find, he said thank you."

"Really?" asked Tom, shocked. "No, you've never told me that before."

"I just think it must be hard for him. It's not like you've gone out of your way to convince him either, is it? It's more like a badly kept secret."

"I suppose." A thought hit Tom. "I could, though, couldn't I? If we manage to track down this Theo lady, then I could. They couldn't help but believe if they met her, if I explained exactly what was going on. I know we don't want the whole world to start believing, but maybe if just my mum and dad did, then surely that would be okay. . . ."

"They're not meant to see ghosts, though."

"What do you mean?"

"Your dad is meant to create mad socks and to read the Sunday papers. Your mum is meant to work in a castle and worry about whether or not you have brushed your teeth. I don't think they're meant to see ghosts. I think they are meant to be normal parents, Tom. Besides," he added, chuckling, "I reckon you'd hate it if they could."

"Why's that?"

"Can you imagine it? We'd be sent out of your room to give you time to do your homework, told off for keeping you up at night. Your mum would be twitching to tell the Screamer to put some clothes on, telling Monty off for talking so loudly the whole time, and running herself ragged trying to get Tike to take a bath."

Tom couldn't help but smile, even though a melancholy hint lingered at the corners of his mouth. "You're right, I know you are. It's just so difficult sometimes . . ." He changed the subject. "So, are you all set for tonight?"

"Ready as I'll ever be. Do you want us to wake you when we set off?"

"No, I think I'd best get some sleep. If this doesn't go as planned, tomorrow is going to be a long old day."

"Okay, well then, wish me luck for later."

"Good luck, Arthur."

"Thanks! Good night, Tom."

"Nanight."

And with that, Tom finally turned off the light.

A Very Important Mission

IT WAS AT THE UGLIEST OF HOURS WHEN TIKE CRAWLED out through Kate's laundry basket and spilled out into her cupboard—that fragile wavering point where nobody is sure if it is very late at night, or very early in the morning. It was still dark, with dawn only just beginning to contemplate appearing, a faint glow reluctantly appearing on the horizon. It wasn't as if Tike could see it, though, hidden as he was among Kate's sneakers, school uniforms, and a rather pretty blue velvet dress that was obviously for special occasions.

"This is crazy!" Tike laughed quietly as he gave Arthur a helping hand out of the laundry basket. Grey Arthur fell ungracefully to the floor, and quickly scrambled to a crouching position.

"I know, I know . . . ," muttered Arthur, trying to peer through the slats of the wooden cupboard door. It didn't work, and he soon gave up. The pair of them were dressed from head to toe in black, like ghostly burglars from a silent movie.

"You're gonna turn me into a Contrary if we carry on like this. If you tell any other Poltergeists what I'm doing . . ."

"It'll be our secret," promised Arthur.

Tike rolled his eyes, but seemed pleased at the reassurance. "Madness," he simply said in response.

"This is the right place? You're sure?" whispered Grey Arthur.

"Trust me." Tike nodded. "I don't think there's a kid at that school I haven't hit on a Laundry Run before. This is Kate Getty's cupboard, all right."

"And you're convinced you've found an exact match of the necklace?"

"Sure as I can be. Can't be that many demonically-ugly-looking-chunky-gold-clown-with-beady-red-eye necklaces knocking around, can there?"

"You'd be surprised. . . ."

"You wouldn't believe how many jewelry shops I had to go through before I found one. Umpteen shops. Finally found it in the dingiest little place ever, next to some big gold sovereign rings shaped like mutant wolf heads. Odd place. Anyway, here it is." Tike rummaged into his pocket and produced the offending piece of jewelry. He held it like you would hold a soiled diaper, grimacing as he dangled it before him. The chain looked as if it had been plundered from a sink and stripped of its plug, and the clown's red eyes caught what little light there was, making it look positively sinister. "She should be grateful it got pinched in the first place. I reckon we'd be doing her a favor by not giving it back. It's well nasty."

"That's not quite the point though, is it?"

"No, I know, but still." He stared at it, shaking his head. "*Ugly.*"

"Okay, so we're in position, we've got the necklace, and Kate's fast asleep. Are you ready to do this?" Arthur asked. Tike took a deep breath, nodded, and then disintegrated into a fit of giggles. "Tike, be quiet!" pleaded Arthur, a smile creeping onto his face no matter how much he struggled to stay composed. "You've got to . . . If she hears us . . . We can't . . ."

And then Arthur started giggling too.

It *was* ludicrous. Here were two ghosts, sneaking into a girl's bedroom in the middle of the night, not to scare her, not to steal her socks, or hide her homework, or do any of the other things ghosts are meant to do, but there in order to haunt her into believing that ghosts don't exist. Tom's master plan was as simple as it was faintly deranged—they were to return Kate's necklace to her, or rather an exact copy of it, in the hope that it would convince her that the dreadlocked ghost she saw was nothing but a dream. Really, they'd done well to get this far without collapsing with laughter. Grey Arthur tried to be serious, tried his hardest to stifle his chuckling, but one look at Tike's face, creased with mirth, tears rolling down his dirty cheeks, made him snort and start all over again. He clamped his hand over his mouth, and with the other gestured for Tike to stop, but it was no use. He had to turn away from him in the end, burying his face in a school shirt that was hanging up in the cupboard, and forced himself to think of one of Woeful William's poems, in order to stop his shoulders shuddering and his eyes from watering with amusement.

"Okay, I'm done," whispered Tike eventually, his voice still thick with suppressed laughter. Tike coughed, took a deep breath, and said it again, managing to sound almost serious this time: "I'm done."

"Promise? Because if you start giggling again, then *I* will, and we'll never even make it out of this cupboard."

"Yeah, I promise. For now. But we'd best get this done quickly, 'cause I don't know how long I can last."

Arthur took a tentative peep at Tike, and when he was certain that Tike wasn't going to set him off again, he turned around properly. "Okay . . . Let's get this over and done with. We need to leave it somewhere that she's bound to find it in the morning."

"Yeah, good luck with that. Her room's a mess."

Grey Arthur frowned and pushed his head out through the closed cupboard door.

It took a monumental effort not to gasp.

Kate's room looked like a bomb had gone off in a clothes factory. The carpet, assuming a carpet even existed, was entirely smothered by a layer, or several, of dirty clothes. Mismatched shoes decorated the surface, like sprinkles scattered on an unattractive cake. Posters covered every inch of wall space and had begun spreading onto the ceiling: posters of boys with shiny smiles and bleach-tipped hair, in bands that Grey Arthur had seen miming to songs on Saturday morning television. A large grimy full-length mirror hung among the posters, and beneath it several boxes of makeup overflowed onto the ground. An armchair rested in among the clothes, half-buried, like an iceberg in a sea of mess. Kate Getty lay asleep among all this clutter, curled up on her bed, snug under a duvet cover printed with pictures of cats, clutching a teddy bear. She stirred, and Grey Arthur quickly pulled his head back inside the cupboard.

"How does she put up with living in such a mess?" asked Arthur.

"And why does she even bother owning a laundry basket?" asked Tike.

Grey Arthur felt the giggles rising again and bit his lip, trying to keep them inside. He took a deep breath, counted to five, and let it out slowly.

"I guess we'll have to put it under her pillow. Make out it fell off when she was asleep."

"Great. 'Cause it won't at all make things worse if she wakes up with a ghost rummaging around under her head."

"Well, have you got a better idea?"

"Not really."

"We'll just have to be extra careful, that's all. You ready to do this?"

"Sure. Let's go."

And with that, Tike and Grey Arthur quietly crawled out through the cupboard door and snuck into Kate's room. Tike favored an army-style crawl, shuffling across the ground on his belly, while Arthur stooped low and scuttled along, hands clawing across the clothes terrain. They had nearly made it halfway across the floor when Kate spoke.

"What's that?" she demanded. Tike and Arthur froze, panicked. It was still dark in the room, but all it would take would be one flick of the bedside lamp, and they would be exposed. Tike deftly leaped behind the arm-chair, crouching out of sight, but Grey Arthur was frozen to the spot with indecision. . . . Tike spotted Grey Arthur's rabbit-caught-in-the-headlights moment and came to the rescue. He grabbed Arthur by the neck of his waistcoat and hauled him behind the chair as well. They paused, hearts racing, waiting to see what would happen next.

"Of course I don't still have the elephant," sighed Kate sleepily. "I sold it back to the circus."

Arthur nearly cried with relief when he realized she was just sleep-talking. He grinned at Tike, but when he saw Tike was, yet again, on the brink of laughing, he tried his best to look serious. If he buckled, even slightly, the pair of them would just crumble.

"Let's go . . . ," muttered Arthur in his best "Don't

You Dare Laugh" voice. Together, the ghostly pair padded quietly to the side of Kate's bed. She looked almost sweet, if you can believe that—eyes shut, a sleepy smile twitching on her lips, hands wrapped tight around her teddy bear. There was something different about her, and for a while Grey Arthur struggled to place it. Tike was obviously thinking the same thing, because he pointed at her face and grinned.

"She's not orange. Dunno why, but I just kind of thought she slept in that orange gunk."

It was true. Without her penned-in eyebrows and her carrot-toned foundation, Kate could pass for an average human girl. She smacked her lips and stirred in her sleep, and both Grey Arthur and Tike instinctively took a step back. Arthur nodded at Tike, urging him on, and Tike reached inside his pocket and pulled out the ugly necklace. Carefully, ever so carefully, playing-Jenga-careful, Buckaroo-careful, he slipped the necklace under her pillow. Arthur watched with bated breath, wary that Kate could wake at any minute. She didn't, though. She breathed slowly, deeply, and in the darkness of the room Arthur could just about make out the telltale fluttering under her eyelids that indicated dreams. Tike slowly retracted his hand out from under the pillow, and like a magician showing off a fine trick, displayed his empty hands to Arthur.

Grey Arthur smiled broadly.

"Time to get out of here," he said.

Milk-floats and Floating Ghosts

AS THE SUN, RATHER HALFHEARTEDLY, BEGAN ITS LAZY crawl up into the sky, Brian Loft was already up and about, and busily at work.

Brian liked to whistle while he worked. Partly it was because it was a habit he'd picked up from his old man, who seemed to spend his entire life whistling "Roll out the Barrel." Partly it was because it made him feel cheerful, even on a bleak January day, at a dismal time of the morning. Mostly, though, it was because there was a shameful lack of a sound system and speakers installed in his milk-float. So, Brian whistled as he slowly trundled down the road, adding his own music to the dawn chorus, the chinking of milk bottles taking up the role of percussion.

It was a perfectly normal Tuesday morning, filled with bushes and birdsong, full-cream milk and neighborhood cats, garden paths and doormats that reminded you to wipe your feet.

And a knight in shining armor, charging down the road, waving a giant sword.

Sometimes the gap between seeing something and that image filtering through to your brain can be very wide indeed. This was one of those times. Brian saw the knight charging down the middle of the quiet road, framed on either side by parked Volvo estates and carefully maintained shrubberies, and for the longest time he just stared and stared, his mind empty. He blinked a couple of times, and again for good measure, then shook his head, his mouth falling open, all whistling forgotten.

His brain had finally caught up.

Brian slammed on the brakes, and the sound of glass bottles colliding into one another filled the quiet English street. The knight was continuing his charge toward Brian, and the milkman noticed with a start that the knight's feet, encased in shiny metal pointed boots, never once touched the road, instead skimming a good few centimeters off the surface. Heavy metal gauntlets encased his hands, gripped tightly around a large two-handed sword, and a visor covered his face, dark slits where his eyes should be.

Brian knew he should probably run. Or scream. Or throw milk bottles at him. Or do anything that you'd expect to do when a gigantic knight charges toward you waving a massive sword, all the while floating above the road. The strange thing is, Brian did none of these things. Brian sat, stock-still, in the front of his milk-float, and just dumbly watched as this knight charged closer and closer and closer toward him. Close enough to see the joins in his suit of armor. Close enough to see the details carved into the blade of the sword. Close enough to realize that it was too late to do anything other than grit his teeth, hold his breath, and wait for this all to be over . . .

Five meters away.

Four meters.

Three meters.

Two . . .

The knight charged straight through Brian. Straight through the milk-float. Brian's hair immediately stood up on end, a seeping cold clinging to his skin, and an odd tingling running up and down his back. He gasped, spinning around in the driver's seat, and saw the knight simply passing through his collection of milk bottles and charging out the other side, continuing his run down the road as if Brian hadn't even existed.

Brian watched, transfixed, terrified, amazed as the knight took a left up Hawthorn Road and vanished out of sight.

Then Brian did what no doubt you or I would do if we were in the same situation.

He fainted.

"Mr. Milkman . . . Hello? Can you hear me?"

Brian slowly opened his eyes, and sat up with a start when he found someone's face not ten centimeters away from his own. The old woman smiled, mouth full of crooked teeth, and pushed her glasses back up her nose. "There you are, Mr. Milkman. You had me worried for a while. I came out when I realized it was gone quarter past six and I still didn't have my milk. Most unlike you to be tardy. Then, here you are, out for the count, parked in the middle of the road. Are you all right, dear?"

Brian frowned, rubbing his eyes. "Yeah, I think . . . I'm sorry I'm late . . . I, erm . . ." He paused, trying to remember what had happened. "I must have . . . erm . . . fallen asleep. I'm so sorry."

"Burning the candle at both ends, that'll do it to you," sniffed the woman as she studied Brian's face. "You ought to be careful. Anyone could have stolen your milk while you were sleeping. I know it's a quiet neighborhood, but you can't be too careful these days, can you?"

"No, no, you're right," agreed Brian, as he straightened himself out. He shook his head, trying to chase away the fuzzy feeling. "It won't happen again."

"I should hope not. You're lucky it's milk and not cheese that you're delivering."

"Sorry?"

The woman grinned as she grabbed a pint of milk from the back of the float. "Gives you funny dreams, cheese," she said, as she wandered back toward her house.

Brian watched her go with a dazed smile.

"Trust me," he called after her, "the dream I had was plenty weird enough as it was!"

And with that, Brian started up his milk-float again and continued on his rounds, his ghostly encounter safely filed away under "Weird Dreams That Felt Real but Weren't." In fact, the only lasting effect it had was a promise to himself to get to bed earlier at night, and to carry a flask of coffee with him in the future to prevent another incident of falling asleep at the wheel.

A Few Hours Later

IT WAS A LITTLE BIT AFTER MUM HAD DONE HER traditional morning routine, and while Tom was up and about getting ready for school, and Grey Arthur looked like a zombie. Not the type of actual Zombie ghost that populates Africa and certain states in America, not patchwork skin and rotten teeth, not terrible smell and sluggish thought, but the type that you see in bad horror films. He moaned, and groaned, and dragged his feet, and his hair appeared even more ghostly than usual. It looked like a wig from a charity shop, a wig recovered from the side of the road, a wig that had seen better days, and to top off the look, dark puffy circles clung to his eyes. Grey Arthur, it seems, didn't cope well with lack of sleep.

"I thought ghosts didn't have to sleep?" asked Tom, scarcely able to hide his amusement.

Grey Arthur yawned. "In the past I didn't bother. Not before I met you. Now I think I've gotten a bit too used to it." He paused, thinking, and then frowned. "My eyes feel itchy."

"Why don't you just go back to bed, then? It's not

like you're coming into school with me today. Not until we know that the plan worked."

"It's a bit hard to sleep in with your mum shouting and opening the curtains," moaned Arthur.

Tom laughed. "Yeah, no kidding. I think that's why she does it."

"Come on, Tom, stop dawdling!" called Mum's voice from downstairs. "You're going to be late."

Grey Arthur threw himself down on Tom's bed, looking very sorry for himself.

"I might go back to sleep for a while. Just a little while. Ballpoint Bill is quite happy hanging out in your shed with Harry for the time being, and the Snorgle seems all right playing with the compost." He grabbed Tom's pillow and rested his head on it. "There's no rush, is there?"

"Not really," agreed Tom. "I'm going to be heading into school with Mildred, to test out whether the plan worked. If it did, then all's well, and she can fetch you and the other Invisible Friends back into school. If it didn't, then at least Kate will only be seeing Mildred again, rather than you with your . . ." Tom remembered last night's conversation and gave Arthur a friendly grin. ". . . grey skin and lopsided ears."

"What can I say?" Grey Arthur chuckled tiredly. "I'm a very ghostly ghost."

Tom turned to the mirror and began carefully doing up his tie. "I'm really impressed you managed to replace the necklace. I wasn't sure if Tike would even be able to track down a copy in time, and so to have managed to slip it back into Kate's room is a pretty cool trick. Course, it doesn't make us any closer to tracking down the Terrible Theo, but still, one less thing to worry about. I mean, that's if it worked. Which I hope it has." Tom frowned and turned to face Grey Arthur. "Does the writing on my head look like it's faded at all?"

But Grey Arthur was already fast asleep, sprawled on Tom's duvet. Tom smiled to himself, gelled his hair down over his forehead, and quietly tiptoed out of the room, shutting the door behind him.

Keeping Everything Crossed

WAITING FOR KATE TO COME INTO SCHOOL SO TOM could speak to her felt a little like waiting for the right moment to kick a wasp's nest—Tom was entirely sure that whatever happened, it wasn't going to be much fun. The more he thought about it, the more he wanted to turn tail and run, but looking down and seeing Mildred's anxious, serious face persuaded him to stay put. She was every bit as nervous as he was. Mildred had volunteered to approach Kate on her own, to test whether Kate could still see her when she wasn't trying to be seen, but Kate had a terrible habit of ignoring people's existence. (Especially if they wore black eyeliner. Or were short. Or tall. Or pudgy. Or skinny. Or had braces. Or had ever bought the same shoes as Kate. Or . . . Well, you catch the gist.) In fact, there were very few people Kate ever did acknowledge, and Tom was one of them. The fact that she chose to grace his life with her presence was not usually a marvelous thing, since it meant he bore the full brunt of her less-than-pleasant personality, but right now it *was* a good thing. In a wasp-nest-kicking kind of way. Besides, he could hardly leave Mildred to face the Kate-Beast on her own. Tom shivered, and adjusted his scarf. The snow had gone, but don't let that fool you into thinking the weather was any warmer. Tom sniffed, feeling his nose starting to drip.

"She's late," complained Mildred.

"She's always late."

"I grow impatient."

"Yeah, me too. I just want to get this over and done with." Tom looked at Mildred. "How should we test if she can still see you?"

"I don't know, Thomas." Mildred pondered the question for a while, staring off into space. "I could pull my head off and throw it at her, see if she recoils."

Tom laughed, and then looked at Mildred's serious expression and realized he wasn't sure that she was joking. "You can do that?" he asked, alarmed.

"I don't know. I've never tried." She started feeling around the base of her neck, making gentle tugging motions, and Tom actually found himself shuddering.

"Please, don't start trying now. I don't think I could cope with seeing you remove your own head. Certainly not so soon after breakfast." Tom chuckled at the thought of Mildred hurling her detached head at Kate, and then felt a pang of guilt when he imagined the terrified look on Kate's face. It was a very small pang, but a pang, nonetheless. "I'll start the conversation, and then mention that you want to talk with her. If she's rude to you, then you know she can still see you. If not, then the plan has obviously worked. Sound okay to you?"

"Indeed." Mildred looked ahead and nodded to Tom. "Kate is approaching, and she isn't alone."

In the distance, Tom could see Kate, linked arm in arm with Isabelle and Marianne, the three of them marching down the road and forcing everyone else to get out of their way. Tom felt his heart begin to race a little. As she got closer, Tom spotted the familiar ugly clown necklace jingling around Kate's neck, and he smiled. At least she had found it. That was half the plan down.

Kate, Marianne, and Isabelle continued their stomp into the school grounds. They were heading straight for Tom and Mildred, and for one horrible second Tom thought they wouldn't stop, that they would just crash straight into him and trample him to the ground beneath their pointy-heeled, non-school-uniform-approved shoes. He braced for impact, but thankfully they ground to a halt just in front of him. Close enough for Tom to see the orange rim around Kate's face. Close enough to see just how many times Isabelle had had her ears pierced. Close enough to smell the overwhelming amount of perfume Marianne was wearing. Close enough to be spat on. Slapping distance. Far too close for comfort.

"Get out of the way, Freakazoid," growled Kate. Tom took a deep breath.

"Go on," urged Mildred.

"I thought a ghost stole your necklace," Tom spluttered, his voice about an octave higher than he had been expecting it to be. He cringed at that. Kate scowled at him, and protectively clasped the chunk of gold menace that she wore. Tom waited anxiously for her response.

"I made that up to test who would be stupid enough to believe me," she snapped. "Well done, Freak Boy, you get the stupid award."

"Yeah, Tom, you're so pathetic," sneered Isabelle.

"What an idiot." Marianne giggled.

"What a loser." Isabelle laughed.

Despite all the insults flying his way, Tom found himself grinning. The smile on his lips jarred awkwardly with the nerves he felt, but it wouldn't go away. So far so good. He had to make sure, though. "So, you *didn't* get visited by a ghost, then?"

"Duh. What did I just say? I had a dream about a ghost, then thought it would be funny to see if anyone would be dumb enough to believe me if I said it was real. Didn't think anyone would be idiot enough to fall for it."

"Apart from Freak Boy," corrected Marianne.

"I-See-Ghosts-Boy," added Isabelle.

"Yeah, Tom, you should look gullible up in the dictionary. It's in there." Marianne chuckled.

Kate sighed, exasperated, and flicked Marianne's ear. "Marianne, you spanner, you're meant to say it *isn't* in there."

"Isn't it?"

"No, of course it is, you div, but what you're meant to say is that it isn't, so he'll look it up, and then you get to call him gullible for checking."

"Oh, right. I get it. That's funny." Marianne giggled. "Go look up gullible. It isn't in there," she ordered Tom. Kate rolled her eyes.

"Are you going to move, or are we going to have to kick you out the way?" asked Kate, glaring at Tom. Tom swallowed nervously. Here came the final test.

"I just . . . erm . . . My friend wanted to talk to you. Mildred."

"Who?"

"You know, pale, dark hair, different-color eyes . . ."

"You mean Gothrah?" asked Kate. Marianne and Isabelle giggled like giddy hyenas. "Yeah, you can tell her when she shows up that she has a new nickname. And tell her I wouldn't be seen dead standing anywhere near that little freak, let alone talking to her. In fact, tell her not to bother turning up to school at all—I don't want to have to share my air with a filthy little goth head like her."

And with that, Kate marched off, *straight through Mildred*, still linked arm in arm with her catty friends. Kate shuddered slightly as she did so, as any human who passes through a ghost does, but Kate being Kate, she still found a way to blame it on Tom.

"Ergh, look at my arms," she declared as she traipsed away. "Covered in manky goose bumps. Just being close to Freak Boy gives me the creeps."

Tom raised an eyebrow at Mildred, who clapped.

"That went well," she said.

"Oh yeah, great," sighed Tom. "I especially liked the part where I got called gullible, an idiot, Freakazoid, Freak Boy, and I-See-Ghosts-Boy."

"But she was unable to see me," replied Mildred. "Which means your plan worked." She flipped open her notebook and began writing down what had just occurred. She noticed Tom peering over her shoulder and explained (at the same time as writing, which Tom found to be quite a neat trick) her notes. "It really is quite fascinating, the human capacity to ignore or reject the supernatural, even on the flimsiest of evidence. I'm tempted to write a book on the matter."

Tom laughed. "Are you calling my plan flimsy?"

"Absolutely," Mildred agreed. "But it worked, which is all that really matters."

"I suppose," said Tom. "At least that's one less problem to worry about. We'd better catch this Theo soon, though, or else we're going to have our hands full."

"Full of what?" asked Mildred.

Tom smiled. "It's a phrase. It means that we're going to be very busy tracking down ghost-seeing humans and convincing them not to believe."

"What an odd phrase. I can't see how that would have been used very often, before this specific situation arose."

"Well, no." Tom chuckled. "It doesn't mean *exactly* that. It just means that we'll be busy."

"I see." Mildred snapped shut her notebook and placed it back inside her black satchel. "Now that we are assured that the plan worked, I shall fetch the other Invisible Friends and reunite them with their humans."

"You do that," replied Tom with a grin. "And, Mildred? Don't worry about what Kate said about you. She's just a bit evil."

"I wasn't concerned, Thomas. *I have a nickname.*" She actually seemed pleased. "I've never had a nickname before."

Mildred strode off in the direction of Tom's house, and while Tom couldn't be entirely sure, he thought he detected a hint of a skip in her step. Tom couldn't even begin to fathom how being given a nickname by Kate was a good thing, but it had obviously appealed to Mildred. He stood, watching her go, the sound of the second bell ringing behind him, when someone tugged his sleeve. Tom nearly leaped straight out of his skin.

"Sorry, Tom, didn't mean to startle you," said Pete, looking half apologetic for making Tom jump and half amused that he did. "You're late today. Were you watching the news too?"

"What? Why would I be watching the news?" asked Tom, confused.

"Oh, I dunno," said Pete. "*Maybe because someone has stolen the crown jewels?*"

A Most Audacious Theft

IT DIDN'T TAKE LONG FOR WORD OF THE THEFT TO SPREAD around the school. It was hard deciphering the truth of the affair, due to the nature of school-ground gossip, but Tom and Grey Arthur managed to slowly piece together what had happened through the time-honored trick of eavesdropping.

"I heard that it was a group of men with guns that stole it."

"That's rubbish. Who'd you hear that from?"

"The caretaker."

"That's not true. It was just one guy with a gun."

"There wasn't a gun."

"It wasn't even a guy. It was a woman."

"It wasn't a woman. It was a guy with dreadlocks."

"It was a *woman* with dreadlocks. Red dreadlocks."

"My dad reckons terrorists stole it."

"What would terrorists want with a crown?"

"To sell it, duh."

"Or keep it. Blackmail the queen!"

"I reckon it was ninjas. Ninjas could steal it, easy. You wouldn't even see them."

Tom and Grey Arthur wandered off together as the conversation steered toward the unlikely realm of highly trained martial arts crown jewel thieves, and who would win in a fight between Beefeaters and ninjas.

"Did you hear that?" whispered Tom to Grey Arthur.

Arthur nodded. "Woman with dreadlocks. Sounds about right."

"It's not good, is it?" asked Tom.

Grey Arthur shook his head. "It's really not good. If she carries on like this, she's bound to get caught. Or rather, they'll try to catch her and fall right through her, which is even worse."

Tom was contemplating that when Tike raced around the corner, with Montague and Mildred in tow, and skidded to a halt just in front of them. His eyes were wide, and he bubbled with excitement.

"Tom! Arthur! Did you hear?" he yelled.

"We heard," replied Tom, as Arthur nodded.

"*Ninjas stole the crown jewels!*"

Where Do We Go from Here?

IT TOOK A LITTLE WHILE FOR TIKE TO GET OVER THE disappointment of realizing that it was the Terrible

Theo, and not a crack squad of highly trained ninja mercenaries, that had stolen the crown jewels.

"I suppose it's still pretty cool that a Poltergeist stole them," he'd muttered as they'd left school that evening. Grey Arthur had frowned at him, and Tike quickly corrected himself. "And when I say cool, I mean bad. Way bad. Terrible."

"It *is* bad, Tike," agreed Montague. "It means that this ghost is hardly flying under the radar."

"She can fly?" gasped Tike. "And she dresses up as a knight. *Coolest. Poltergeist. Ever.*"

"She can't fly," said Tom, before looking to Monty for confirmation. "Can she?"

"Honestly, Tom, I have no idea. I doubt it, though."

Tom was the first to navigate his way through the unruliness that was Mrs. Scruffles's front garden. In summer, autumn, and spring, thick leaves hid away the worst horrors, but now everything was reduced to its most basic of elements—sticks with scratchy thorns, stubborn evergreens with spiky leaves, and a thick layer of damp rubbish that usually lurked out of sight. The path was exposed as a scramble of broken bricks, mismatched tiles, and a feeble scattering of gravel. Add to this a thin layer of ice, and you were in potential-broken-ankle territory. Tom took careful, measured steps, arms held aloft like a nervous tightrope walker, while the ghosts followed behind. He reached the door and sighed with relief at the fact he had managed to make it without going head over heels. Grey Arthur leaned past him and knocked loudly at the door. Tom stomped his feet, rubbed his arms, breathed warm air onto his fingers, all the things you do to keep warm in January in England, while he waited for Mrs. Scruffles to come to the red, peeling, sad-looking front door.

When it swung open, it revealed not Mrs. Scruffles, but Agatha Tibbles. The hefty Persian cat mowed loudly at them and then turned around, wandering down the corridor toward the kitchen, bushy tail swishing behind her.

"I think we're meant to follow," Monty said, gesturing for Tom to go inside. Tom dutifully obliged, taking time to rid his shoes of all the dirt they had gathered on that short trip down the garden path. He shuffled and twisted and jiggled on the doormat until he was certain that he'd rid himself of the worst of it, and then he ducked in through the open doorway into the warm, welcoming comfort of Mrs. Scruffles's home. The smell of baking, and biscuits, and just a hint of *cat*, wafted down the corridor to greet him.

Mrs. Scruffles was sitting at the table, poring over a book, when they came in. Black bin liners were gathered around her chair, like Santa's sacks, each full to overflowing with even more books. She smiled cheerily, if a little wearily, and gestured for them to take a seat. Not that there was any seat free, decorated as they were with a topping of sleeping cat, so it ended up with Tom, Mildred, Arthur, Monty, and Tike scooping up armfuls of feline and relocating them onto their laps. Harry milled about in the doorway, testing out his claws on a scratching post. An audience of kittens watched him, transfixed.

"Sorry about not coming to meet you at the door. Poor manners, I know," apologized Mrs. Scruffles, as she pushed her reading glasses back up her nose. "I didn't want to lose my place—I'm wading through this chapter at the moment, trying to see if it can help us."

"And can it?" asked Tom, hopefully.

Mrs. Scruffles smiled sadly and shut the book. "Doesn't look that way." She removed her glasses, letting them dangle from the neck cord, and rubbed her eyes. She looked tired. "Long day," she explained.

"Did you see the news?" asked Tom.

Mrs. Scruffles nodded, her expression serious. "Oh yes. I saw. We've got quite a crisis on our hands, haven't we?"

The table was already laid, and Tike wasted no time in tucking into the pile of chocolate bourbons. The big teapot was stowed away under a large, chunky-knit tea cozy, ready and waiting for their arrival. Grey Arthur grabbed the pot and began pouring for everyone.

"How did it go up in London with Freddie? Has he managed to track down Theo yet?" Arthur asked, as he topped up Mrs. Scruffles's cup of tea. She smiled gratefully and took a sip.

"It's not the best of news, I'm afraid."

"Can't he help us?" asked Tom.

"Well, about that . . ." She took a deep breath and shook her head. "He's not there."

"What? He's not been stolen again, has he?" cried Tike, alarmed.

Mrs. Scruffles looked momentarily perplexed, until she realized that Tike was referring to the Collector saga. "Oh no, no. Nothing like that. Turns out, he's on an exchange trip. It's a once-yearly thing—the Contraries from England go over to America, and vice versa."

"An exchange trip? Is there no way to get him back?" Monty asked, twitching his mustache thoughtfully.

"Well, I managed to talk to their chairwoman, a lovely Zombie lady from New Orleans. She's looking after the Victoria Station Lost and Found Department while he's away . . . Once I explained the predicament, she agreed to send word back home, but the problem is she's not sure how long it will take to find him."

"Why's that?" asked Grey Arthur.

"Oh, it's some odd thing they do over there. All the ghosts meet up, and then a spirit animal guides them to somewhere entirely random where they have fires, exchange stories, sing songs, bond as a group. Was Carl's idea, as far as I can tell."

"Carl?" asked Monty.

"A Contrary Screamer," explained Tom. "The Calming Whisperer. He's a bit . . . hippie."

"Figures," muttered Tike.

"So could an American Contrary not assist us?" suggested Mildred.

Mrs. Scruffles smiled. "Oh, they all offered, which was terribly kind of them. I'm just not sure what use they will be. There's a Banshee who likes to sing happy songs at weddings and Bar Mitzvahs, a Thesper who can't act, a ghost who is convinced he is a spirit animal stuck in human form, an obsessive-compulsive Poltergeist who sneaks into people's houses at night and tidies up, and a Sadness Summoner who somehow manages to make all humans in the vicinity uncontrollably happy. And of course, there's Alison, the chairwoman, who is just quite a chatty, friendly, likable Zombie. They're all very lovely ghosts, but I'm afraid I can't see them being much use in our current situation."

"So, what is our course of action now, Mrs. Scruffles? Must we wait for Freddie to return?" Mildred asked, pushing her straight black hair behind her ears. It was something Mildred tended to do when she needed to think. How tucking your hair away helps the thinking process was beyond Tom, but he'd noticed it was something girls do.

Mrs. Scruffles sighed heavily. "Time isn't really on our side, Mildred. Things have escalated somewhat. I'm afraid we can't afford to just sit and wait. . . ." She pushed the book she had been reading to one side and rummaged through the nearest black bin liner. The book she removed was called *Ancient Britain—A*

Druidic Domain. It was an obscenely large book, and it smelled of the section of a library where only academics dare to tread. Mrs. Scruffles tapped the front cover. "It wasn't an entirely wasted trip. I spent the night at the London library, scouring through all the resources they have on Druids, but it's just all so frustrating. I took a leaf out of Tike's book, and, well . . . *borrowed* . . . as many books on Druids as I could find, but all the information is so watered down or vague. He said, she said, they said . . . Imagine that over hundreds of years . . ."

"You weren't able to find *anything* of use?" Tom asked, shocked.

"Oh, if you want a love potion, or a sleep potion, or something that will make you smell like a deer for a month, then I'm all set, but it seems the grander spells never quite made it to the books. Apparently the Druids were quite a secretive bunch." A rather bold tabby cat started drinking out of Mrs. Scruffles's teacup, slurping enthusiastically. She shooed it away halfheartedly and carried on drinking. Tom grimaced. "I've been thinking about this a lot, an awful lot, Tom, and I'm not sure that you'll like the conclusion I've come to."

The ghosts exchanged concerned looks over the table, as Mrs. Scruffles traced her ghostly finger around the rim of her teacup, lips pursed, eyes distant. She sighed and looked up.

"Maybe," she said, a resigned tone in her voice, "all this is a sign. Maybe the Druids' magic being forgotten or lost over the years, Freddie being away, Theo escaping, perhaps this is just the way it's meant to be. Maybe we're not meant to be able to stop this. . . ."

"And maybe it just means Tom shouldn't put his sticky hands all over weird, magic stones," countered Tike.

"I thought we were saying that was a coincidence!" complained Tom.

"Whatever," replied Tike with a mischievous shrug. "Of course we're meant to stop this. We're Invisible Friends. We can't be Invisible Friends if all and sundry can see us, can we?"

Ghost logic. Usually it made Tom feel like he was going to have a nosebleed when he was subjected to too much ghost logic, but this little gem from Tike was different. Tike grinned at him, and Tom grinned back.

"He's right, Mrs. Scruffles," agreed Grey Arthur. "We shouldn't give up. There has to be a way. Just because we haven't found it yet, doesn't mean there isn't one."

"You're right, Arthur," agreed Mrs. Scruffles. "I'm sorry. It's just been a long day. A momentary lapse in positivity. Tell us what you want us to do."

Grey Arthur faltered. "Me?" he asked, shocked. "Why me?"

"You were the one that said we could find her. Where do you want us to start?"

Grey Arthur flashed a panicked look at Tom, who nodded encouragingly at him. He bit his lip, humming to himself, eyes fixed on a distant point. His lips moved silently as he ran through ideas in his head. "O-kay . . . ," he said hesitantly. "Okay. I've got it. Mildred, you help Mrs. Scruffles with going through the books. Two heads are better than one, after all."

"It would be my pleasure," replied Mildred. Arthur grinned at her, and then turned his attention to Montague.

"Monty, do you know Essay Dave?"

"Not personally, but I've heard of him. Top-class paperwork Poltergeist, isn't he?"

"That's the one. I was wondering, if I give you his address, if you could pop up and have a word with him, let him know what's going on. Who knows, he might have some old Druid books lying around his office. It's worth a try. We can trust him, and I'm sure he'll want to help—after all, it would make his job much tougher if humans could see him."

"I'll get straight on it," agreed Monty.

"Tike, can you ask around your friends, see if a new insanely strong Poltergeist has shown up on the scene?"

"Will do, gov'nor," replied Tike with a wink.

"Me, Tom, and Harry will head back home. Tom can have a look on the computer, see if he can spot any more sightings, anything that might help us narrow down a location. If we find anything out, we'll get back to you, otherwise we'll meet back here tomorrow after school to catch up on what we've discovered."

"See. That wasn't too difficult, was it? We have a plan," Monty replied with a broad smile.

Perhaps plan wasn't quite the right word. Technically, it was a plan to help them think up a plan, the most rudimentary of ideas, a few tentative steps in the right direction, while remaining firmly in the dark. But that is, after all, how most plans start, and Grey Arthur consoled himself with the thought that it was a lot better than simply giving up. They just had to hope that they worked out what was happening before the human world did.

When Things Go from Bad . . .

"'*I WOZ OUT IN DE PARK 2DAY WHEN I WOZ GRABBED by a leprecorn and he did steal my hat and then I ran cos I woz scared and he ate my hat and then I woke up in a bush. LOL,*'" read Tom, shaking his head with dismay. "This is useless, Arthur. All these people are mad."

The three of them were crowded around Tom's dad's computer, desperately searching for a lead. When they had started looking, there had still been just a hint of light left in the day, but now night had well and truly established itself, and the room was dark. The glow from the screen threw an unnatural light onto their faces, accentuating the frowns they all wore. They were frowning with good reason, too. All they had found so far were examples of people who seemed to type with a fist, WHOLE OUTBURSTS IN CAPITAL LETTERS, and stories that were so ludicrous that Tom had to keep checking to make sure they weren't remnants of April Fools' jokes.

"What about that one?" asked Arthur, pointing at the screen. "Ghost spotted in woodland."

Tom clicked on the link and growled, "Nope, not helpful. *I was in the forest trying to get sticks for my snowman, because he needed arms, and all the sticks nearby I could find were either too fat or too short, or didn't have little twiggy fingers, which is what the snowman needs, because otherwise how would he do up his scarf if he didn't have fingers—*'"

"Skip to the end," interrupted Arthur.

Tom laughed and raced through. "Blah blah blah, *'found the sticks I needed,'* blah blah, *'tall scary bony ghost,'* blah blah. No good. Not even a hint of dreadlocks or a knight costume. I think we're wasting our time."

"What about that one? Ghost spotted at Stonehenge?"

Tom dutifully clicked on the link, and then blushed as a photo of himself popped up. He quickly closed the page.

"I think we can safely say that's no help to us either."

The Harrowing Screamer moaned in disappointment.

"Don't worry, Harry," said Grey Arthur. "We'll get there in the end."

"Oh, here we go . . . I've got a response from Claudia. . . . And, great, another dead end. She says that she appreciates us keeping her in the loop, but she's glad to report that all the ghosts that have been reported recently have been either the result of over-active imaginations, or just people trying to get their five minutes of fame on television."

"Well, that is good, in a way," said Arthur, trying to

be encouraging. "Good in the absolutely-no-help-to-us way, but good that the Terrible Theo isn't trying to pop up on TV again."

"Unless you count *Crimewatch*," replied Tom glumly.

"Well, yes, there is that . . . ," admitted Arthur. "But on the upside, there's so many different versions of that story floating around, and not once have I heard the newslady say they are looking for a tall, dreadlocked *ghost*. As long as they still think she's human, then we're fine."

"Ish."

"Ish," Arthur agreed. "Come on, Tom, you're going to start turning blue and reading poetry at this rate. Chin up. Perhaps the others are having more luck."

They weren't.

To Worse . . .

DURING THE TIME TIKE WAS DASHING AROUND THE country, interrogating every Poltergeist he knew (with absolutely no success), Mildred and Mrs. Scruffles had drunk about a gallon of tea each, eaten an entire tin of assorted cookies (including the silver wrappers around the orange cream ones), read through nineteen books from beginning to end, and they were also still no closer to finding anything even vaguely useful. The cats were trying their best to be helpful, but since their interpretation of helpful involved rubbing against the books, walking across the pages as you tried to read them, and sometimes bringing in mice to liven up the proceedings, their efforts didn't actually contribute much.

Mildred shut the book she was looking through and shook her head.

"I am beginning to wonder if this is an exercise in futility," she muttered, rubbing her eyes. "Everything is contradictory—the Druids built Stonehenge, the Druids didn't, the stones themselves are magical, the stones have no power at all—and not one single mention of how to reseal a ley-line, or diminish the visibility of the Terrible Theo."

"I must admit, I'm not having much luck either," sighed Mrs. Scruffles, as she removed Carrot Cake from the table for the third time in as many minutes. As soon as his feet hit the floor he bounced back up again, surprisingly nimble for a cat of his years, and began rubbing his scent all over Mildred's book. Mildred left him to it. She looked at Mrs. Scruffles, her pale face even more serious than usual.

"Did you know there used to be wolves, wild, in England?" she asked.

Mrs. Scruffles looked up from the book, confused. "I did, yes. Why are you telling me this?"

"They hunted them to extinction, because humans were frightened of them and thought they were evil."

"I don't think it's quite so simple," said Mrs. Scruffles

softly, realizing Mildred's implication. "Wolves also used to steal livestock."

"Poltergeists steal all the time."

"It's not the same."

"Is it not?"

Mrs. Scruffles sighed softly and pushed her book to one side. "That was a long time ago, Mildred. Things change. Humans change." She smiled at Mildred. "Besides, you're not a wolf. I picture you as more of a cat. A very serious cat."

"And Harry? What would he be?"

Mrs. Scruffles didn't answer that question. Instead, she smiled gently at the little, scared-looking Faintly Real who was perched at her table.

"Let's just keep on looking, shall we?" she said, pushing aside a finished book and reaching for another. "Let's not worry about anything like that until we have to. Besides, right this very second, Monty is visiting Essay Dave. If anyone can help us fix this, it's Essay Dave."

To Dismal . . .

"LOOK," SAID DAVE, AS HE RECLINED IN HIS CHAIR, shiny-shoed feet perched on his paper-strewn desk, "I appreciate everything you ghosts did for me, freeing me from the Collector, and believe me, I really don't want humans to be able to see me, but I'm just not sure how I can help you."

Monty stared at the stacks of paper, giant teetering monoliths of information, that cluttered the office. The neon light, still defiantly broken, flickered overhead, caused shadows to appear and vanish, giving the room a slightly surreal feel. He rubbed his eyes, trying to force away the nagging strains of fatigue.

"There has to be something here, *anything*, that can just shed a bit of light on the situation. How the Druids managed to seal the ley-line, who this Theo is, where she might be hiding out—any insight at all would be helpful. We're grasping at straws, so the tiniest bit of help you could give would at least be something."

Essay Dave adjusted his tie with the words TOP SECRET emblazoned on it, and sat up, swinging his feet back to the floor, his paper suit rustling as he did so.

"What you're looking for simply can't be found. The Druids never committed any of their magic or knowledge to paper. I'm good at my job, really good, but even I can't steal something that never existed in the first place. If you are hoping to find a way to throw this Terrible Theo back into Stonehenge and slam the door shut, then you need to start thinking of an alternative plan, because that magic is well and truly lost. I wish I had better news, I really do, but I'm being brutally honest here." Essay Dave looked at Monty thoughtfully, his expression darkening. "I hate to be the one to say this, but have you contemplated that there is nothing you can do? That this set of actions, now set in motion, can't be undone?"

"We're trying not to come to that conclusion," admitted Monty. Dave nodded, and twisted a silver pen between his fingers as he mulled over Monty's response.

"How long do you think we have at this rate, before enough people believe and then convince everyone else? I mean, one person here, one person there, isolated eccentrics, easy to dismiss, but if this builds momentum . . . How far are we from that crucial tipping point?"

Monty sighed. "How long is a piece of string? We've managed to stop one girl believing so far, and Claudia managed to persuade her human colleagues that they were just victims of a hoax, but who knows how many others will have seen the Terrible Theo by now. Even if only one in a hundred who see her realize that she is a ghost, then eventually those numbers will add up to something substantial. We can carry on trying to trick people into not believing, but there's no guarantees that that approach will always work, no guarantees we'll even be able to find all those humans affected, and anyway, all the while Theo is loose, it will be like King Canute trying to order back the tide."

"It's a fairly grim outlook," murmured Essay Dave. He tapped his desk with the pen, rattling out a marching beat, and chewed his lip. Montague waited, hopefully. Finally Dave laid down the pen and crossed his arms. "The best I can do is offer to help organize the evacuation when the time comes."

"*Evacuation?*" spluttered Monty.

"Of course. If everyone in England starts believing, starts seeing, then the best we can do is offer to relocate the ghosts here to another country. Some might embrace this new way of life, but there will be plenty who simply won't be accepted into the human world, nor would want to be."

"And where would we go to?" Monty found his voice rising with distress, and he took a breath, deliberately forcing calm back into his words. "The earth is so much smaller these days. If England believes, then it won't be long until the rest of the world does."

"Then we keep on moving until there is nowhere left to go."

Monty had come to Essay Dave's office full of hope, genuinely expecting to be handed a piece of paper, old paper, yellowed paper, a piece of paper containing answers, directions, enlightenment, something that would fix it all. Instead he'd been met with a rather unhelpful dose of reality, pessimism, and hard truths. Monty wandered over to Essay Dave's office window and peered through a gap in the blinds at the London view. Outside, the human world glowed brightly in the night, office blocks studded with the light from windows where tired workers lingered late, cars trundling through the roads below, orange pools of illumination gathered like puddles beneath streetlamps, people hurrying about their lives, walking their dogs, meeting a date, wandering home, people walking simply because they had nowhere else to go. Essay Dave drifted to Monty's side.

"I know. It will be a shame to leave it all behind. It's beautiful, isn't it?" Dave said quietly.

"Actually," admitted Montague sadly, "for the first time, it looks quite scary. There's so many of them out there, with no idea what's about to happen. I wonder if they're ready for us."

"I think the bigger question is whether we are ready for them . . . ," muttered Dave. Outside, a police car screamed past, throwing blue traces of light across the walls, sirens wailing. Dave watched quietly as Monty let go of the blind, shutting out the world below. "Listen, Monty, it might not come to it. Just because I can't help you, doesn't mean that nobody else can. We need to prepare for every possible outcome, that's all."

"I know, I know." Montague nodded. "It's just a lot to think about. You take it for granted, don't you, that everything will just stay the same, and then when a big change like this looms on the horizon, it feels like the carpet has been ripped out from under your feet." He smiled wistfully. "When I was younger, I used to dream about humans being able to see us. I used to picture the applause as I performed onstage, the TV interviews, people stopping me in the street to get my autograph."

"And now?"

"I guess age has dragged some realizations in its wake. They'd be more likely to scream and run than clap and fawn. Also, and I think this is key—I'm not just thinking about myself anymore. I've got a human to look after, friends to worry about. . . . I guess I'm starting to see the bigger picture." The two ghosts stood, dwarfed by the stacks of paper dotted around them, and for a while the only noise was the rasping breath of an electric heater, and the hum of the neon lights.

"It might not happen," said Dave finally.

"It might not," agreed Monty. "Let's just cross our fingers that Tom has got better news than I have."

And Back Again

"I GIVE UP," CRIED TOM, PUSHING THE COMPUTER mouse away and leaning back in his chair. He rubbed his eyes and blinked in an exaggerated fashion. "It's useless. Utterly useless."

Grey Arthur was lying on his back on the floor, legs propped up against the wall, studying his grey toes as they dangled above him. The Harrowing Screamer seemed to have fallen asleep standing up, or at least it appeared that way. For the last hour he'd been making small, frequent, odd noises that sounded very much like snoring. Every now and then his fingers would twitch, and he'd sway slightly, but other than that he was pretty much out for the count.

Tom heard the door to the study creak open. Dad peered in, the glow from the hall carving a wedge of light across the carpet to where Tom was sitting.

"I thought I heard you talking. Weren't you heading up to bed ages ago?" he asked, as he groped around inside the door frame for a switch. He found it, and the room burst into light. Harry woke up with a start, hands instinctively springing to his face, protecting his eyes from the brightness, and Grey Arthur rolled into a sitting position. Tom winced as his eyes took their time to get adjusted.

"I was . . . I mean, I am. I just got distracted," replied Tom. The words became tangled up with a yawn he couldn't hold back, making his voice stretch and warp as he spoke.

"You shouldn't sit at the computer in the dark. It's bad for your eyes," chastised Dad gently. "What are you doing, anyway? Homework?"

"Research."

"Going well?"

"Not really. Was just about to call it a night."

"Seems like a good idea to me," replied Dad. "You look exhausted." He paused, a broad smile growing. "Hey, did your mum tell you the good news?"

"News?" asked Tom, confused. "What news?"

"Turns out that petition worked! Think your woman Claudia's autograph was the final straw. The trucks are going to take a different route to the theme park. No more dust all over the garden, no more cracks appearing in the road, and no more early mornings being woken by rumbling sounds—not that that ever affected you, Mr. Dead-to-the-world-before-nine-o'clock-in-the-morning. It's finished. We won." Dad beamed proudly at Tom.

"That's great, Dad, but isn't the theme park nearly finished anyway?"

"Well, yes, it opens next week, but that's not the point."

"It isn't?"

Dad smiled, that small, knowing, adult smile of a parent about to impart a tidbit of wisdom. "No, the point is we made a stand and didn't give up. When you're a bit older, you'll realize you can't win every battle, but that doesn't mean you shouldn't try for all it's worth, and that doesn't mean that you shouldn't celebrate even the tiniest victories. So your mum and I have shared a rather nice bottle of wine, and raised a toast to a week's worth of annoyed truck drivers going the scenic route to work." He grinned triumphantly at Tom.

Tom nodded, smiling back. "Thanks, Dad."

"For what?"

"For the advice."

Dad looked pleased, if a little bemused, by Tom's earnest appreciation, but then Dad had no idea of just how much was going on behind the scenes. He nodded at Tom, touched by the father-son moment that had just passed.

"Go on, you, up to bed."

Tom didn't need much persuading. He dragged his feet up the stairs and collapsed on the bed, too tired to even brush his teeth. Grey Arthur was just as bad, and he slipped beneath the bed without a word, and was asleep as soon as his lopsided ears hit the Pretty Betsy Doll pillow. By the time Dad came up to check on Tom, he was already sound asleep. Dad pulled the covers over him, and quietly turned off the light.

"Good night, Tom," he whispered, as he gently pulled the door closed.

Strangers in the Night

TOM WOKE UP TO THE SOUND OF ARGUING. IN THE darkness he could make out Grey Arthur's voice, but the two others—one male, one female—sounded familiar, though he couldn't quite place them.

"I said, put them back," Arthur snapped.

"Look, we're here to do you a favor," said the boy.

"Tike said to come by if we stumbled across anything odd," said the girl.

"Least you can do is hand over some socks for the hassle," the boy added.

"You can't take them. It's winter. His feet will get cold," Grey Arthur explained.

"Foot. His foot will get cold. We only ever take one," retorted the girl.

"Oh, come on. Tom was nice enough to free you from the Collector. Least you can do is leave him some matching socks."

"Yeah, and before that we helped free him when he was all tied up in that hut, which makes us even-stevens," complained the boy.

Tom turned on the bedside light and winced as everything flooded with brightness.

"What's going on?" he asked thickly, voice still choked with sleepiness.

Grey Arthur shrugged apologetically. "Sorry to wake you, Tom. You've got visitors."

Tom sat up and rubbed the sleep from his eyes. Blearily, he struggled to make sense of what was happening. The boy ghost had a mop of scraggy blue hair, held out of his face with a green rugby sock, and the girl ghost had bright orange hair tied up in pigtails. Both wore outfits made from stitched-together socks. Tom recognized them immediately.

The Mischief Twins.

"Hello, Mike. Hello, Miranda," he said tiredly.

"Evening, squire," chirped Mike.

Miranda quickly dropped a stash of socks from her hand and stepped in front of them, hoping Tom wouldn't notice.

"Evening, Tom," she said.

"What time is it?" Tom asked, fumbling for his bedside clock. He groaned when he saw it.

3:18 a.m.

"They say they've got some important news to give you," Grey Arthur explained.

"Yeah, your man Tike asked us to keep our eyes peeled in case we bump into anything unusual on our rounds," Mike said. "And to let you know if we did."

"And we did," said Miranda. "And so here we are."

"Okay, okay . . . ," Tom said. His brain felt like a pile of mulch, and he struggled to think of what to say. He slapped his face, trying to shake loose the remnants of sleep.

"Your human's gone odd, Arthur . . . ," whispered Miranda.

"*Odder*," corrected Mike.

"Okay!" said Tom, finally regaining limited use of his brain. "What's going on?"

"Tike said you're on the lookout for a Poltergeist, yeah? Some, like, über-Poltergeist, on a mega stealing spree?" Mike asked. Tom nodded.

"So, we decided to go off the beaten track on the Laundry Run, just see what we could find," Miranda said, picking up the story. "So, we take a few more lefts than usual, throw in a couple more rights, and . . . Bingo."

"Bingo?" repeated Tom.

"Bob's your uncle," nodded Mike. "Some serious Poltergeisting going on. Like, crazy ghosting.

Probably even a gold-plated kitchen sink in there somewhere."

"In where?"

"I dunno," said Miranda. "Some warehouse place. Wrote down the directions for you." She threw a scrunched-up piece of paper at Tom, who carefully laid it out on the bed. "Thought you could go check it out."

"'Turn left at the pile of tartan socks?'" read Tom. "What kind of directions are these?"

"Laundry Run ones. Duh." Mike and Miranda shared amused looks. Tom blushed. How was he meant to know?

"Tom can't do the Laundry Run," Grey Arthur said. "Is there another way there?"

"Tike said Tom was ley-lining left, right, and center chasing after the Collector bloke. If he can do that, then he can Laundry Run. We've no idea how you'd get there otherwise. It's all a bit random. Two exits next to each other, and you could crawl out hundreds of miles apart. The laundry basket next to Tom's? Pops out somewhere in Scotland. The one on the other side? Some mad old beardy man in Newcastle. Great socks there. Well worth a trip."

For some reason, it didn't surprise Tom in the slightest that Poltergeist travel would be more chaotic than any other method. If it was straightforward and organized, it wouldn't suit them.

"Nice pajamas, by the way, Tom. And I like your head tattoo." Miranda chuckled. Tom turned even redder, and retreated farther under his duvet, one hand obscuring his still visible head graffiti.

"Right, then, job done. Say hello to Tike for us," Mike said, and he waved cheerily at Tom. "Have fun."

"Wait. You're not coming?" Tom asked.

Miranda laughed. "No way. Thanks to Arthur, we're at least three socks down, and running late. Besides, all this heroic stuff is a bit too serious for us."

"If you need some socks pinched, or a toilet bowl covered with clingfilm, then give us a shout," agreed Miranda. "But we're a bit keener on causing chaos than fixing it."

And with that they turned and plunged headfirst into Tom's laundry basket and were gone. It's amazing how much quieter a room can seem without Poltergeists in it.

"What now?" asked Arthur, sitting down on the edge of the bed next to Tom. "Do you want to go back to sleep?"

"Nah, I'm awake now. Might as well go fetch the other ghosts and check it out."

Tom got out of bed and pulled on his sneakers. Pajamas and shoes might not be the best attire for ghost hunting, but Tom was a bit too tired to go rummaging through his wardrobe for something more suitable. He went to ask Arthur's opinion on whether he'd need a coat, but Arthur was already gone. Tom shrugged and pulled on a hooded top. That would have to do.

Now he just had to stay awake long enough to see this through.

And Now for Something Completely Different

GREY ARTHUR RETURNED TO FIND TOM IN HIS SNEAKERS, hooded top, and Mr. Space Pirate pajamas, slumped facedown on his desk, fast asleep.

"Tom . . . ," he whispered. "Tom . . ."

"Oi! *Tom!*" shouted Tike. Tom sat bolt upright and wiped the dribble from his chin. Hopefully nobody noticed.

"I'm awake!" he said, not too convincingly. "I was just resting my head."

"Course you were," said Tike with a wink. "You just drooled down yourself for fun."

Mildred, Montague, the Harrowing Screamer, Tike, and Grey Arthur all stood in the room, ready to go. Tom stood up, trying to straighten out a kink in his neck from falling asleep in an odd position. Something cracked, and Grey Arthur winced, but Tom felt much better afterward.

"Right, then . . . so we're going on the Laundry Run, yeah?" asked Tike. Tom nodded apprehensively. "So, who here's been before?"

Grey Arthur lifted his hand, but everyone else's stayed down.

"Well, that should make things interesting . . . ," Tike muttered. "Care to explain to our newbies how it's done, Arthur?"

Grey Arthur shrugged. "You just jump into the laundry basket, and sink down into the network. That's it, really, isn't it?"

"Pretty much," agreed Tike. "It's well easy to get lost down there, though, so you all need to stick together. Last thing we need is Tom going walkabout and crawling out into some girl's bedroom."

"Hey, why would it be me that gets lost?" asked Tom, a little annoyed. The Invisible Friends shared quiet looks, but nobody answered. Tom huffed. "I might be really good at the Laundry Run. You never know," he muttered.

"Here's the map, Tike," Arthur said, changing the subject. "Does it make sense to you?" Grey Arthur handed over the scrap of paper, and Tike read it, occasionally nodding.

"Turn at the tartan socks . . . follow the crawlspace down by pink mohair cardigan . . . sharp right at unwashed stench . . . Easy peasy. It's really not far."

"I need someone to stay behind, just in case Mum and Dad get up in the night to check on me," announced Tom. "They shouldn't, but if they do, I'd rather know than crawl back into a massive argument about where I've been going in the middle of the night."

"Consider me volunteered," intoned Montague. "I can't say I'm overly excited at the prospect of crawling through filthy underwear. I'll stay on guard, let you know if you get caught out. I can even make a fake human shape in the bed for you."

"Oh yeah, out of clothes, good idea," agreed Tom.

"Clothes . . . clothes it is, then. I was going to use papier-mâché, but clothes is probably easier."

Tom grinned.

"Right, then," Tike said, jiggling on the spot, "I'll go first, then you, Tom, then Arthur, Mildred, and, Harry, you can take the back. Okay, Tom, you gonna get dressed before we go?"

"This is what I'm wearing."

"Riiiight. Okay. Watch what I do, and copy." Tike sprinted up toward the laundry basket, leaped in the air, tucked his knees to his chest, and vanished inside. Tom chased after him and peered into the basket. There was no sight of the Poltergeist.

"Tike?" Arthur called.

"Come on, slowcoach," came a muffled response, from deeper within the laundry basket than should be possible. Tom lifted the laundry basket and looked underneath it, but all that was there was carpet and fluff. He didn't know what he'd been expecting to see, to be honest. He placed the laundry basket back down in place. Tom pulled a strange face, a mix of nerves, excitement, sleepiness, and bemusement, and took a deep breath. Carefully, he stuck one leg inside the laundry basket. It squished various items of clothing out of the way, and then came to a firm stop as he reached the bottom.

"I don't think I'm going to fit," he complained.

Arthur smiled encouragingly at him. "Put both legs in. Plenty of room."

Tom sighed, but did as he was told. The result was, rather undramatically, Tom, standing up to his waist in his laundry basket.

"This is stupid," he muttered.

"Try crouching down inside, Thomas," instructed Mildred. Tom tried, but instead of fitting in, he heard the wicker basket straining as he bent it out of shape. He nearly lost his balance, and had to windmill his arms frantically to stay upright. He caught hold of a shelf and hung there, precariously balanced.

"Okay, change of plans. Monty, I'll stay here, you can go in my place," Tom said.

"Jump," said Monty.

"What? How am I supposed to jump? I'm stuck inside a stupid laundry basket."

"You stepped in, hesitantly, slowly. Tike jumped in. Maybe that's what you're doing wrong. So, jump."

"I don't think it's that at all, Monty. I just think humans and laundry baskets don't mix. But, if it makes you happy . . ."

Tom held on to the shelf and made an awkward half-jump inside the laundry basket. He managed, within the tight confines of wicker, to raise himself slightly off the floor, but the strange part was, he never landed.

Tom plummeted through the ground.

All That Glitters

As Tom fell through the laundry basket, he'd briefly wondered if this was how Alice had felt after recklessly pursuing the white rabbit. He'd tried to slow his fall by clawing at the walls, but clothing had just broken free and descended with him. Tom had just enough time to wonder about the best way to land (knees tucked? legs bent?) but not enough time to put it into action, and he plopped to a halt on a mass of springy woollen sweaters. It was a surprisingly comfortable landing.

He'd arrived in what looked to be an alcove made mostly of laddered tights. They twisted and intertwined to form walls, and while it was quite fascinating to see, there was also no denying the overwhelming whiff of feet that accompanied it. Tike was standing in the center of the space, studying the map. Tom heard a screeching noise from above, and managed to roll out of the way just in time to stop Arthur landing through him. Mildred followed, a more dignified entrance than Arthur's, and the Harrowing Screamer fell in shortly after. He landed perfectly, managing to stay standing, but tatters of clothes hung from his claws where he had obviously tried to slow his fall too.

"Welcome to the Laundry Run," Tike had said as he spun about, trying to get his bearings. Mildred was already taking notes. Something caught Tom's eye, and he rushed over to pick it up.

"My sweater!" he'd cried as he held it. "I put it in the wash months ago. I've been looking everywhere for this."

"Yeah, sometimes things come along for the ride when a Poltergeist goes through your basket. Leave 'em down here long enough, and they just get absorbed into the walls. Pretty neat, really."

Tom had wrapped his sweater around his waist, determined to spare it the fate of wall absorption. It made him wonder just how many clothes he'd lost this way in the past, hitching a ride with a Poltergeist to tumble into this secret network of passages. Maybe that's where his Star Wars pajamas had ended up when he was a kid.

Tike had finally decided the right way to go, and gestured toward a small crawlspace, only just big enough to go through on all fours. Tom had sighed a bit—it wasn't as if he was claustrophobic, but still, the thought of being trapped in a tight smelly space didn't exactly thrill him either.

"Okay, Tike," Tom had said. "Lead the way."

"Don't be such a pansy," Tike had replied.

"It will be okay, Thomas," Mildred had whispered.

"I'll be right behind you," reassured Grey Arthur.

The Harrowing Screamer had just hissed. Encouragingly? In amusement? It was really hard to tell.

That was the annoying thing about ghosts. Hearing by emotion made pretending not to be scared nigh on impossible. Tom thought about trying to argue that he wasn't worried at all, but realized there wasn't much point. He just took a deep breath, nodded, and chewed his lip, in that order.

"Ready?" Tike had asked, and before waiting for Tom to reply, he'd scurried off through the small hole. Tom threw himself down on all fours and took after him.

It was pretty much every bit as bad as Tom had imagined it would be. There was scarcely enough space to move, let alone other necessary human actions, such as breathing. The floor was soft and spongy beneath him, but every now and then he'd hit a patch that was crispy, or possibly worse, sticky, and he would have no choice but to drag himself through it. Tom quietly swore to himself that, after today, he would never let himself get talked into traveling by laundry again. It was claustrophobic, hot, and smelled unbearably of musty socks and damp sports gear. He took a breath, and nearly inhaled a pair of swimming shorts, and it took a monumental effort not to retch. He fished the offending pair away from his mouth, and grimaced at the taste of chlorine. Yes, it was for the good of the Ghost World, and mankind, and blah blah blah, but it stank, and brushing against all these clothes made Tom feel like he might explode from all the static electricity. Next time, the ghosts could go ahead, and he'd get a taxi to meet them at the other end. Or cycle. Or jog. Anything! Anything but this. He scuttled forward, careful never to lose sight of Tike's grubby sneakers. The thought of getting lost in here was terrifying.

The clothes began to change, the farther in they went. There were bands of style—one section consisted of nothing but white trousers, white socks, white hoodies, white pants. At the end of this section lay a pile of tartan socks, just as Mike and Miranda had said, and here the path split in two. Tike briefly consulted the map, and then hurried down the left passage. The next section it led into obviously belonged to some kind of hippie student—coarse hemp materials in rainbow colors, tie-dyed skirts, and a faint whiff of sandlewood incense. If the rooms are an indicator of the person who lives above, Tom wondered what his chasm of tights said about the person that lived in Aubergine Road before him. Maybe, in time, it would change to be decked with school shirts, PE shorts, and knitted sweaters from Grandma. Tike whistled to get Tom's attention. A pink, mohair cardigan was embedded in the wall, and Tike looked at it, nodded, and then continued down the sloping path. Another stage, and this person obviously didn't believe in deodorant, or baths, or removing their clothes until they fell off of their own accord. Tom's eyes watered, and he tucked his hands inside his sleeves so he wouldn't have to touch anything.

"Isn't this wicked?" called Tike from in front. Tom didn't answer. He was afraid that if he opened his mouth, he might actually be able to taste what he could smell. Chlorine was bad enough, but this would probably give Tom some weird lurgy, or make his tongue wither. He shuffled onward, trying not to breathe too often. For a brief second, he lost sight of Tike's feet, and blind panic gripped him. Visions of being trapped here rampaged in his head, living off what food had been dropped down Unhygienic Man's clothes, building a bed from unwashed pants, resting his head on a pillow made from crispy socks. He scrambled forward at speed, and quickly caught up.

Never, never again, he said to himself. Leave the Laundry Run to the Poltergeists.

The corridor, if you could call it that, curled round sharply to the right, and as Tom followed it he realized that Tike had stopped. The ghost twisted around, and grinned impishly at Tom.

"I reckon we're here. Look at this. Got to be the place."

Tom peered past Tike and gasped. Beyond the layer of grimy clothes they were currently wading through, everything changed. Skirts with shiny sequins glinted, tops dressed with mini crystals gleamed, silver and gold trousers, like something from an eighties music video, were twined into the clothing walls. If Aladdin had opened a charity shop, Tom imagined this is what the clothes aisle would look like.

"Is everyone else still behind you?" Tike asked. Tom craned around and saw Grey Arthur shoveling socks out of the way, a horrified look on his face.

Tom smiled. At least it wasn't just him who was finding this less than enjoyable.

"Looks that way," Tom replied. Tike nodded.

"Right, then. Exit should be around here somewhere. Takes a bit of a knack, finding the way out, so best you steer clear and leave it to the pro." Tike cracked his knuckles and ruffled his hair for good measure. Tom, quite happy to leave Tike to it, leaned against the wall to catch his breath.

And fell right through it.

It was like being caught in a fabric avalanche, and Tom tumbled, twisted, spun, and slid through multitudes of clothes. Sequins tugged at his skin, rending tiny scratches, and something with hooks instead of buttons latched into his hair. A velvet scarf, deep royal purple, tangled round his neck, and Tom frantically clawed at it to break loose.

The floor slammed into Tom, and he lay there, sprawled, winded, dressed like a hyperactive child unleashed in a dressing-up box. The purple scarf still clung round his neck, a silver corset jutted out from where it was caught in his hair, and round his ankle were a pair of glittery tights. Tike fell out next to him, and Grey Arthur, Mildred, and the Harrowing Screamer weren't far behind. Tike and Arthur took one look at Tom and burst out laughing. Tom scowled.

"Don't frown at me!" Tike chuckled. "I told you to wait, but oh no, you had to be all impatient."

"I fell!" protested Tom.

"If you say so." Tike stared at the scarf and smirked. "Purple's really not your color."

"Don't be mean, Tike," said Grey Arthur, shaking off the giggles. He smiled kindly at Tom. "I think it looks nice."

Tom growled and tugged away at the clothes that were draped around him. The Harrowing Screamer helpfully cut through the tights tangle with one swift slash from his claws. Just for good measure though, he turned the tights into shreds, presumably for the same reason a kitten destroys rolls of kitchen towel—just because he could. Tom struggled to his feet and tried to regain a little bit of dignity while studying where they were. Mildred stood at his side, looking up at him, her odd-colored eyes as somber as ever.

"Do you believe this to be the correct location, Thomas?" she asked.

They were in a large warehouse. The windows were boarded up, and judging by the amount of cobwebs that spanned the closed door, it hadn't been in proper use for a long time. Dust smothered the floor, and Tom realized his hands were filthy from where he fell. He brushed them clean on his pajama bottoms. He briefly contemplated how it was possible to fall *up* out of a laundry basket, and when it made his brain twinge, he gave up, instead concentrating on his surroundings. It was gloomy inside, and it was taking a while for his eyes to adjust to the light. Slowly, details further away presented themselves. It was as if the room were expanding before him, black fading to grey, then shifting into focus—the pile of shiny, pretty, sparkly clothes that crowded around a large laundry basket; cardboard boxes, stacked around the edges of the space, boxes with gnawed corners, and indecipherable labels. At the far end of the room, the polished floor caught the light, glinting subtly. Tom shrugged at Mildred, and edged forward. Everyone followed.

As Tom got closer, he realized it wasn't simply the floor that caught the light. It was what was *on* the floor. A chunky layer of gold, necklaces, bracelets, rings, coins, every treasure you could ever hope to find within a pirate's chest, smothered the ground. A glass chandelier hung from the ceiling, looking out of place among the dusty boxes, its droplet crystals scattering reflected rainbows across the floor.

"I think so, Mildred," Tom whispered, in belated response.

The treasure floor surrounded a golden chair, and in it sat a most striking-looking Poltergeist. She was picking at her teeth with the pointy end of a scepter, and reclining in a spectacularly laid-back fashion among all the grandeur. Her hair was bright, fiery red, and fell in huge matted dreadlocks to her waist. Some of her dreads had large bulges in them, like snakes trying to digest an ambitious meal, and Tom rather suspected that if you were to take a knife to them and slice one open, coins and gems and heaven knows what would come cascading out of hiding. Her clothes were a total mishmash of contrasting colors and styles—a heavily beaded green ballgown, sparkly orange tights, shiny red shoes that looked like she had just mugged a wicked witch, a punkish silver belt studded with spikes . . . Her arms were weighed down with assorted bangles, and each one of her fingers boasted so many rings that it was a wonder that she could even lift them, let alone bend her digits in any way. To top the look off, she wore a horrible gold clown necklace with glowing red eyes—Kate's necklace—and perched on top of her dreadlocks, a token of elegance among her tatty hair, rested the crown jewels.

"I think I'm in love," sighed Tike. Grey Arthur nudged him to pay attention.

"How do!" she called, waving at her guests. For a mystical, ancient, powerful criminal ghost, she gave a surprisingly friendly greeting. This wasn't what Tom had been expecting at all. She threw the scepter aside, and it landed with a resounding clank on the floor. "Don't mind the mess, I'm just getting settled in. It's all a bit sparse at the moment."

Sparse? *Sparse?* thought Tom. If this was sparse, then he dreaded to think what she was building up to. Tom had read stories about dragons hoarding less treasure than this.

"It just takes a while to get back into the swing of things," she carried on, throwing her dreads over her shoulder, out of the way. "Been out of practice for a while. Call it an enforced holiday."

"I was under the impression that you were imprisoned," Mildred said. Tom looked at her, shocked. Trust Mildred to call a spade a spade. He was waiting for the Poltergeist to get annoyed, but to his relief she laughed.

"That's putting it bluntly. No sense of humor, those Druids. It's all *you've stolen everything I own*, or *you've bankrupted the country again, and now we have to go to war to steal some other kingdom's gold*. Wah, wah. Bunch of whiners, the lot of them. Look at me, Eliza Nimble, trapped for all those years, and you don't see me moping around. All's well that ends well, eh?"

Tom noted that she didn't call herself Theo. He frowned, not sure what to make of that.

"I don't think it's going that well. That's what we need to talk to you about," Grey Arthur said. "You're causing a few problems. . . ."

The Poltergeist sighed. "Great. Here we go again. I knew you'd turn up eventually. Too good to be true, it was. You Druids look a lot different these days, though. I assume the queen's got her knickers in a twist about her missing hat? I guess some things always stay the same. . . ."

"Not exactly," Tom said. "We're not Druids, for a start. A lot has changed since you, erm, *went away*."

Mildred stepped up to the task of reciting the abridged version of umpteen centuries' worth of missed history, while Grey Arthur and Tom nodded seriously, Tike swooned, and the Harrowing Screamer grumbled at how shiny everything was. Mildred, in her best teacher impression, spoke of science, and the ignoring of ghosts, of the way the two worlds drifted apart, of horses and carts turning to motorbikes and cars, of lanterns to street-lights, of huts to skyscrapers, and finally, of a boy who can see ghosts, a TV psychic who really was a ghost, and then finished the tale with the Invisible Friends standing before her. Eliza Nimble sat back and tutted thoughtfully.

"So . . . ," Eliza muttered. "Humans can't see ghosts anymore?"

"That's right. All apart from Tom. But he's a one-off," Arthur explained.

"That's hilarious!" roared Eliza, her dreadlocks shaking as she laughed. "I mean, I knew humans were dumb—no offense, Jon."

"Tom," corrected Tom.

"Tom. But seriously? They just spend their whole lives not seeing us anymore? Talk about making a Poltergeist's job even easier. This is going to be a cakewalk. Cheers for coming here to fill me in. I appreciate it."

Tom balked. "That's not quite what we meant to do."

"It isn't?" she asked.

"Not quite," admitted Tom. "See, the thing is, for some reason, being trapped in the ley-line all that time has made you a bit different. As in, normal-humans-can-see-you different. We're actually here to persuade you to stop. You've got to return all this stuff you've stolen and steer clear of humans."

"Now, Jon . . ."

"Tom," corrected Tom again.

"Tom. *Where would be the fun in that?*"

Tom looked at his ghostly friends, unsure how to respond. He raised his eyebrows at Tike, silently appealing for help.

"Don't look at me. It's a fair point," Tike replied. Tom sighed.

"It's not meant to be fun. It's meant to be the right thing to do." Tom explained feebly.

Eliza threw her head back and laughed again. The crown nearly fell, but she grabbed it just in time. "The right thing to do? Now *that's* entertaining. Have you ever met a Poltergeist before?"

"Tike is a Poltergeist," Mildred responded. "And yet he manages to curtail his activities."

"Oh, really?" Eliza snorted. "Is that why he's stealing from me?"

Everyone turned to look at Tike, who threw his hands in the air, feigning innocence. A tiara and a Fabergé egg tumbled out from the bottom of his tatty sweater. The little Poltergeist shifted guiltily.

"I was just gonna make sure they got returned to their owner," he explained, as he nudged them aside with his scuffed sneaker. "Besides, it's not stealing if it's already stolen, is it?" Tom rolled his eyes.

"Look, can you just give us a few days?" he begged. "You've waited this long, a little longer can't hurt. You can always steal it all back if we don't work out a compromise, and in the meantime we can help you catch up on all the stuff you've missed—TVs, computer games, watches, I'm sure there's loads you don't know about."

"And what do I get out of this? It sounds like this is for your benefit, far more than mine. A history lesson is hardly the most tempting lure for a Poltergeist, and it took me ages to steal all this. Seems daft to just give it all up."

Tom looked at the Invisible Friends.

"We will persevere to make you invisible," piped up Mildred. "Surely, being the only Poltergeist that is visible would cause you problems in undertaking your hauntings?"

"I've never known any different," Eliza said dismissively.

"Okay, no, that's a fair point," agreed Tom, thinking quickly, "but think how much easier it would be, how much more fun you could have, if no humans could see you? And the way things are, all the other Poltergeists have a bit of an unfair advantage over you, don't they?"

"I suppose . . ." Eliza nodded thoughtfully, as she tied her dreadlocks into knots, and then untied them again. "So, essentially, what you're proposing is a truce? Just for a few days?"

"Just a few days," agreed Tom.

"And if you can't fix this, even if I'm still visible, I'll be free to go? No secret plans to try and throw me back in the ley-line?"

"Scout's honor." Tom nodded. Eliza frowned, not understanding the reference.

"That means he promises," explained Grey Arthur.

"Okay, then," she said, jumping up from her chair.

"Wait. You said okay?" Tom had never actually thought that she'd go along with it. Now he wasn't quite sure what to do.

"Yeah, okay. You can show me what's what, tell me what's valuable these days, let me in on all the gossip, work on making me invisible (which sounds like it might be in all our best interests), and in exchange I'll let you temporarily rehome these belongings with the humans that I nicked them from, and I'll lie low for a bit. Deal?"

"Deal!" yelped Arthur, diving in front of Tom and nodding enthusiastically. He shook hands with Eliza, and the sound of bangles jangling filled the air as he wobbled her hand about. Tom smiled queasily. It all sounded so very easy, but the more he thought about it, the more it worried him.

How do you entertain an ancient Poltergeist?

What did she mean by "*temporarily* rehome"?

How would they keep their promise to try to turn her invisible?

And where exactly do you store a ghost that humans can see?

English Hospitality

MRS. SCRUFFLES OPENED HER FRONT DOOR A CRACK, revealing feet wedged inside fluffy slippers, grey hair wrapped in rollers, and a paisley dressing gown tied round her waist. The dawn had just broken, and bird-song carried cheerfully in the crisp, cold morning air. She peered down at Tom, confused.

"Isn't it a bit early for you to be popping over?" she asked, rubbing her eyes. "Do your parents know you're out?"

"Yes, it is, and no, they don't," replied Tom apologet-ically. "It was a bit of an emergency. We didn't know where else to go."

Mrs. Scruffles popped her head out of the open door and looked past Tom at the ghosts gathered on her doorstep. She spotted Eliza, resplendent in her beaded ballgown and bright orange tights, and her eyes widened.

"I think you'd better get inside," she said urgently.

Mrs. Scruffles put the kettle on, and everyone crowded into the kitchen. The cats immediately swarmed around Eliza, and she sat down, cross-legged, on the floor with them, fussing as many as possible. Some braver cats took opportunistic swipes at her dreadlocks, and others clambered onto her lap. Tike was staring at the Poltergeist with undisguised admiration, while Mildred was helping Mrs. Scruffles by laying the table. Harry played with a ball of string that the cats had lost interest in.

"Where's Monty?" asked Mrs. Scruffles, as she threw an entire box of tea bags into her large teapot.

"Back at Tom's, staying watch in case Tom's parents

work out he's not there," answered Grey Arthur. He was sitting at the table, patiently waiting for the tea to brew. Mrs. Scruffles ruffled his hair affectionately.

"You did well finding her. I'll have to thank the twins too, next time I see them." She placed a plate of jammy cookies down on the table, and Grey Arthur snatched one away. "I'll phone the nice Zombie lady who runs the American Contraries in a bit and see if she can set her obsessive-compulsive Poltergeist the task of tidying the warehouse and returning all the items to where they belong. It's a bit beyond her normal tricks of dusting shelves and bleaching work surfaces, but I'm sure she can muddle through."

Tom was slumped at the opposite side of the table to Grey Arthur, scarcely able to keep his eyes open. He yawned and picked up a cookie too, but couldn't find the energy to eat it.

"A cup of tea will soon wake you up, Tom," Mrs. Scruffles said.

Tom shook his head. "I don't want to wake up. I'm really quite looking forward to crawling back into bed. I can get at least another"—he looked at the grandfather clock and couldn't help but groan—"three hours' sleep before I'm meant to get up."

"Okay, then. Well, we'd best sort out what we're going to do quickly, before you pass out on my kitchen table." Mrs. Scruffles set out cups for everyone but Tom, and poured out the tea. Mildred and Tike took their places at the table. Harry, as ever, preferred to stand, and Eliza seemed quite distracted by the feline onslaught, and so stayed put.

"Now, I understand the terms of the agreement are that Eliza will stay out of sight for a few days and allow us to return the items she has stolen so far, on the condition that we help her get up to date with the changes to the world that have taken place, keep her entertained, and work on a method to somehow make her invisible. Is that all?" Mrs. Scruffles said *all* in such a way as to make them realize that they had agreed to far more than she was entirely happy with. It certainly was a lot to promise. Assorted nodding occurred around the table. Mrs. Scruffles looked thoughtful. "The history lesson is one thing. The invisibility is a whole different arena, and something that I will continue looking into. However, another big question remains: How am I meant to keep her entertained?"

Mildred put her hand up to answer the question. When Mrs. Scruffles looked at her, she picked up her black satchel and placed it on the table. "I took a detour via Holly's house. I have brought Monopoly, Snakes and Ladders, and Mousetrap," Mildred informed her.

"That's very thoughtful of you, Mildred." Mrs. Scruffles took a sip of her tea. If she was thinking that it would take more than that to entertain a powerful Poltergeist, she was polite enough not to say it. "I'll hit the books while Tom is catching up on his beauty sleep, see if I can't find some more answers now I've got the Terrible Theo to help point the way."

Tom sat upright with a start, having heard his name. "Did you say something?" he asked sleepily.

"Nothing for you to worry about, Tom." Mrs. Scruffles twisted in her chair and turned to face Eliza Nimble. "Eliza, forgive me if I'm being a bit intrusive here, but I was just wondering if you could explain where you've been since you made that appearance in the knight's outfit and terrified those poor humans. Not that I'm judging you, not at all, you weren't to know, but it'll just help us work out if there are any other people we need to track down."

Eliza looked at Mrs. Scruffles, confused. "Since I did what now?"

"You know, the whole sword-waving thingy you did," explained Arthur.

Eliza looked thoughtful, and then burst out laughing. "Oh, superb. So it's not just me that's visible. How funny."

"Someone else escaped with you?" asked Mildred, alarmed.

Eliza shrugged. "Well, obviously. You wouldn't catch me dead in a knight's suit of armor. Far too hard to make a quick getaway with all that clanking. Good old John Method. And you thought you had your hands full with me!" Carrot Cake sprawled next to her, exposing his belly, and Eliza tickled him. He twisted on his back, paws waving in the air, and Eliza chuckled heartily.

"Who is John Method?" asked Grey Arthur.

"He's a Thesper. Got locked up the same time as me. Amazing ghost. Can impersonate just about anyone. A little cuckoo though, bless him, but aren't most Thespers, really? The villagers got all annoyed because he would take on the role of anyone he felt like, and nobody would be able to tell them apart. Not even John. He'd get so caught up in the role, he'd actually believe he was that person. Caused endless confusion. So, when they couldn't work out how to deal with it, they just chucked him in the ley-line with me, and sealed the door. Bit mean, really. Not entirely his fault."

"So, we now have to find a second ghost? And you're both known as the Terrible Theo? Because that just makes things complicated."

Eliza looked at Mrs. Scruffles and laughed. "Talk about Chinese whispers," she said, shaking her head with amusement.

"What do you mean, Chinese whispers?" asked Grey Arthur. "What does China have to do with all this?"

"You hear a name, you pass it on, they pass it on, they pass it on, and over the years it changes and changes. It's not the Terrible Theo at all. It's Trio. Tr-ee-oh."

"Trio," repeated Mildred. "Meaning *three*."

"Three?" spluttered Grey Arthur, alarmed. "Wait. There were *three* of you trapped?"

"Oh," said Eliza, smiling sweetly. "You haven't bumped into the Eldritch yet?"

Revelations

"THIS COMPLICATES MATTERS SOMEWHAT," SAID MRS. Scruffles finally.

"Oh yeah, just a tad," replied Tike, with as much sarcasm as he could muster.

"Well, you asked. Don't shoot the messenger," Eliza said, as she scooped Puddles off the floor, sniffed him, and then placed him down again rather abruptly.

"Eliza, we need you to tell us everything you know," said Mrs. Scruffles as she handed the Poltergeist a cup of tea. Eliza smelled it, dipped her tongue into it, shrugged, and began to drink from the cup. She finished it, and handed it back to Mrs. Scruffles, who quickly topped it up.

"Fine. Not sure how much more there is to say, though."

"What is the Eldritch?" asked Mildred. She had her notebook out, pen at the ready.

"He's the Screamer," Eliza replied, knocking back her second cup of tea. "This stuff is good," she added approvingly.

"Well, that's just perfect," complained Tom, suddenly feeling awake. "An ancient, visible Screamer strutting around England. That's just what we needed."

Eliza shook her head. "No, not *a* Screamer. *The* Screamer. The first. The original. The rest are just pale imitations."

The Harrowing Screamer made a moan of complaint from the corner of the room, where he was busy playing with Agatha Tibbles.

"I'm not saying it to be rude. I'm sure when you're not hugging cats, you're entirely terrifying"—she didn't look convinced—"but this ghost . . . he's something else. It wasn't just the humans that locked him away, although they certainly didn't complain when he was suggested. The other ghosts agreed that, for the humans' sake, myself and John could be locked away, on the condition that the Eldritch was thrown in with us. Nice, huh? Imagine a Screamer so frightening that even ghosts can't bear to be near him."

Tom swallowed dryly. This was getting worse by the second.

"Can you tell us what happened with the ley-lines? How they managed to trap you?" asked Mrs. Scruffles.

Eliza frowned. "It's not exactly my fondest memory." She paused, hands drifting to her dreadlocks, where her ringed fingers deftly spun, tangled, and untangled them as she spoke. "I was off near the coast, relieving some travelers of some rather beautiful shiny objects, when suddenly I hear weird voices carrying on the wind. Really weird, sound all disjointed, echoing, and then there was the mist. Coasts get misty, that's nothing new, but this? This wasn't right. It got really thick, really quickly, so I can't see a thing. Next thing I know, the mist clears, and I'm miles away, standing in the center of Stonehenge, surrounded by all these seriously angry-faced men and women doing all kinds of seriously angry magic, and I can't budge an inch. I'm begging, I'm pleading, even promised to give back everything I'd stolen, but it didn't make a scrap of difference. They'd already made up their mind. Some big bloke with a big stick shouted out one last word, and that was it. The ley-line just swallowed me up. I tried to get out but . . . well, you know the rest. The door was firmly shut." She sighed, brushing the layers of gathered cat hair from her ballgown before looking up and forcing a smile on to her lips. "Still, all's well that ends well, huh? I'm out now."

"This ritual . . . ," said Mrs. Scruffles gently. "Is there anything more you can tell us about it?"

Eliza laughed, a short sharp bark. "So you can put me back? Sorry, lady, but there's no way I'm telling you one little shred of information that might help you lock me back inside there. You all seem very nice, but that human's voice"—she bobbed her head over to Tom, who was oblivious, eyes half shut—"positively screams with worry every time he mentions humans being able to see me, and I know only too well what desperate people will do to make a situation easier."

The Invisible Friends sat in guilty silence for a while. Until they'd met Eliza, there was no denying that their first priority, their first instinct, had been simply to throw the Trio back inside the ley-line and seal it up again, and they'd dedicated all their energy into working out how. They hadn't even seriously contemplated reversing the visibility until Mildred had thrown it onto the table, one last desperate rise in the stakes to persuade Eliza to come along with them. Now, meeting her, talking to her—she wasn't evil, like the Collector, wasn't cruel, like Dr. Brown . . . she was just a ghost who loved her job a little too much, a Poltergeist who specialized in a rather unpopular field. Grey Arthur shifted uncomfortably, an awkward heavy spiked feeling lodged in his chest.

"What was it like?"

Tike's voice, quieter than usual, softer than normal, cut across the room. Eliza looked at him, tilting her head, her dreadlocks swishing across the floor.

"What was what like?" she asked.

"Being trapped. All that time. What was it like?"

Eliza looked at Tike thoughtfully before responding. "Terrifying, at first. I was the last ghost captured, so the others were already inside when I arrived. Imagine being trapped inside a short tunnel of ley-line with the Eldritch. John and I cowered at one end, the Screamer at the other, for what seemed an eternity. It was better, if you could call it that, during the day, but at night . . . You can't even begin to understand how powerful he was when the light had gone. After a while . . ." She caught herself and laughed. "I say a while, like it was no time at all, but maybe it was months, maybe it was years, maybe even longer, but after a while the terror fades. It has to. It was always there, chewing at the back of everything, but you learn to cope with it. The worst thing about it all, though, or possibly the best, wasn't being stuck in there with the Eldritch. It was that the door was never fully shut. You could always see a thin sliver of the outside world, and sometimes voices, sounds would carry through. Arguments, battles, laughter . . . You'd catch glimpses of the world changing—clothes, uniforms, weapons—and some days it was wonderful to know everything outside still existed, and sometimes it was torture to see everything you were held away from. John and I would try to keep up, I'd listen to how the way people spoke altered through the years in those little snatched fragments of conversation, and he'd try to mimic the people and ghosts that walked past." She smiled fondly. "He loved the knights, did John. It was a happy time when they were around, if happy is the right word. I think they appealed to his sense of the dramatic. Anyway, that's what it was like.

"Then, one day, the ground shakes, and the doorway just falls open. That massive stone that had held us in place slammed to the floor, and there it is. The outside world. For the longest time we simply stood and stared. Then, we ran, the three of us, just ran and ran and ran, just picked a random direction and fled as fast as we could." She smiled at Tike, and nodded. "I know, you're probably thinking that it's odd that we stayed with the Eldritch, but after all those centuries of being trapped together, I guess it just seemed right to stay as a three. Besides, it's not his fault, is it? We are what we are at the end of the day. So we hid, the three of us, the Terrible

Trio as you call it, and we waited for the Druids to come and hunt us down and put us back inside. Heaven knows how long we waited. Time becomes a little meaningless when you've spent as long as we have locked away. Eventually, we realized nobody was coming." She smiled at Tike, her eyes shining happily. "So that was it. We said our good-byes, and we set off into the world again. I followed a Poltergeist I stumbled across, discovered the Laundry Run—something we never had when I was younger, at least, not in the form it is now—and the rest is history."

"Do you have any idea where the others would be now?" asked Grey Arthur.

Eliza shrugged. "Round here is John Method's old haunting ground, but exactly where he is, or even *who* he is by now, is anyone's guess. If he's out of character, you needn't worry about him scaring humans—no one would even give him a second look—but you'll have a mighty hard time finding him. If he's in character, well, let's put it this way: that ghost certainly knows how to work a crowd, so he'll be easier to find, but you could have one almighty mess on your hands. Heads you lose, tails I win, eh?"

"Pretty much," grumbled Grey Arthur.

"And the Eldritch? Well, he never had a place to call home—as I recall it, everywhere he settled he'd get chased out of by villagers with burning torches, so he could literally be anywhere." Eliza paused and looked intently at Mrs. Scruffles. "So, come on, then, I've been honest with you, even if I have skimped on a few of the details. Perhaps you can be the same with me. Do you have even the vaguest clue how to turn me back invisible, or was that never really part of the plan?"

Mrs. Scruffles placed her cup down on the table and looked kindly at Eliza. "Originally, no, that wasn't even something we had considered. Meeting you has changed things somewhat, I won't deny it. What stays the same, though, is the fact that we simply can't leave visible ghosts roaming the land. This is a very different world to the one you left behind, and we don't believe it would end well for humans or for ghosts if the two were to merge again."

Eliza nodded, understanding. "I guess you'd better start working out a plan to help me blend in with all the normal, invisible ghosts, then, hadn't you? Because I didn't escape one prison to get trapped in another one, even if it does have lots of cats to keep me company, and sweet warm brown beverages to offer. I'm a Poltergeist, always have been, and always will be, and there's only so long I can go without stealing shiny things before my palms start itching." Eliza looked across the table to where Tom had rested his head on a doily and was busy dribbling. "I think the human has succumbed to sleep."

Grey Arthur looked at Tom and grinned. "Yeah, it's been a long old night for him. We should probably get him back before his parents realize he's missing. Come on, Tom, time to wake up." Tom sat up, his forehead creased, his eyes bleary, and for a while he looked dumbly around the room, struck by that postsleep disorientation you get when you wake outside the confines of your own room. Slowly, the haze cleared, and he remembered where he was.

"What did I miss?" he asked. "Is everything fixed yet?"

"I believe we are some way from achieving that goal, Thomas," Mildred informed him, handing him a napkin to wipe the dribble from his chin. Tom took it sheepishly. "But we are making progress."

"Progress," muttered Tom tiredly. "Progress is always good. Can I go back to bed now?"

"Of course you can, Tom," Mrs. Scruffles said, rising from the table to see him to the door. "Grey Arthur and Harry will see you home. The rest of us will stay here. We have work to do."

So Tom dragged himself home, sticky mouth, weary legs, wincing at the bright daylight, as Grey Arthur and the Harrowing Screamer escorted him. Pajamas aren't exactly the best attire for keeping out the January cold, and Tom was shivering from head to toe by the time he arrived back home. Grey Arthur plunged through the front door, and after checking that the coast was parent-clear, unlocked the door to let Tom inside. Quietly, Tom made his way up the stairs, feet straddling the very outskirts of each step to avoid the dreaded creaking, and finally he threw himself down on the bed, pushing Monty's huddle of sleeping human-shaped clothes onto the floor. He was awake long enough to rid himself of his shoes and sweater, and then quickly immersed himself in the warmth of his duvet.

"You were gone ever such a long time—I was getting worried. How did it go?" asked Montague, as Tom curled up in bed. Harry made an optimistic-sounding howl, and Grey Arthur nodded.

"One down . . . ," he whispered. "That's the good news."

"And the bad?" asked Monty. Tom was already asleep, and Grey Arthur busied himself tidying away the mess he had left in his wake. He threw the top into the laundry basket, placed Tom's shoes out of the way, and scooped up the clothes from the floor.

"The bad news is, there's still two to go." Grey Arthur sighed. "And it gets worse."

"How can it possibly get worse?" asked a rather incredulous Monty.

Grey Arthur smiled, a thin lopsided smile, a brace-for-impact smile, a bearer-of-bad-tidings smile.

"One of them," he said, "is a Screamer."

No Rest for the Weary

MORE THAN ANYTHING, THE NEXT MORNING TOM WANTED to sleep in. If you could have offered him an electric guitar, a private gig with Cold Fish, a walk-on part in a James Carefree movie, any of these things that filled Tom's list of Best Things That Could Possibly Ever Happen to Me, right at that very moment, he would still have preferred to sleep a little longer in his warm, comfy, familiar bed, curled up underneath his duvet.

It wasn't to happen though.

Instead, Tom woke up to see Eliza Nimble standing in his bedroom, with Grey Arthur, Mildred, and Harry at her side. Tom practically launched himself out of bed, bounding over to the door, throwing himself in front of it to prevent anyone from walking in.

"She can't be here!" he hissed, gesturing wildly at the dreadlocked ghost. "What if my parents see her?"

"Relax, Tom. Your parents are out for the day," explained Arthur, as he jumped onto the bed. "Your mum has got an extra shift at the castle, and your dad has got some kind of sock conference up in London."

"They do?" asked Tom, confused. "How do you know this and I don't?"

"Erm, maybe because I pay attention to what they say?" Arthur responded with a grin.

Eliza was already exploring Tom's bedroom, and Harry followed her, growling lowly when it looked like some of Tom's belongings might go astray. She raised her hands, trying to look innocent.

"How did you get here?" Tom asked.

"Don't worry, Thomas. No humans saw her," explained Mildred. "Mrs. Scruffles went out first thing this morning to buy a laundry basket so we could travel without being seen."

Tom glanced over at his own laundry basket and sighed. He'd have to think about getting a lock for it someday, if a lock that could keep Poltergeists out even existed. Maybe just a doorbell instead, so at least he could get a bit more warning. Eliza was studying Tom's treasured marble collection, and he dashed over and quickly moved them to a safe distance away. Shiny objects and Eliza didn't seem to be a good mix.

"Okay, fair enough, but that still doesn't explain *why* you're here," he muttered, throwing his action figures hastily into his drawer.

"I was bored," Eliza replied. "Mrs. Scruffles, Montague, and Tike are busy trying to work out where the other two ghosts might be, so I thought we could pay you a visit. Mildred seems to think you can help us work on, oh, what are you calling it?"

"De-visibilization," Mildred said, lifting a stack of books and weird props out of her little black satchel and placing them onto Tom's desk. "We're still working on the theory that the length of time they were trapped in the ley-line has somehow left residual magic on the Terrible Trio, and it is this magic that is contributing to their visibility, enhancing their ghostly potence."

"And in English?"

"I'm covered in magic," sniffed Eliza, studying her hands with visible disgust. "Ley-line magic. And it doesn't seem to want to come off."

"Really?" Tom had asked. "*Not even with soap and water?*"

And that was how their first attempt at de-visibilization (a word Mildred had concocted for the occasion) took shape.

Eliza had glared, Grey Arthur had giggled, Harry had hissed in an amused fashion, and Mildred had thought it was definitely worth a try.

Now, it has to be said that there is not a Poltergeist alive that enjoys a bubble bath (with the possible exception of the American Contrary), and Eliza hated every rose-scented moment of it. Tom, Grey Arthur, Mildred, and Harry waited out on the landing, having set Eliza up with a lovely warm bath and some fresh, warm towels from the airing cupboard. In return, they were treated to a series of wails, complaints, howling, language that wouldn't have been out of place on a battlefield, and pleading to be spared her bubbly fate, all shouted through the closed bathroom door. Eventually, a very grumpy-looking Eliza appeared in the doorway, draped in a floral bath towel, her long dreads dripping wet, and a scowl on her face that would curdle milk and make newborn babies cry.

"So?" she growled. "Am I fixed? I'd better be fixed."

Everyone shrugged in response.

"No idea. All of us can see ghosts anyway," Tom replied.

"Indeed. The only way to know is by exposing you to conventional humans. If they see you, then we know that it has not worked," explained Mildred.

Eliza rolled her eyes. "Fine. I'll go get changed back into my dress and pop outside, then."

"Erm, about that . . . ," said Arthur.

It had been decided, while Eliza was soaking in the bath, that sending out Eliza dressed in a ballgown, red shoes, orange tights, and studded belt probably wasn't the best idea. If the plan didn't work, if humans could still see her, it was far better that they saw a Faintly Real-like ghost, a ghost trying at least to be a little bit normal, rather than one that looked like a rainbow had been sick on her. It had taken rather a lot of persuading, but Tom had agreed to let Mildred raid his mum's wardrobe to find something a little bit more suitable to wear. She'd picked out a rather nice, rather plain brown dress, though you wouldn't have known that by the way Eliza recoiled in horror when presented with it. Tom thought she might actually throw herself on the floor and have a full-fledged temper tantrum, and it took another good ten minutes before she could be coaxed into her new attire, and then another five before she agreed to actually leave the house and approach humans. It probably didn't help that Tom and Arthur had snorted with laughter when they first saw her in it, but really, that was as much down to her grumpy expression as it was to the ill-suited clothes.

Eliza finally wandered outside the house, lurking out front in Tom's garden, under strict instructions not to walk through any walls, not to hover, definitely not to steal, and to strike up a very normal, very human conversation with anyone who walked past. Tom, Grey Arthur, and Harry waited in the lounge, net curtains twitching, as they anxiously watched her progress.

Five minutes, and one conversation later, she marched back, rang the doorbell, and waited to be let in. "The old woman with the scrappy dog says the weather is very mild, actually, for this time of year, but warned me that, even so, I'll get a cold if I continue to go outside with wet hair." She scowled at Tom. "I hope you're happy. It didn't work. I bathed for nothing."

So, back to the drawing board it was, and on to plan B.

And then C.

And D.

E, F, G, H, I, and J didn't work any better either. They forced Eliza into ley-lines, hoping that traveling on them would somehow *suck* the magic back out of her and return it to the ley-lines. It didn't. They tried an invisibility spell that Mildred had found in an old book about witches, but that only succeeded in making the kitchen and Eliza smell like rotten eggs (which, oddly, she preferred to the smell of rose bubble bath). Tom spent an age spraying the whole place with air freshener, so that his parents wouldn't ask too many questions when they came home. They tried visualization techniques lifted from a book called *Be What You Want to Be Through Harnessing the Power of Your Mind*. That was a painful hour of Grey Arthur saying things like "Picture yourself in a meadow full of flowers" and Eliza telling him that this was the stupidest thing she'd ever heard of.

Apparently, Eliza was a little too old for New Age therapy techniques. They tried rubbing Eliza with crystals, making her wear camouflage clothing, dousing her with invisible ink, making her run around on the spot for ages in the hope that she was invisible when tired (she wasn't—she was irritable when tired); they tried making her drink gallons of water in the hope of "flushing" the magic from her system. . . . They even fetched Montague to try a spot of hypnotism (he'd played a hypnotist once onstage, so he was the closest they had to the real thing). He twisted his mustache into dramatic points and waved a pendant in front of her for about ten minutes while intoning "LOOK INTO MY EYES." Eliza ended up stealing the pendant when Monty was briefly distracted, and she refused to give it back, calling it a payment for putting her through his act, so that plan was also written off.

Eventually, they retreated back to Tom's bedroom and decided to call it a day.

"Perhaps," Mildred had said, as she returned Eliza's favored outfit of many colors, "there is no quick solution to this problem. It is possible we may just have to wait for it to fade of its own accord."

"And perhaps it's here for good," moaned Eliza. "You ever considered that?"

"Well, let's just cross that bridge when we come to it," said Monty gently. "No point getting ahead of ourselves."

"Hello?" called a voice from downstairs. Mum's voice. Tom looked at Grey Arthur in horror.

"*I thought you said she was out for the day?*" he asked.

Grey Arthur looked as shocked as Tom did. "She is. I mean, she's supposed to be. She's back early," he said anxiously. "Okay, Mildred, Monty, Harry, you need to get Eliza out of here, now. Go, Tom. I'll tidy up all this mess."

"Tom, are you in?" came Mum's voice again. Tom looked at Arthur, who was busy scooping up armfuls of crystals and invisible ink cartridges, camouflage clothing and books on witches.

"Go on, Tom, before she comes up here to find you," said Arthur.

Tom nodded and headed out of the door.

Here We Go Again

"You're back early, Mum," called Tom as he trotted down the stairs. He wandered into the kitchen, where Mum was sitting at the table, having a cup of tea.

"It wasn't that busy, so Janet said I should go home early. Too cold for the tourists. Well, most of them. Actually, considering the castle was practically empty, we had quite an eventful day." Mum paused, sniffing. "Does the kitchen smell weird to you?"

"Eventful day?" asked Tom, quickly changing the subject. The last thing he wanted to do was explain why the kitchen smelled so very sulphurous. Out of the corner of his eye he spotted a bundle of abandoned crystals, and stealthily pocketed them before Mum could notice. "What happened?"

"Well, we had a bit of a medical crisis at work. A young girl, foreign I guess, didn't seem to speak a word of English, was found wandering around the graveyard."

"And that's a medical emergency?" asked Tom, puzzled.

Mum rolled her eyes. "Hold on, I haven't gotten there yet. Anyway, this girl . . . She really wasn't dressed for the weather, beautiful dress (if a little tatty), bare feet . . . don't think she was all there, if you catch my meaning." Mum nodded at Tom, and Tom nodded back to show that he understood. "The poor little mite was so cold that she'd literally turned blue. Head to toe, *blue.* Hypothermia, that's what they call it. See, you think I'm fussing when I make you wrap up warm, but there's a good reason why I worry."

Alarm bells had started ringing for Tom. "What was she doing?" he asked, trying to keep the concern from his voice. Mum gave him a look that said she was saving the weirdest for last.

"You won't believe this. . . ."

"Try me . . . ," insisted Tom.

"*Singing.* She was singing. I know, sounds crazy, doesn't it? The cold makes your brain go all odd, I guess. She wouldn't go inside either, refused to budge. I brought her out a cup of tea, and a blanket, but she didn't even touch it. In the end I had to go, but I left Janet looking after her. I even offered to run her down to the doctor's, but Janet said she would take care of it, and that I should just head off home."

No wonder Janet sent Mum home early. The last thing she wanted was Tom's well-meaning mum putting her hands through a ghost.

"I've got to go," Tom said, standing up, his chair scraping noisily across the kitchen tiles.

"Already? I've only just got in. I was hoping we could spend some time together."

"I know, I know, Mum. I'm sorry. I'm having dinner at Mrs. Scruffles's house."

"You never said."

"I must have forgotten. I'm sorry, Mum. I don't want to leave them waiting. . . ."

Mum scowled. "Go on. Go. But don't make a habit out of this, Tom. You need to let me know if you're eating elsewhere."

"I will. Next time. I promise. Say hello and good-bye to Dad again from me. I'll see you later."

Tom turned and dashed out of the front door, pausing in his stride only enough to grab his coat and his hat, and wedge his feet into his still-laced-up shoes.

"Tom!" called Mum after him, but the only response she got was the sound of the front door slamming. She sighed and stared at her cup of tea. "Don't be back too late. . . ."

Following a Lead

TOM CROUCHED IN THE FRONT GARDEN, HIDDEN BY A bush, and started throwing small pebbles up at his own bedroom window. It took an eternity, and Tom had exhausted his small stone supply and begun hurling small sticks and even a lump of chewing gum by the time Arthur realized what was going on and poked his grey head out of the window. He noticed the chewing gum stuck to the glass, and pulled a disgusted face.

"I think people use stones because they don't stick," he informed Tom. It was then, and only then, that the weirdness of the situation seemed to filter through to Arthur. "Why are you hiding in a bush?"

"*I think I know where John Method is. We need to go. NOW,*" whispered Tom. Grey Arthur made a silent "ohhhh" expression, and hurled himself out of the closed window. He fell to the floor, slower than a human would, but still without even an ounce of grace. He picked himself up, dusted off his hands (for effect, more than anything), and grinned at Tom.

"What are we waiting for?" he asked.

"I think we should pick up Monty before we go. Something tells me an ex-Thesper could come in handy," replied Tom, and he crept out of the garden, stooped low, worried that his mum would see him. He practically rolled out of the gate, and pushed his back against the garden wall, safely out in the street. Grey Arthur floated through the wall and patiently waited while Tom acted like a very amateur soldier trying to avoid detection. Eventually, assured that he was far enough away from the house not to have to explain why he wasn't already eating dinner with Mrs. Scruffles ("I was throwing stones up at my window to get my Invisible Friend's attention" didn't seem like the best thing to say, and Tom would rather not have to think up a lie), Tom straightened up and started speed walking.

"Let's just hope we get there in time . . . ," he said breathily, as his legs carried him as fast as they could.

And so it was, exactly twelve minutes and one leyline later, that Tom, Grey Arthur, and Montague Equador Scullion the Third stood before the familiar sight of Thorblefort Castle.

"I can see why John might be attracted to this place . . . ," muttered Monty, his eyes still firmly drawn to the castle. "It certainly has a dramatic flair." For a while, the three of them stood, transfixed, watching the clouds scrolling across the sky, feeling the small specks of water that threatened full-fledged rain, admiring the crumbling stonework, the empty windows, the smell of damp grass, soft moss, and *history* heavy in the air.

Suddenly, Grey Arthur and Monty looked at each other, alarm clear on their faces, and without saying a word began charging across the drawbridge. Monty took long, purposeful strides, and Grey Arthur's little legs worked overtime to keep up.

"What's going on?" yelled Tom, as he took off after them.

"Can't you hear it, Tom?" cried Arthur, as he sped into the distance.

"Hear what?"

"*We're too late!*"

Two for the Price of One

THE INSTANT THEY RAN INTO THE COURTYARD THE bracing sea wind rolled over the walls to greet them. It nearly tore Tom's scarf away, and he struggled to bring it back under control, numb fingers working slowly to grab hold. The wind was so cold, and so strong, that it stung tears from Tom's eyes, and instantly threw color into his cheeks. He leaned into it, body angled at nearly forty-five degrees, each step an effort, while the ghosts ran ahead without so much as a second's hesitation. He pushed on, ignoring the burning sensation building in his legs, ignoring the way the wind threw flecks of dirt into his face, just simply struggling to catch up with his ghostly friends.

Finally, Tom staggered to a halt next to where Monty and Grey Arthur stood, lungs aching, legs wobbly, face flushed, as the true magnitude of the scene in front of him unfolded. Tides of sadness flowed over him, tugging at the corners of his mouth, dragging sighs from him, but the crushing melancholy was kept at bay by a sense of overwhelming shock.

Sorrow Jane was sitting on the low, crumbling wall of the cemetery, her pale moonlight-colored hair twisting and dancing in the wind. Her delicate blue bare feet dangled beneath the ragged ends of her deep blue dress, a dress that shimmered mesmerizingly with thousands of tiny lights. She turned to see her approaching guests, her watery eyes greeting Tom's, her fragile blue face poetically sad, and with an elegant finger she pointed toward the old yew tree.

Tom followed the direction of her hand, and found himself shaking his head, struggling to understand the scene that lay before him. He'd had his suspicions, but even so, seeing it before him made his mind spin slightly, as if gravity had just eased up a notch.

Sorrow Jane was *also* sitting beneath the old yew tree, her dress draped across its muddy roots, her delicate blue skin starkly outlined against its gnarled bark. Thin, pale arms wrapped around her dusty blue knees, hugging them close to her chest, and she was singing, a beautiful song in forgotten words, that chimed, and rose, and danced in the wind. Beside her, untouched, was a mug of tea, and a folded blanket, the type made of coarse material in sludge colors that you see on TV, draped over recently rescued people, remnants of Tom's mum's well-meant offers of help.

That wasn't the most shocking part.

Not by a long shot.

Not far from the second Sorrow Jane, abandoned on the floor, were the remains of a picnic. The tablecloth was carefully laid on the ground, the hamper knocked over, its contents spilled onto the courtyard. Discarded napkins twisted on the breeze. A single apple weighted down a paper plate, with plastic cutlery scattered beside it. Sandwiches were left, half-eaten, dropped to the floor midbite. It was like the picnic version of the *Mary Celeste*.

Only this time, the people weren't missing.

They were still very much here.

"Stay behind me, Gertrude!" bellowed a red-faced man who was cowering over by the old well. His back was pressed up against the curved stone wall, and with one hand he was gesturing for his wife to move behind where he was crouched. With the other hand he was waving a Thermos menacingly, or at least, as menacingly as you can wave a Thermos, in the direction of the second Sorrow Jane. "I'll protect you, honey! Just get away from it!"

Gertrude had taken her husband's advice, and even gone farther—she was busy trying to scramble up onto the roof of the well, tights snagging, fingernails breaking, shoes scuffing, all the while wailing in a way that would make a Banshee proud.

"Hit it, Graham!" she screamed, as she threw herself up higher. The old tiled roof that covered the well groaned under her weight, but held fast. "Hit it! Make it go away!"

John Method had found his audience.

"Tom Golden, thank goodness you're here!"

Janet, Mum's colleague, a closet Faintly Real, rushed up to greet them. Tom hadn't even noticed she was there. She looked more stressed than Tom would have thought possible. Her bright red hair was swept away from her face in a bunch, revealing tired, anxious lines around her green eyes. "Tom, Arthur, Monty, I'm so glad to see you! I have no idea what's going on. She, *it*, this fake Sorrow Jane, she just showed up, and . . . People can see her, Tom! I sent your mum away, I tried to keep all the humans away, I thought they'd all left but I just . . . I just turned my back for two minutes, I swear, and this couple, they must have been here already, and honestly, Tom, I did my best, I really did, but they just must have set up here when I wasn't look-ing, and I . . ." She paused and took a deep breath. "*They can see her, Tom.* They can actually see her. It's not good. They've gone crazy."

Tom looked over at Monty and Grey Arthur. Grey Arthur's face was a terrible mixture of shock and sad-ness, watching these two adults scream and point and threaten the ghost that appeared before them.

"Kill it, Graham!" shrieked the woman, as she removed one of her shoes and hurled it at the imitation

Sorrow Jane. It passed straight through her with hardly a flicker. "For crying out loud, Graham, kill it!"

"I don't think I can, sweetheart!" he yelled desperately in response, as he grabbed loose stones off the floor and threw them toward the blue ghost. They flew harmlessly through, skimming across the ground on the other side of the fake Sorrow Jane, but that didn't deter him from trying again. And again. And again. The real Sorrow Jane watched on, her beautiful face painfully sad, while the fake Sorrow Jane sat, oblivious to everything, lost in song.

"Stop it!" screamed Grey Arthur. He dashed away from Tom's side, throwing himself between the blue ghost beneath the tree and the hysterical couple. "Please, stop it! Stop! She hasn't done anything wrong!"

Upon seeing Grey Arthur, the woman screamed. She threw her head back, and the rawest, most grating, terrified noise escaped her mouth. Her husband hurled his Thermos at Arthur, and when, just as with the fake Sorrow Jane, it traveled straight through, flickers ebbing through Grey Arthur like ripples through water, the woman screamed again. His eyes wide, locked on Grey Arthur, Graham frantically felt around for more rocks to throw, clumsy fingers blindly exploring. He found one, and, clutching it tight, raised his hand, braced to throw again.

That was the moment everything changed. The woman began to cry, huge sobs, mascara smearing down her face, and the man began to cry too, fat tears rolling down his red cheeks. The stone he was clutching fell from his hand, and he dropped to his knees, shoulders shaking. Tom felt it too, a surge of grief washing over everything, pitching and shifting in the air.

The real Sorrow Jane looked down as this scene unfolded, her deep blue eyes fixed on the two humans, and the sadness that radiated out from her grew stronger by the second. Crystal tears rolled silently down her face as she watched. Tom couldn't blame her for crying. Truth be told, even without the world's strongest Sadness Summoner there, he'd have felt like crying too. There it was, happening right in front of them, everything the ghosts had feared. It wasn't invitations to barbecues, or being served tea in a café, it wasn't rolling out the red carpet and making friends, it was two humans, terrified, lashing out because they were so scared, unable to truly understand what was going on. And there, in the middle of it, looking heartbroken, was Grey Arthur.

Monty seized the opportunity while Gertrude and Graham were crying, and rushed over to the fake Sorrow Jane. He grabbed her by the wrist, and led her to her feet.

"Janet, we need to get out of here. Now," he said urgently.

"Erm . . . Okay, okay, follow me." Janet began running across the courtyard. With one hand grasping the fake Sorrow Jane, Monty put his other arm around Arthur, and ushered him away, ghostly hand gently squeezing Grey Arthur's shoulder, that little reassuring touch. Dumbly, Grey Arthur allowed himself to be led away, wiping the tears away from his grey face with the edge of his sleeve.

Which just left Tom.

For what felt like an age, he simply watched the crying couple, watched Sorrow Jane, lost in thought. He'd realized that what they were trying to achieve was important, but it was not until now, this very moment, that he realized just how big a change one ghost could make. Part of him wanted to be angry with the couple, angry at them for reacting the way they did, angry at them for not coping better, angry at them for the way they screamed at Grey Arthur, angry at the hurt, heartbroken look on Arthur's face when he'd seen the way the humans looked at him, even angry at them for having the ludicrous idea of a nice picnic in January, but he couldn't. Not really. Part of Tom felt every bit as sad for them as he did for the ghosts. It wasn't their fault they were scared. Nobody ever *chooses* to be scared. And now, seeing them cry their hearts out, not understanding why, lost to everything but that crushing feeling of sadness that Sorrow Jane wrapped around them, Tom couldn't feel even a shred of anything other than miserable.

"You need to go, Tom." Janet's voice at his side startled him. She smiled tiredly at him, a smile that was anything but happy. "They're waiting for you by the exit. You've got to go."

"What about them?" Tom asked in a small voice.

"It's okay, Monty explained everything to me. I know what I need to do. I'll take care of it."

"How?"

"I'll . . . I'll tell them it was all a new display we were installing, part of History in Action, or something. Holograms that show you how people used to live."

"That'll work for Sorrow Jane and Monty, but what about Grey Arthur? They saw him, too."

"I'll say that the equipment is still a bit glitchy, and that some of the images aren't working properly."

"And the crying? How will you explain why they are crying?"

Janet sighed. "I'll think of something, Tom. Leave it to me. You need to go." She paused, and looked up at the wall where Sorrow Jane was still sitting. "You too, Jane. I'll take it from here. Thank you for your help, but I think it's probably best if they only see Faintly Reals for a while. . . ."

Sorrow Jane didn't acknowledge that she was being spoken to, but quietly did as requested, serenely floating down from the wall and disappearing into the grounds of the cemetery, out of sight. The thick, cloying air of sadness faded away, and Gertrude and Graham began to recover from their induced misery, sniffing, wiping away tears, and looking around, confused.

Tom nodded quietly at Janet. "Thank you," he said.

"Not at all. Just go and sort this out, Tom. And look

after Arthur for me. Poor lad could do with a friend right now."

"Yeah. Will do," he agreed. With a sickly feeling in his stomach, Tom began jogging out toward the entrance.

A Friend in Need

ARTHUR AND MONTY WAITED BY THE DRAWBRIDGE for Tom to join them. Montague still had his arm placed protectively around Grey Arthur's shoulders, and even as Tom approached he could see the faint blue hue that colored Arthur. Before them stood a ghost who was entirely different from the fake Sorrow Jane that had sung in the graveyard, and it took a second for Tom to understand why.

Before them stood John Method.

Just as there are people who are amazingly nondescript, so are there ghosts. If you were to talk to John when he was out of character for thirty minutes, and then look away, if someone were to ask you to describe the ghost you had just spoken with, you would struggle to recall even the most tiny detail. He was just so *abnormally* average. Average height, average build, bland features in a regular-shaped face, mousy brown conventional hair, plain clothes . . .

even the way he spoke was stripped of accent and inflection, and anything that might bestow even the faintest hint of personality. John Method was, quite simply, instantly forgettable. He smiled amicably at Montague.

"How did I do?" he asked. His voice was so very dull that it was an effort to concentrate on what he was saying. Tom found his attention wandering by the second word, and had to chew his lip to stop his focus drifting back to the bundle of misery that was Grey Arthur. "Was I good?"

"You were magnificent," replied Monty, with all honesty. "A true marvel."

"How did you get him to turn back?" Tom asked.

Monty shrugged. "It was simple really, once you think of it. How do you signal that a performance is over? All it took was a round of applause."

Tom turned his attention back to Grey Arthur, who was staring at the ground, lost in contemplation. "Are you all right, Arthur?" he asked. Arthur nodded, just a small bob of the head.

"I'm fine," he said. He didn't sound fine. "I just want to get out of here."

"Did I get the singing right? Because the singing is always tricky," asked John, seemingly oblivious to the chaos he had caused.

"The singing was perfect," said Montague, letting go of Grey Arthur and slowly steering John out of the castle. "That's why we want you to come with us.

We have some friends who would be interested to see what you can do."

"You think they'd like it?" John asked.

"They'd love it," replied Monty.

"You don't think they'd want an encore, here at the castle, before we go?" John asked.

"You know how it works, John. Always leave them hungry for more."

"That's true . . . ," agreed John, as he was shepherded across the drawbridge. The sun was setting behind them, and tall shadows stretched ahead of them, thrown out of shape by the wooden slats. "Would you like to see my knight act? I've been told it's very good."

"Maybe later," said Monty gently, as he steered the Thesper toward the shimmering ley-line portal in the distance.

"If it was so good, then why are you all so miserable?"

Monty sighed, stroking his mustache. "It's a long story, John. We'll explain it as we go. We just need to get moving."

They wandered out onto the grassy banks that surrounded the moat, and the entrance to the ley-line patiently waited and throbbed before them. With no further ado, Monty ushered John Method into the waiting ley-line. The rainbow colors quickly engulfed the second member of the Terrible Trio, and with a quick nod of his head, Monty dived in after him.

"Two down," said Arthur, his voice just scarcely

more than a whisper, as if he hadn't the energy to push the words free. He stepped into the ley-line and vanished out of sight.

Tom nodded to himself, allowing himself a brief moment's respite before he followed.

"One to go," he replied, before throwing his weight into the pulsing colors.

Early to Bed, Early to Rise

IT WAS PAST SEVEN BY THE TIME TOM FINALLY DRAGGED himself home. It wasn't explaining the situation to John that had taken all that time (in fact, he had been quite excited that his performance could have such a profound effect on the human world, but not in the slightest bit surprised—it seemed quite natural to a Thesper that his acting could create such a ruckus), but it was watching John go through his repertoire that had taken so long. Tom had been secretly pleased, though—the knight was the single coolest thing he had ever seen, even in the rather humble setting of Mrs. Scruffles's kitchen, and it went a long way toward shaking off the fug of misery that was clinging to Grey Arthur. It didn't take long for his usual grey color to return, chasing away the miserable Sadness Summoner blue, as John moved from impression to impression. The wailing monk was a little disturbing, his rendition of a king very impressive, and his impromptu mimicry of Tom (right down to the confused expression) even had Mildred laughing out loud. The two Toms had faced each other, mirror-images of bemusement, identical even down to the fading lettering on the forehead, and Grey Arthur howled with disappointment when Tom started frantically applauding to bring it all to an end. There was something exceedingly disconcerting about seeing someone *be* you (although Tom was slightly intrigued to see what the back of his head looked like).

Eliza was happy to be reunited with her old friend, and the pair of them swapped stories about what they had been up to since they last spoke, and they laughed about all the inadvertent chaos they had left in their wake. Mrs. Scruffles fed Tom, since he had missed his dinner to go and collect John, but for someone who loved to entertain, she really didn't prepare for full-fledged meals. Tom had a mighty dinner of pickled onions, mushy peas, and a tin of mystery meat that he didn't dare ask too many questions about. It filled a hole, though, and he was grateful for that, even if it did make his tongue feel strange.

However, for all the merriment, and dubious nutrition, and amusement, there was a weighty problem at the center of everything—they were no closer to de-visibilization, and no closer to tracking down the Eldritch, and now, thanks to John Method's little performance at the castle, they had witnessed firsthand just how much was at stake. It wasn't so much a problem solved as a problem postponed. John and Eliza, nice as they were, weren't going to stay forever in Mrs. Scruffles's company, forsaking their ghostly calling. If they didn't work out a solution soon, things were bound to take a turn for the worse.

This thought was gnawing at Tom as he carried his weary legs up the stairs to his room, Grey Arthur at his side. He flopped down on the bed, exhausted.

"We're getting there, aren't we, Arthur?" he asked as he kicked off his sneakers. Grey Arthur smiled in agreement. "I'm sorry that they were so mean to you at the castle. They didn't mean it. They were just being . . ." Tom struggled to find a word.

"Human. I know, Tom. I'm fine. It just came as a bit of a shock, that's all."

"I'm glad you're okay," Tom said, forcing himself to sit up. He grinned at Arthur as he grabbed his pajamas out from under his pillow, and with an effort stood up, and disappeared onto the landing. As he went, Grey Arthur let his smile fade. They *were* making progress, but with the Eldritch still on the loose, he couldn't help but worry that they weren't making progress fast enough. If a ghost like that makes an appearance, the world is going to sit up and take notice, and they still didn't have even the faintest clue where he was. Today had been the most terrible experience of his ghostly life—that look on their faces, that look of total, absolute horror—and it was something Grey Arthur was desperate never to have repeated. Not for him, not for any ghost. Tom wandered back in, pajamafied, toothpaste froth still clinging to his lip, and Grey Arthur threw his smile back in place.

"Good night, Tom," he said cheerily, hiding his gloomy thoughts out of sight.

"Good night, Arthur," Tom replied, throwing himself down heavily on the bed. "See you in the morning," he muttered, as he trailed into near immediate sleep.

Grey Arthur nodded in agreement, his frown sliding back into place as he crawled beneath the bed and set up for the night. He closed his eyes and tried to force away all the memories from that day that were churning and whirling and racing around his head. Pictures, flashes, echoes of the shouting, they all tangled up his thoughts, no matter how hard he tried to replace them with counting sheep, or Space Pirate adventures. Eventually, though, the thoughts slowed, his mind drifted, and Grey Arthur fell asleep.

Which was just as well.

With what was coming, they were going to need the rest.

A Sunday Morning in a Northern Wood

"DO YOU HAVE THE CAMERA, JAZMINE?" ASKED JARED AS he bounded through the wood, his older sister in tow.

His dark blond hair, sculpted into small spikes, bounced cheerfully with every step.

Jazmine moaned. "Yes, I still have the camera. I had it last time you asked, and the time before that, and I *still* have the camera," she complained, as she had to break into a trot to keep up with him, and then screeching as her long golden hair snagged on a branch and had to be tugged free. Broken twigs crunched under her feet, and the morning light filtered through the branches overhead reluctantly as the pair crashed through the woodland. "Are you going to tell me what this is about?"

"I've told you already," Jared replied, pausing briefly to get his bearings before setting off again at speed. Jazmine sighed and chased after him.

"You're not still going on about that, are you? Ghosts don't exist. How many times do I have to tell you?"

"You'll see . . . ," was all he said in response. Jazmine rolled her eyes. Jared was a nice enough brother, as brothers go, but he had what all the teachers politely called "an overactive imagination." She had only gone along to humor him, but now, looking around the dark, shadowy woods, she was beginning to regret it. She stopped, and when Jared realized she wasn't following, he stopped as well.

"Let's head back, Jared. I don't like it here. It feels creepy."

"Precisely!" he said triumphantly. Jazmine didn't feel triumphant. She felt a little scared. The woodland they had started off in had been just a normal, nice, run-of-the-mill-type forest, with mushrooms, and strange smells, and chattering birds. Somewhere along the line, though, this had changed. The trees seemed taller, more gnarled, uglier, and all the birdsong had stopped. It even felt darker, as if the light wasn't trying so hard to reach the ground.

"Come on. I believe you. Let's head back," she begged.

"No, you don't. You're just saying that," replied Jared. "Look, it's just a little farther. There's a big mansion, all run-down, which is where it hangs out. We just need to get one photo, and then I promise, we can go." He grinned cheekily at his sister, who sighed, but nodded.

"Okay. But as soon as you realize that you're just being an idiot, we're going home, okay?"

"Course," he agreed.

Jazmine slowly walked up to her brother, small steps, anxiously looking around. When Jared had first told her his tale of a menacing ghost chasing him as he searched for "the perfect snowman arm sticks," she just expected him to get bored and drop the subject, but he hadn't. Instead, the more she told him off for lying, the more he'd insisted it was true. Out here, it was easy to see how Jared's imagination had gotten the better of him. It really did seem like the perfect haunted wood— quiet, dark, with strange scratching noises on the outskirts of your hearing, tugging your attention to vacant spaces. Goose bumps crawled up her arms, and she tried to rub them away.

"Creepy," she muttered. Jared nodded knowingly and led on.

"We're close," he whispered. "Get your camera ready."

A horrid scream roared through the forest, and it took a massive effort for Jazmine to stay put and not run. It set her teeth on edge and hurled shivers up and down her spine, and then, as quickly as that, it was gone.

"See!" said Jared. "I told you we're close."

"Foxes," replied Jazmine nervously. "That was just a fox."

"Yeah, right. Don't be stupid."

Jazmine punched him on the arm, and he winced.

"I'm not stupid," she growled.

"You are if you think that was a fox."

Jazmine went to punch him again, but stopped at the last second.

"Heh . . ." She laughed. "You flinched."

"I did not," denied Jared. "It's called reactions, and it's a good thing, because without them . . ." He trailed into silence, his mouth left open, color draining from his face.

"Stop goofing around, Jared. It's not funny," ordered Jazmine.

Jared didn't respond. He stayed, staring at a point in the distance, his breath racing. Slowly, Jazmine turned, camera in hand, to see what he was looking at.

Then she screamed. A full-bodied, total scream, one that simply powered out of her without thought.

The creature screamed back.

The next thing she knew, she was racing through the woods, Jared at her side, faster than she knew was even possible, legs pounding beneath her, hands clawing branches away, adrenaline surging through every inch of her, forcing her on, faster, farther, through the woods, lungs dragging in huge gasps of air, surging onward. They emerged on the outskirts of the wood, gratefully bursting into the light, and both bent over, hands on knees, lungs aching, legs wobbling, eyes wide, faces pale. They looked at each other, each a mirror of the other's scared expression, and Jazmine shook her head, scarcely able to believe what she had just seen.

"Told . . . you . . . ," gasped Jared, in between rasping breaths. Jazmine nodded dumbly. "Did . . . you . . . get . . . a . . . photo?" he asked.

With trembling hands, Jazmine studied the camera. It took a while for her to hold it steady enough to see, but finally, with tremendous effort, she did. At the top, the dial read: PHOTOS TAKEN: ONE.

Jazmine smiled shakily at her brother.

"Yes," she replied. "*I did.*"

A Sunday Morning in Aubergine Road

TOM WOKE, BLEARY-EYED, TO SEE GREY ARTHUR STANDING over his bed, grinning at him, a glass of orange juice in his hand, ready to help Tom kick-start the day. With a small jump, Tom realized the Harrowing Screamer was also in his room, standing at the far end of his bed. He was doing something strange with his claws, and it took Tom a second to realize he was waving. Tom took the glass of orange juice from Grey Arthur with a smile, and waved back at Harry.

"Morning," he croaked. He took a sip, wet his throat, and had another go at talking. "Morning," he said, far more convincingly this time. "You're up early."

"We've been up for aaaaaages," said Arthur, plonking himself down on the bed. "We've been over to Mrs. Scruffles's house already. Everyone's there. Tike's been harassing John until he does his knight impression, Eliza's been stealing all Mrs. Scruffles's cutlery (she's stirring her tea with a wooden spoon, since everything shiny has gone missing), Mildred's been working on a new theory of de-visibilization, and Harry and I have been trying to work out where the Eldritch could be. So far, we've narrowed it down to England."

The Harrowing Screamer moaned, and Grey Arthur corrected himself.

"And possibly Scotland, or Wales."

Tom nodded and took another sip of orange juice.

"Claudia has been in touch, and given us all the haunting reports she's been sent at *Exceedingly Haunted Homes*. We had a look through, and most of them are a bit, you know . . ." Grey Arthur twirled a finger round his head while rolling his eyes. "But some might be worth looking into, now we know what we're after. I brought them over, figured we could have a look through together."

"And what are you going to do, Harry?" asked Tom.

"He's our paper shredder, aren't you, Harry?" said Arthur affectionately. "So your mum won't find whole reams of reports on ghosts in your room, and go off on one of her speeches."

Tom couldn't help but smile, especially when the Harrowing Screamer twitched his claws for emphasis. Grey Arthur and Harry looked at Tom, fidgeting excitedly, and Tom took the hint.

"Okay, okay, I'm getting up. You two are worse than my mum," he complained, as he threw aside his duvet.

"Great. Go grab yourself some breakfast, and we'll set everything up. There's no time to waste," said Grey Arthur, clearing off some space on Tom's desk. Tom shook his head as he wandered out of the door. Some days, his life felt stranger than others.

A little while later, Tom drifted downstairs. His mum was outside, hanging out the washing (Tom had no idea why she bothered, as at this time of year it just ended up frozen solid, but she persevered regardless), and Dad was sitting at the table with his gallon of tea, and his mountain of newspapers.

"Morning, sleepyhead. Feel better for an early night?" he asked.

"Much," agreed Tom, as he deftly retrieved the cartoon section from the middle of Dad's reading material. He plonked himself down at the table, grabbing a box of cereal and a bowl.

"Anything exciting happening in the world?" he asked.

Dad shrugged. "Depends on your definition of exciting, I suppose. The crown jewels have shown up— turns out it was just a training exercise to test the Beefeaters' reactions, that went a bit wonky. I dare say someone's getting a right telling-off over that."

Tom stifled a laugh. A training exercise? As lame excuses go, that was right up there with the best.

"Anything else?" he asked. Dad flipped back over the pages he had read.

"Royal scandal (now there's a surprise), corrupt politicians, a robbery, article on why Britain is getting fatter, sales of night-lights are up two hundred percent in the Wolverhampton area, pictures of a certain celebrity leaving a nightclub, blah blah . . . I think we can safely say that nothing too exciting is going on," concluded Dad. Tom smiled, relieved. As long as there were no headlines proclaiming the existence of ghosts, then everything was okay. For now. "Anyway, what's all this interest in the news? Usually you just steal the comics, and that's it."

"I guess I'm just growing up," said Tom in his most mature voice. Dad smiled, impressed.

"So we'll be fighting over who gets to read the papers first soon, eh?" Dad chuckled, pushing his elbows out and guarding his newspaper.

Tom grinned. "Well, I don't think you have to worry quite yet," he admitted, as he filled his bowl to overflowing with milk and Mr. Space Pirate Hoops.

And so that was how Sunday started.

How it ended, in the middle of a gloomy forest, trapped in an abandoned mansion with the Eldritch, with TV crews bearing down on Tom and the Invisible Friends, and nowhere to go, well, that takes a little bit more explaining.

When Things Go Wrong

THE HARROWING SCREAMER TOOK ON THE ROLE OF paper shredder with gusto, which was just as well, as there were obscene amounts of paper to go through, and none of them were useful for anything other than turning into confetti. Hours slowly dwindled away, lost in reading, and scowling, sighing, and shredding.

"This is getting us nowhere," complained Tom eventually. "We shouldn't just be sitting around doing nothing. We should be out there, looking."

"Just wandering the streets, going '*Here, Screamer, Screamer*'?" asked Grey Arthur. Tom reddened, realizing how daft his suggestion was. "I know you're getting frustrated, but we'll work it out eventually. We always do."

"But it's just taking so long," huffed Tom, throwing yet another useless report toward Harry, who readily caught it on one claw, and proceeded to whittle it down to nothing.

"Well, let's take a break, then. Read a book, pop the telly on, whatever."

Tom stood up from the desk, took a brief second to admire the amount of cuts his fingers had accumulated (when would someone get round to inventing paper-cut-free paper?), and wandered over to the telly. He switched it on, and with a humongous sigh, flopped down onto the bed. The news was on, and Tom moaned, scrambling around to find the remote.

"... *in Wolverhampton, following reports of a terrifying creature prowling the area* ..."

The name Wolverhampton immediately nudged a memory, and Tom sat bolt upright. It was something his dad had said earlier that day, something he read from the paper. . . .

"... *sales of night-lights are up two hundred percent in the Wolverhampton area* ..."

In that moment, whether it was intuition, sixth sense, or a leap of deductive reasoning, Tom knew.

He knew where the Eldritch was.

"Arthur, Harry," he hissed. "You need to see this."

The TV presenter was standing on the edge of woodland, clutching an umbrella that failed to protect him from the worst of the weather. He looked about as grumpy as you could possibly get without swearing.

"Good evening," he said somberly. "I am here on the outskirts of Manor Woods, the site where two young children encountered a terrifying creature earlier on today. We are lucky enough to have them here with us tonight. Jared, Jazmine, in your own words, can you talk us through what happened?"

The two children grinned excitedly into the camera, each jostling for best position.

"Well, first off, my sister didn't believe me, which is why we went back with the camera," said Jared.

"That's a lie. I did believe him, which is why I went along with the camera, to get proof," said Jazmine.

"You're such a liar! Anyway, I'd seen it before, but nobody believed me." He said that pointedly, glaring at his sister. "So I wanted to go back, even though it was really scary."

"And so we're wandering in, and hear this awful scream."

"Which meant we were close."

"Really close. And then we saw it, just standing there, staring at us," she said dramatically.

"Can you explain for the viewers at home what you saw?" asked the presenter, looking seriously into the camera.

"Sure can. It was tall. Six feet."

"Seven feet," corrected Jazmine.

"Maybe eight feet tall. Really scrawny. Sharp teeth."

"Long, twisted claws."

"It was all so quick, though. Next thing I know, we're

outside the forest. We just ran and ran until we were out," said Jared, as Jazmine nodded, before adding triumphantly:

"Not before we got a picture, though."

"And what do you think it was?" asked the presenter. Jared and Jazmine looked at each other before replying in unison:

"*A ghost.*"

Grey Arthur gasped.

The camera panned back to the TV presenter, who was smirking in an "Aren't children amusing?" way. "The children may well think they have seen a ghost, but we have wildlife expert Dr. Olly Dimble here, who has studied the photograph, and has a different opinion. Dr. Dimble, care to enlighten us?"

The camera zoomed out to include a wiry, bearded man in the shot. He looked like he was enjoying his moment in the spotlight, and paused in a very intellectual fashion before answering.

"I would love to. Having studied the picture, I can in fact tell you that what we are looking at is a large cat, undeniably a panther."

"And the fact that he is walking upright?" asked the presenter.

Dr. Dimble nodded, pleased that he had asked the question. "The fact that he is roaming upright leads us to believe that this is in fact an escaped circus panther, trained to walk on its hind legs. The long, twisted claws would have occurred after prolonged periods of walking in this manner, as usually the length of the claws is reduced by the natural wear and tear taking place when climbing or walking. In the circus, this animal would have had someone to clip his claws—in the wild, with nobody to undertake this task, they have grown beyond normal limits. His scrawny build, and the fact that he approached these children, leads us to believe that he is malnourished, and may be acting out of character due to his hunger and inability to hunt for himself. He may also be trying to protect his territory. We believe he may have been abandoned here by the people who used to live in the mansion, and so may well shelter there when he isn't hunting."

"Thank you," said the presenter. "For those of you at home tuning in late, here is that photo once more."

Tom, Grey Arthur, and Harry waited with bated breath.

It was the most blurred, out-of-focus, vague photograph you could imagine. Only the faintest outline, the most smudged of images, the most indecipherable of shapes, could be made out. Tom and Grey Arthur laughed with relief.

That is, until Dr. Dimble continued talking.

"We just want to reassure the public that we are doing everything we can to capture this creature. The whole forest has been sealed off, with no way for this panther to leave unnoticed. Reports of wild cats loose in Britain have been going on for many years, and this offers us our first real chance to trap one. We have camera crews positioned all around the forest, and at first light we intend to tighten the circle, closing the net if you will, eventually cornering this creature. When this happens, we will be in the privileged position, *for the first time ever on live television*, to show the nation the capture of this splendid animal, and offer irrefutable proof that big cats really do roam our countryside." Dr. Dimble grinned enthusiastically down the camera.

The TV presenter smiled. "We all look forward to seeing that tomorrow. This is Ted Brandy, reporting from Manor Woods, Wolverhampton. Good night."

Tom turned off the television and waited for Grey Arthur to say something.

Anything.

"Not good," said Grey Arthur finally. "That's not good at all."

Countdown to Chaos

"WE NEED TO MOVE. NOW," SAID ARTHUR, BEGINNING THAT familiar anxious pacing of his. "We need to gather everyone up and head out there as soon as possible. If the Screamer gets caught on television, if everyone sees it, if they manage to record proof . . . Oh, Tom, this could be terrible. You saw what happened at the castle. Imagine that, happening all over the country, all at once. There's no way we could undo that. That would be it. Done. Forever." Arthur stopped pacing and looked determinedly at Tom.

"Nope. I don't even have time to stay here and pace. We've got to get going and try to get the Eldritch out."

"Sounds like a plan," agreed Tom. The Harrowing Screamer howled enthusiastically.

"Okay, then. Well, what are you waiting for, Tom? Get your shoes on."

"What?" Tom spluttered. "You want me to come with you?"

"Of course I want you to come with us." Grey Arthur looked confused. "Why wouldn't I? You're like our resident expert."

"On what? Screamers? Arthur, I hadn't even seen a ghost until only a few months ago, so I don't know why you think I'm—"

"No, no," interrupted Arthur. "On being scared."

"Oh," said Tom in a small voice. Being an expert on being afraid didn't strike him as a particularly good thing. Thomas "Cowardly Custard" Golden. As titles go, he thought he might even prefer Freak Boy to that.

"It's not an insult, Tom," added Arthur kindly, spotting Tom's crestfallen face. "It's just, you humans, you get scared by so many different things—loud noises, spiders, heights, mice, small spaces, wasps, the dark, dogs, ghost stories . . . There's not much that can scare a ghost, Tom. It's not something we're used to. I mean it. We could really do with your help. I can't even imagine what it's like to be that scared, Tom. What do you do?"

Tom chewed his lip, contemplating what Arthur had said. He was right. Tom had just never thought much about it before. His mind flitted back to that very first encounter at the castle, where a Screamer had approached him in the dungeons, then to the night when the Harrowing Screamer had first shown up in his bedroom, and a slow smile crept onto his face.

"What is it, Tom? That's your 'I Have a Plan' smile. What's going on?"

Tom nodded at Grey Arthur and the Harrowing Screamer. "Let's not waste any more time, then. We've got a ghost to rescue."

"So, you're coming? Oh, Tom, that's great news."

"I need some time to pack, though, and you need to go tell Mrs. Scruffles what is going on, work out how we're going to get to Manor Woods, and find a way for my parents to let me stay out tonight. That part won't be easy, especially since I have school tomorrow."

"I'm sure Mrs. Scruffles will work something out," replied Arthur with an eager grin.

Tom smiled uneasily. "I wouldn't be so sure of that. My parents aren't going to be happy about this."

Manor Woods

TOM WAS WRONG.

His parents were very happy indeed when Mrs. Scruffles turned up on their doorstep an hour later to announce that Tom was having a sleepover with Mildred.

"That's brilliant news!" Mum had said.

"Of course we don't mind the short notice!" Dad had said.

"No, we really aren't angry that tomorrow is a school day!" they had agreed.

It might strike you as unusual that they were so accommodating to this last-minute request, but then you wouldn't know, just as Tom's parents didn't know, exactly why they were so happy.

Mrs. Scruffles cheated.

As she stood on the doorstep, doing her very best human impression, concentrating to be as Real as possible, unseen behind her stood another American Contrary, the Sadness Summoner whose blue hue was the color of tropical seas and summer skies, the ghost who made everyone near her uncontrollably happy. Tom's parents couldn't have been annoyed if they tried.

It was a little unfair, but this was a very important mission, and sometimes you're allowed to be a little bit unfair for the greater good. You just shouldn't make a habit of it.

So, with Tom packed, the route planned, the Invisible Friends gathered, and Tom allowed to stay out, all it took then was for all of them to jump into the nearest ley-line and get thrown out on the outskirts of Manor Woods.

The sun had set by the time they arrived, and a full,

pockmarked silvery moon hung above them, framed in a cloudless sky dusted with stars. It was beautiful, but the setting sun had dragged with it what little heat there was, and the night was bitterly cold. Tom, Grey Arthur, Montague Equador Scullion the Third, Mildred Rattledust, Tike, and the Harrowing Screamer were all crouched a discreet distance away from the outskirts of the forest, hiding behind a bush. Strictly speaking, Tom was the only one who *needed* to crouch, since Tom was the only one likely to be spotted, but they all did it anyway so that Tom didn't feel too much like the odd one out. The whole forest had been hastily sealed off with the kind of barriers workmen put up to stop you falling down manholes, and signs, placed at regular intervals, warned KEEP OUT—WILD CAT LOOSE IN AREA. That, in itself, wouldn't have been a problem to get past. What *was* problematic was the fact that, every hundred meters or so around the barrier, members of the TV crew stood watch, flashlights in hand, video cameras at the ready, in case something stirred in the darkness of the woods.

"This would be so much easier," sighed Monty, "if there was a ley-line that ran into the forest. Or a Laundry Run into the mansion. Or anything."

"Perhaps that is why the Eldritch chose this location, Montague," replied Mildred, her mismatched eyes fixed on the manned barrier ahead. "For its remoteness."

It made sense. After being chased from pillar to post by ghosts and humans alike, before finally being banished, it was hardly surprising that the Eldritch would choose to settle somewhere that wasn't easily accessible. In many ways, it was a good thing—it was the reason why he had taken this long to get spotted. If he hadn't chosen to chase the two children away, they might never even have realized he was here. At this very moment, though, this lack of access was a definite hurdle. With no supernatural way in, it meant that they would have to walk in, and out again, which was easier said than done. Easy enough for the invisible ghosts—a little bit more taxing when you included the highly visible Tom, and the rather attention-drawing Eldritch.

Tom shivered quietly at Arthur's side. He'd wrapped up warm, but not as warm as he would have liked— happy as his parents were, it still might have aroused their suspicions if he'd left the house for a quiet sleepover outfitted like he was going on an Arctic expedition. With cold hands, he rearranged the rucksack on his back for the umpteenth time, and curled his toes inside his shoes, just to try to force some life back into them.

"Whatever we're going to do, can we do it soon? My fingers are going to drop off if we stay here much longer," he whispered.

Grey Arthur looked briefly alarmed, but then he smiled. "That's one of those expressions, right? Like 'I could eat a horse'?" he said hopefully.

Tom shook his head. "Nope, it's one of those things

that can really happen if human fingers or toes get too cold. It's called frostbite."

Grey Arthur's eyes grew wide. "Okay . . . okay . . . Don't panic, everyone, but we really need to get a move on. *Tom's fingers are beginning to fall off.*"

Tom felt like telling him it wasn't *that* urgent, but decided that anything that could get them moving was a good idea, even if it was the fear that Tom was going to end up with stumps for hands. There was no point sitting around, just staring at the woods. The longer they waited, the bigger the chance that something could go wrong.

"I believe I have a solution for getting us inside the perimeter," Mildred informed them. "However, it will only work once. We will have to think of an alternative plan to extract ourselves."

"That'll do," said Tike, cracking his knuckles. "We'll work the rest out as we go."

Mildred nodded. She stooped low next to Tom, her mismatched eyes level with his. "When you get the opportunity, run through the barrier, Thomas."

"What about you?" Tom whispered.

"I will rejoin you later." And with that, she stood up, pale hands quietly smoothing away unseen creases in her black skirt. Tom watched curiously.

Mildred took a deep breath and concentrated. Her brow furrowed, her fists clenched, her eyes closed, Mildred Rattledust threw all of her energy into becoming Realer. Her pale skin slowly became less cloudy, her outline became less hazy, and her unique touch of black freckles appeared across her nose, one after the other. Her lips twitched, a faint outline of a smile, and shaking loose her fingers, and opening her eyes, she nodded at Tom. Tom nodded back, impressed. She was definitely getting better at appearing Real. One final touch was added—she closed her eyes tightly again, took another deep breath . . . her black school uniform shuddered out of existence, and in its place appeared an exceedingly somber pair of pajamas. They were black-striped cotton, and although they had just been magicked into existence, looked as if Mildred had spent a good hour ironing them first. The icing on the cake came when, with a twist of her wrist, Mildred's sinister, threadbare monkey materialized, its drooping eye gazing out toward the waiting men, and she clutched it like a bedtime comforter. If they hadn't been hiding out of sight, Tom would have clapped. She waved quietly good-bye to Tom and the remaining Invisible Friends, and, in a slightly dazed and haphazard fashion, her free arm sweeping before her, began walking toward the barricade.

Two men with flashlights were positioned about fifty meters directly ahead. Mildred weaved toward them, with sleepy, faltering steps. It seemed like an age before they spotted her, but when you are waiting anxiously, even seconds drag. The beams of light from both their flashlights immediately settled onto Mildred.

Tom held his breath, and he felt the ghosts at his side

tense as well. Being in a direct light like that would test even the most seasoned of Faintly Reals, let alone Mildred. They needn't have worried. She held her ground, defiantly silhouetted, and everyone let out a collective sigh of relief. Mildred was definitely Real enough to be seen. So far, the plan, whatever it might be, was working. Caught in her own, personal spotlight, Mildred suddenly stopped in her path. She stretched, she rubbed her eyes, she yawned, and she peered blearily at the men, who were staring back at her in confusion.

"You all right, love?" one called out to her.

"Where am I?" she muttered. The men raced toward her, concerned, abandoning their posts.

"What are you doing out here at this time of night?" Tom heard one of them ask.

"What? Where?" cried Mildred, swooning on her feet. With one hand behind her back, she began frantically pointing toward the now unmanned forest barricade. Tom took the hint, and, low to the ground, quiet as possible, began to creep forward while Mildred kept the men distracted. She made a great act of looking at her surroundings as if for the first time, and being shocked. "I must have sleepwalked. How disagreeable."

"Sleepwalked?" repeated the second man. "There's no houses for miles!"

"It's possible I ran," replied Mildred. "That would explain how I covered so much ground." She yawned again for effect, as the two men looked at her dubiously.

Tom ducked beneath the barrier, creeping along,

hands clawing through the cold muddy ground. For a while he continued at a slow pace, fearful of making any noise, but as soon as he felt he was far enough away from Mildred and the two men, he threw himself upright, breaking into a sprint, the silvery moonlight leading a crooked path as he weaved and bobbed through the trees. Mildred's voice carried through the woods, but eventually the distance between them grew enough that all that could be heard was the wind rustling through the trees' bare branches, Tom's feet crashing through the woods, and the sound of his own breathing. Satisfied that he had put enough distance between himself and the TV crew, Tom ducked behind a tree, backpack pressed up against the rough bark, and struggled to get back his breath. The freezing cold air meant that every time he exhaled, a cloud of smoke hung before his face, but after running like that, Tom felt baking hot. He loosened his scarf and unbuttoned the top of his coat, actually enjoying the cold air against his skin. Grey Arthur, Monty, Tike, and Harry waited next to him, none of them out of breath, none of them even mildly affected by being hot or cold. Tom grinned tiredly at them, but they didn't smile back. Grey Arthur, Tike, and Monty were looking around at the woodland, concern etched across their faces. Even Harry seemed on edge. He bristled defensively, flexing his claws, a low rumbling growl escaping him.

Tom frowned and looked at the woodlands, trying to see what the ghosts were picking up on.

Something felt subtly wrong about it all. Something in the angles of the trees, the shapes the branches took, the way the stars seemed thinner, fewer, dimmer here, that niggled at him. Even the full, bright moon that had hung over them at the outskirts of the woods seemed to be muted and subdued. Grey Arthur noticed Tom's expression, and nodded.

"I think it must be because we're close to the Eldritch," he said, in answer to Tom's unasked question. It wasn't a reassuring response. If this was how it felt just being in the same area as him . . . well, that didn't bear thinking about. Tom smiled determinedly, brushing away the mulch and dirt that stuck to his hands after crawling through the barrier.

"Let's go," he said, as bravely as he could muster.

The farther into the forest they walked, the worse it got. They had started walking evenly spread out, a steady pace, heads held high, but within a few minutes they were clustered together, small, timid steps, heads constantly turning, twitching, tilting, straining to pick out the odd noises that grated through the heavy quiet. The stars above grew fewer and fewer, glittering dimly, like dying fairy lights, and the moon that had glowed healthily and heartily now was tainted with a sickly yellow sheen. The trees seemed to take on faces, an image that you would catch out of the corner of your eye, a snarling mouth formed of branches, a gnarled hole that looked like a menacing glare, a bush that would take on the shape of a Screamer, but when you looked directly at them, the image would vanish, like a magic eye painting that you couldn't quite grasp. The warmth Tom had felt from running had slowly faded away, and now he was shivering uncontrollably, although he couldn't be entirely sure whether it was due to the cold, or nerves.

They pressed onward in silence, nobody feeling much like talking. The branches of trees and bushes seemed to shift to make progress slower, snagging on Tom's clothes, scratching his skin, roots grappling at his feet, trying to trip him. The ghosts were unaffected by these physical changes, drifting through the forest untouched, and Tom struggled to keep up, hands held close to his chest, eyes warily scanning from side to side as he walked. There was a constant sensation, burrowing at the back of everyone's mind, of being watched, and that feeling only grew heavier, and heavier, the farther in they walked. It would have been enough to deter even the most intrepid of travelers, to persuade them that the woods were no place for either human or ghost to be, but Tom and the Invisible Friends were spurred on by the thought of daybreak, of television crews crashing through the woods, of homes throughout the country being broadcast live footage of a cornered Screamer, of how the neat divide between the two worlds would break, and deep down the truth of it was that they were more scared of that than anything the Eldritch could throw at them.

Tom wasn't sure how long they walked. Time felt as warped and skewed here as the woods themselves, and he wouldn't be surprised to discover that hours had gone by, nor surprised to discover it was just minutes. The Real World, the familiar world of humans, had been whittled away, and the supernatural soaked everything through and through.

Suddenly, the trees thinned, the woods retreated, and there before them, in all its horrific glory, stood the abandoned mansion.

Walking into a Nightmare

IT WAS WORSE THAN ANY OF THEM COULD POSSIBLY HAVE imagined. Tom gasped, and instantly fell back a few paces. Tike began breathing rapidly, grubby hands nervously ruffling and unruffling his black-and-white streaked hair. Harry whined, a high-pitched, bracing noise that set Tom's teeth on edge. Monty put a reassuring arm around Grey Arthur's shoulders, but his face was drawn, and his eyes seemed impossibly wide. Grey Arthur remembered Eliza's words—"*You can't even begin to understand how powerful he was when the light had gone*"—and finally, he realized the true depth of what she had been saying.

The mansion might once have been beautiful, picturesque, but what stood before them now had been tainted beyond all recognition. It was weeping black shadows from smashed windows, like tears sprawling down a broken face. The stonework was warped and corrupted, decaying rot chewing into its surface. All the grass that surrounded it, a lawn that in the past would have been striped in vibrant greens, was withered and dead. Bushes that were once lovingly sculpted into birds and animals now took on unnatural shapes, jutting claws, grating angles, cloaked shades that guarded the way ahead. There were no stars in the sky that framed this scene, and the yellow moon colored everything in a sickly palette. The front door of the mansion had simply rotted away, splintered shards of soggy wood cluttering the entrance, and from within came a low, haunting scream, which seemed to shake the whole building.

"That's rather disconcerting," came a small voice from beside Tom. He turned and saw Mildred, back in her normal attire of a black school uniform. She retained her sinister monkey, though, clutching it within her pale hand like a threadbare comfort blanket. Tom grinned at her, a wild grin that showed more teeth than normal.

"Mildred!" cried Grey Arthur, launching himself from Monty's side and crushing her in a ghostly bear hug. "Thank goodness you're here."

"I did tell you I would rejoin you," she said, her voice muffled from within Grey Arthur's grasp. "I would not let you face the Eldritch without me."

The joy of their reunion quickly vanished, though,

smothered by the horror of their surroundings. Smiles faded, mouths becoming taut thin lines, faces falling into anxious frowns. The mansion loomed ahead of them, their final destination, the place where the legendary Eldritch, the original Screamer, was hiding, and not one of them wanted to take a single step closer to it. Another scream tore out of the building, and Tom shuddered.

"My mouth has taken on an undesirable dry texture," said Mildred quietly.

Tom nodded. "Yeah, that happens."

"And my hands are shaking."

"Yeah, that happens too."

"I think I'm beginning to understand why the other ghosts agreed for the Eldritch to be locked away," muttered Monty, his eyes constantly locked on the dark, rotten doorway in the distance. "Being scared like this is deeply unpleasant."

"We'll be fine. Don't worry," said Grey Arthur, looking up at Monty. "Tom has a plan. Don't you, Tom?"

"I do," agreed Tom. Now was as good a time as any to put it into action. He swung his rucksack off his shoulder and placed it down on the floor. With unsteady hands, he wrenched open the zip, then gestured dramatically to the contents within.

"Flashlights?" cried Tike, unable to hide the disappointment in his voice. "*That's* your master plan? Flashlights? What are we going to do? Make shadow puppets at him until he agrees to come along with us?"

"I hate to say it, but I kind of agree with Tike, Tom. What use are flashlights?" asked Monty.

Tom had been hoping for a better response than this. Perhaps they'd been expecting a magical anti-fear talisman, or a mystical Screamer dispeller, instead of a bunch of flashlights raided from Tom's house, run on nothing more supernatural than batteries. "Something Grey Arthur said got me thinking," Tom explained. "Remember when we were at the castle, Arthur, and that Screamer was waiting for me in the dungeon? The first thing I did, when my legs would listen, was run upstairs into the light. Same thing when Harry showed up—Dad heard me shouting, and he came and turned on the light, and then every-thing wasn't so bad. Something Eliza said as well, she said that the Eldritch is a lot more powerful at night-time, and she said that the villagers used to chase him away with burning torches. Well, we can't wait for daytime, and we don't have any burning torches, but these plastic ones should do. I've got one each. It was short notice, so some aren't very good—that one is my bike light, and that's one you strap to your head when you go camping—but they should do the trick. *Hopefully*."

"Why didn't you give them to us sooner, Tom?" asked Monty.

Tom shrugged sheepishly. "Because I'm not sure how much batteries are left in them."

"Well, that's reassuring," sighed Tike, as he leaned

in and grabbed the biggest flashlight, the one Dad used for searching in the garage at night. He looked at the Harrowing Screamer, and the long curling claws that weren't exactly designed for flashlight holding, and pulled out the camping light for him, fastening it around his head. Harry gnashed his sharp teeth, apparently not too happy about having a light source attached to him, but allowed Tike to continue. "There you go, Harry. You look stupid as anything, but if it does the trick, I suppose . . ." He handed Mildred the flashlight from Mum's car, Monty the flashlight from Dad's, Grey Arthur the bike light, and Tom the final flashlight, a bright green tacky affair with Mr. Space Pirate illustrations printed on it. Tom zipped up the bag once more, throwing it onto his back. All the flashlights switched on okay, which was a good start, even if some did need some persuasive tapping.

"I guess we're ready to head in, then," said Tom, staring at the haunted mansion before them.

"I guess we are," agreed Grey Arthur.

Nobody wanted to make the first move, though. For a good minute more, they stood in silence, listening to the screams that seeped out of the mansion, watching the shadows drip down its surface, transfixed by the way the dimensions of the place seemed to warp and shift before your eyes.

It was Harry who summoned his courage first. With a bloodcurdling scream, he forced himself forward, his old bones clicking reluctantly, a pool of light bouncing before him as he walked. The others quickly followed, as much because they were afraid to be left behind as they were keen to move forward.

The lawn, which would once have been springy and healthy, squelched uncomfortably as Tom walked across it, clutching at his shoes, making every step feel like walking through moldy glue. The towering bushes that lined the way ahead, crafted into unpleasant shapes, shifted and altered out of the corner of his eye, tugging relentlessly at his attention. When Tom shined his flashlight on them they would remain stock-still, but as soon as the light drifted away, the writhing and stretching would begin again. Tom tried his best to just concentrate on reaching the doorway, one step, another, deep breaths, and the Invisible Friends did the same. They moved on, closely huddled together, Tom at the center, white knuckles clutching his flashlight, constantly struggling to get his breathing under control. He'd had nightmares more pleasant than this, and at least during those there was the potential to wake up.

They marched through the dead garden, across the withered lawn, past the warped bushes, and finally drew to a halt by the entrance, the mansion looming imposingly above them. Bats fluttered around the building, silhouetted by the yellow moonlight. It was the ultimate haunted house, something dragged from the scariest ghost story you had ever heard, told on the darkest of nights, in the lowest of whispers.

And they had no choice but to go in.

The wooden steps that led up to the door were spongy and rotten, and they groaned and gave slightly under Tom's weight. The ghosts simply floated silently behind him, but Tom had to consider every step he took, testing his weight before moving onward, terrified that the wood wouldn't carry him, would crumble beneath him, and he would plunge through the slats and vanish out of sight. He held his breath as he climbed higher, and gave a short-lived sigh of relief when he finally reached the top. Grey Arthur drifted to his side, his grey ghostly face pinched with fear, and he nodded at Tom, who nodded back.

"This is it," Tom whispered.

"This is it," Arthur agreed.

Tom glanced behind to make sure all the Invisible Friends were still with him before he went on. They were. Pale, scared, and anxious, but there. Mildred was gripping her toy monkey tightly, her other hand holding the flashlight, the beam shaking from where her hands were unsteady. Tike and Harry stuck closely together, staring quietly at the doorway. Monty swallowed dryly, holding his flashlight up high as he tried to peer into the darkness that lurked within the entrance. Tom nodded to them, and they nodded back.

They were ready to head in.

No Turning Back

THE FRONT DOOR HAD SIMPLY ROTTED AWAY, A FEW sodden pieces of wood clinging to a rusty hinge, the rest collected at the entrance in piles of musty-smelling splinters. Tom kicked the pile, trying to clear a way through, and couldn't help but screech when his foot revealed maggots crawling beneath. His foot jerked instinctively, sending fat, pale grubs cascading through the air.

"It's okay, Tom!" cried Grey Arthur, a little too shrilly to be convincing. Tom nodded dumbly, his mouth too dry for words, and shook his foot again, to make sure there were no creepy-crawlies left on him, and then once more, for good measure. He stepped carefully over the remaining pile, an anguished look on his face, and took his first step into the mansion. The others weren't far behind.

Inside was even more disturbing than outside: something Tom wouldn't have thought possible if he wasn't seeing it for himself. A long corridor stretched ahead, the walls of which bulged and sagged, veins of rot marbling the surface. Tom harbored a suspicion that if he was to touch them, they would collapse, and he held his arms close to his side, keen for that not to happen. The carpet they walked on was sticky and smeared with tarry black shadows that clung to the soles of Tom's shoes. Portraits jutted out from the walls, painted in dark, moody colors, hung on rusty nails, and the horrifying faces that lurked inside had eyes that moved, following their progress. Grey Arthur made a concerted effort not to look at them, as he didn't like the way his stomach jolted when they looked back. Instead, he hurried along at Tom's side, swinging the light of his bike light ahead, trying to make out where this corridor was leading. The flashlights did little to push back the dark, feebly illuminating the path ahead only a few scarce meters at a time. A spiral staircase appeared before them, emerging out of the darkness, but it led to nowhere, abruptly ending in a tangle of contorted wood. Things fluttered out of sight, noises scratched, and Tom's heart raced so fast that he was concerned that it might break through overexertion. Mildred linked arms with Monty at the back, Tike and the Harrowing Screamer next, with Tom and Grey Arthur bravely forging the way ahead. It felt like they walked for miles, impossibly far, and Tom began to wonder if they were ever going to reach the other side, whether they would be trapped in here forever. That thought made his heart lurch. He sucked in a deep breath of stale, musty air, and pushed on. They would have to come to a stop eventually. They just had to.

And they did.

The light from Tom's flashlight settled on a door in front of them blocking the way. Tom had never seen a door that he would describe as terrifying before. Not until now.

The door writhed and twisted as they watched, constantly shifting, knots in its wood appearing and vanishing like gaping mouths, and shadows seeped out from underneath its frame, puddling around their feet. A scream howled from the other side, shaking the door on its hinges, and instinctively everyone took a step back.

"I think this is it," whispered Mildred.

"I don't know if I can do this . . . ," muttered Tike, looking anxiously at Tom.

"We'll be fine," Tom found himself saying, unable to drag his eyes away from the door. "As long as we stay together, we'll be fine."

"I'll be right next to you, Tom," muttered Grey Arthur. "I promise."

Monty put his arm around Tike protectively, and nodded. "We're ready," he said quietly. "Let's do this, before we change our minds."

Mildred gave Harry's arm a reassuring squeeze, and walked right up to the door. With one hand holding her monkey, and one hand clutching her flashlight, she took a deep breath, and nudged the door open with one of her black patent leather shoes.

Facing Defeat

THE ELDRITCH, THE FINAL MEMBER OF THE TERRIBLE Trio, stood in the middle of what was once the Great

Hall, waiting for them. Tom was vaguely aware of the surrounding room—a chandelier, tall dark windows, grimy walls—but these were just minor details that fluttered at the far reaches of his attention. The Screamer made sure of that.

Nightmares have a vagueness of shape and form, indistinct horrors that mill just outside the grasp of normal vision, and the same was true for the Eldritch. Like a normal Screamer, he was a merging of shadows and bone, but such a simple description doesn't do justice to what stood before the Invisible Friends and Tom. He was tall, eight feet, maybe nine feet tall, and the shadows that draped across like skin were tattered like a rotten cloak, revealing the awful bone frame that lurked inside. His mouth was a black, oily hole, threaded through with teeth like broken glass. His claws, hanging from long, slight hands, curled menacingly, and his feet ended in the same abrupt twists of sharpness. The air around him was heavy with the smell of rot, and damp, of earth and lightning, and it left an acrid taste in your mouth when you breathed. Tom became slowly aware of a sound of terrible screaming, and it shocked him to realize that he was the one making it.

The flashlights the Invisible Friends grasped were horribly useless in the face of such a creature. The light simply dwindled away, pathetic shreds of illumination that wavered hopelessly before the Eldritch.

All logical thoughts vanished.

Everything was swept away on a tide of uncontrollable panic. The Harrowing Screamer was clawing at the walls, trying to find a way out, lost in a blind terror. Mildred was dumbly tapping her flashlight, her expression frightened and lost, as if somehow she could will the light into being stronger. Monty cowered in the corner, his body shielding Tike, his flashlight abandoned on the floor, feebly spilling light. Grey Arthur remained at Tom's side, his mouth working silently, his eyes wide, his grey color fading to white, and at the back of his mind Tom realized that Grey Arthur's hand was clinging to Tom's sleeve, trying to drag him away. Tom couldn't move though. He wanted to. More than anything, he wanted to, but the sight before him locked every muscle in his body in place, and all he could do was stand and watch in silent horror.

The Eldritch threw back his head, threw open that awful mouth, and screamed.

Instinct finally caught up with Tom and hurled him into motion, but it was too late. The Eldritch had closed the gap between them and now stood not a meter away. As Tom darted forward, a skeletal, shadowy hand shot out to greet him, claws effortlessly threading through the material of Tom's coat. The Eldritch hoisted Tom into the air, suspended by threads of ripping wool, legs kicking frantically but helplessly at nothing. Tom's hands clawed blindly at where his coat was snagged, but he was unable to free himself. Small, desperate sounds of shock escaped Tom's mouth, instantly drowned in the madness of the room.

No human had ever been this close to the Eldritch. Not at night. No human had been brave, or foolish, enough to even try.

Once, when Tom had been very young, a bird had flown into the house. Lost, disorientated, scared, it had thrown itself again and again and again against the closed window, wings hammering against the glass, feathers flying. The memory surfaced, scurrying across Tom's thoughts, as his heart pounded inside his chest every bit as frantically as that trapped bird against the window. Pins and needles crept into Tom's fingertips and began slowly twining their way up his hands. Black began soaking in around the edges of his vision, and he felt his eyes begin to roll up into his head as the crazy fluttering in his chest continued. The Screamer stared at him, watching curiously as Tom struggled in his grasp, his heart pounding so quickly he was afraid it would break.

"Arthur . . . ," Tom called weakly. "Help . . ."

Grey Arthur was trying, ghostly hands wrapped tightly around Tom's trouser-leg, trying to pull him back down to the ground, but he was no match at all for the Eldritch's strength. Shadows danced across the floor, snaking defiantly across the abandoned flashlight beams. The walls seemed to shake, trembling with every sound the Eldritch made. Reality waned, and left nightmares in its place.

Tom kept forgetting to breathe. Hung there, caught

like a fly in a web, feet twitching, the phrase "scared to death" marched into his thoughts and refused to leave, rattling around and around and around. Except now, Tom knew it wasn't just a phrase, knew it wasn't just something you say but something that felt like a terrifying inevitability.

"Arthur . . . ," he called, his voice thick and distant. If Arthur called back to him, Tom couldn't hear it.

They weren't enough. The Invisible Friends, for all their good intentions, weren't enough to confront the Eldritch, to stop the television crews from finding him, to stop the inevitable belief in ghosts. They'd tried, thrown everything they had at it, but they simply weren't enough, and this was how it was all going to end, miles away from home.

That was the thought running through Tom's mind, the second before the lights came on.

Illumination

A GIANT CHANDELIER, SUSPENDED ABOVE THE ROOM, burst into beautiful, glorious light, electricity humming through its dusty crystals, sending fragmented rainbows dancing across the dark space. The light tore the shadows from the walls, forcing reality back in at the seams, chasing away the supernatural horror and, in that moment, the worst of the fear was swept aside.

Tom fell to the floor and lay there, gasping for breath. Grey Arthur rushed to his side, crouching over his friend, ghostly face wretched with worry. Tom shakily nodded to show that he was okay, though the truth was he still felt far from it. He dragged in heavy lungfuls of air, and laid one hand over his heart, glad to feel the frantic beating slowing to a less dangerous pace. Sensation slowly crept back into his fingers, and he flexed them to chase the last of the numbness away. Tom's thoughts caught up with him, and he scrambled to his feet, first looking around for the Eldritch, who had retreated into the farthest corner, then to see where the other Invisible Friends were, and then looking dumbly up at the glowing chandelier. He looked at Grey Arthur quizzically, but Arthur seemed every bit as surprised as he was.

Throughout the mansion, lights clicked, flickered, and spluttered into life, washing away the darkness. The shadows slowly retreated, the walls sighed as they straightened out, the portraits with the sinister eyes became pictures of the countryside, painted in pastel colors, mottled with mildew and faded with age. Reality, emboldened by the restored lighting, struggled once again to assert itself. The sinister noises disappeared, the constant feeling of being watched lifted, and the door of warping wood became simply a door again. In the middle of the forest, the abandoned mansion stood in an unkempt garden, glowing like

Blackpool illuminations. No longer tainted, no longer terrifying—simply a run-down, neglected building once more, full to brimming with light.

Back in the Great Hall, the Eldritch howled forlornly, his claws shielding his eyes. He seemed somehow diminished, shorter, less imposing, and the fear that radiated from him failed to bite as deeply. No longer wrapped in darkness, he was just a regular, good old-fashioned Screamer. He pressed himself as far as possible into the corner, moaning lowly.

"How . . . ?" muttered Tom, as he stared around the room.

"No idea," breathed Grey Arthur. He was grinning giddily, and quickly looked to see that everyone was okay. "I'm so glad you're all right, Tom. For a second there I thought you were . . ." Arthur trailed into silence, not wanting to put it into words. Tom understood.

"I thought I was too," he agreed.

"I don't think he meant to hurt you, Tom."

"I know. I got that impression too. Not much of a consolation when your heart is about to explode, though. Is everyone else okay?"

"Looks to be," replied Arthur.

Harry, for quite possibly the first time in his ghostly existence, looked happy to be somewhere bright, his claws raised gratefully in the air, shardlike teeth glinting happily. Montague was brushing off his cloak, and Tike was getting to his feet, staring dumbly at the glowing chandelier. Mildred wandered over to the

window to pick up her toy monkey, having accidentally sent it flying in all the chaos.

Tom looked at the Eldritch. In bright light, Tom
almost felt sorry for it. It actually seemed scared, its
twisted back pressed hard against the wall, its smoky
eyes wincing at the brightness, a strained, sad howl
escaping from its blackened mouth. He took a step
toward it, and it flinched, arms raised protectively in
front. Tom didn't blame it. After being chased away
for its whole supernatural life, then being banished
for all that time, it was a small wonder that it was
afraid of people and ghosts alike. Tom stooped, as
close to it as his courage would allow. It might have
been just a regular Screamer in bright light, but it was
still a Screamer, nonetheless, and the memory of
what it had been in the pitch-black still whirred
inside his chest.

"There are people coming here to find you. We have
to get you out. Do you understand?" he asked.

The Eldritch's shardlike teeth chattered in response,
garbling a moan.

"I think we'll take that as a yes, Tom," replied Monty.
The Harrowing Screamer murmured in agreement.

"Great," replied Tom, flashing a grin at Grey Arthur.
"We did it! We actually did it. Everything is going to
be all right, Arthur. We've still got plenty of time until
daybreak."

Tom and Grey Arthur shared a smile, Tike cheered,
Harry hissed happily, and Montague clapped.

There was one Invisible Friend, though, that didn't join in the celebrations.

"Thomas . . . ," said Mildred, from her position at the window. She'd already gathered her toy, but still stood, transfixed, looking outside, a ghostly hand pressed up against the window. "I think we may have a problem."

Incoming

TOM FROWNED AND DARTED OVER TO JOIN HER. IT TOOK a while for his vision to adjust from the brightness of the Great Hall to the darkness of outside. He framed his eyes with his hands and stared out of the window. Lights flickered in the distance, orbs darting, weaving, bobbing between the trees. As they drew closer, Tom realized they weren't orbs at all, but beams of light, crashing through the woodland toward the mansion, sweeping across the forest floor, but it still took a little while for Tom to process what he was seeing.

Flashlight.

People with flashlights.

Television crews with flashlights.

Heading this way.

"They must have been alerted by the light from the mansion and are coming to investigate," explained Mildred.

"We've got to get out of here!" Tom cried, turning round in panic.

"There is no time," replied Mildred. "If we leave now, they will see us."

"And if we stay here, they definitely will!" he screeched. He dashed to the doorway, peering out into the corridor. In the distance, he could hear raised voices floating in through the open entrance, indistinct sounds that didn't quite form words. The camera crew were close. Mildred was right—if they ran out now, they would definitely get spotted. To go through all this, only for the Eldritch still to get seen . . . Tom felt like screaming through sheer frustration. Just when everything seemed like it was starting to go right. His nails dug into the wood of the door frame as he tried to work out what to do. Think, Tom. Think . . . Think!

"This way!" he yelled finally, throwing himself out into the hallway at speed. The Invisible Friends and the Eldritch followed close behind. From outside, through the gaping open entrance, the sound of voices, now close enough, clear enough to be understood, traveled to greet them.

"*Hello? This is Dr. Dimble, filming with Northreach news. Is there anybody there?*"

Tom skidded to a halt in the hallway, the carpet gathering beneath his feet. The spiral staircase, the one that had previously seemed to end in a tangle of wood, now, in the bright glow of the restored electricity, led up to a landing. Tom grinned wildly, a tiny grain of hope still intact.

"This way!" he shouted, racing up the stairs.

It has to be said, spiral staircases are not designed to be raced up. It takes a long time to get anywhere when you are effectively running round in steep circles. Tom powered on, though, legs twinging, lungs aching, hurtling upward as fast as humanly possible. He threw aside his flashlight, his beloved Mr. Space Pirate flashlight that he'd had since he was seven, and used both hands to grab hold of the rail, anything to help him go faster.

"Hello? Is anyone there? We saw the lights on, and we wanted to make sure you're okay. It's not safe to be here! There's a wild panther loose! Hello?"

Tom finally reached the top and began speeding down the corridor, ghosts still in hot pursuit. He pushed open doors as he ran, door after door, stopping just briefly to peer inside before shaking his head and powering onward. One door, two doors, four doors, six . . .

"Come on, Tom! Just choose one!" yelled Tike, as he ran behind him. "They're already coming up the stairs!"

Tom pushed open another door, looked inside, and instead of sprinting on, he ran into the room and slammed the door shut. The ghosts plunged through the closed door to join him.

They were in a bedroom, or what had once been a bedroom. A decrepit four-poster bed, a mash of exposed springs and mice nests, draped in spiderwebs, stood in the center of the room, and a moldy chest of drawers was perched next to it. Damp wallpaper was slowly peeling off the walls, black mold gathered in the corners of the ceiling, and a single, bare lightbulb hung in the center of the room, fizzing as it glowed. It had been a long while since anyone had slept here. Grey Arthur looked quizzically at Tom, who was already up by the chest of drawers, shoulder pressed against its side, red-faced as he frantically tried to push it across the room.

"What are we doing, Tom?" Arthur asked.

"Help me . . . move it . . . ," Tom gasped, still out of breath from running, "across . . . the door."

Monty and Tike leaped across the room to assist, and made short work of moving the chest of drawers across the doorway, forming an impromptu barricade. Satisfied that the door was now sealed shut, Tom leaned his back against the rickety piece of furniture, taking huge gulps of air, his face flushed. He smiled shakily at the gathered ghosts.

They didn't smile back.

"We're in a bedroom, Tom. We're trapped in a bedroom with the Eldritch, with a TV crew breathing down our necks," said Tike, confused. "What kind of rubbish plan is this?"

Improvisation

"I'VE GOT AN IDEA," TOM WHISPERED AS HE PUSHED himself upright again and began scouring the room.

"Is your idea to get caught on national TV, miles away from your home, with an ancient visible ghost?" demanded Tike. "Because that's what's about to happen."

There was a thumping noise at the door, and Tom nearly leaped out of his skin.

"Hello? We know you're in there. We just want to talk to you," called a voice. "I need to let you know that we're filming, and we want to ask you a few questions."

"Whatever your idea is, Tom, I think you'd better get on with it," said Montague urgently.

Tom nodded, continuing his search with greater speed. The thumping continued, louder this time. Tom threw himself to the floor, looking underneath the bed, and then shook his head and got up again. The thumping got even louder, as if they were trying to break down the door.

"*Tom* . . . ," Arthur said.

"I know, I know . . . I'm looking for a laundry basket. If we can find one, then we can get out of here," he explained.

Tike howled. "There ain't a Laundry Run to here, Tom. It's the first thing I checked before we headed out. If this is your master plan, then we're stuffed."

The chest of drawers began to shift away from the door with each thump, and Grey Arthur, Monty, and Tike quickly leaped to push it back in place. The Harrowing Screamer and the Eldritch both moaned softly, puddles of shadows gathering at their feet.

"*Tom!*" cried Arthur.

There was a cupboard door, built into the wall, and Tom tugged it open. Mice scurried quickly into holes in the woodwork, disappearing in a flurry of squeaks, but Tom didn't pay them much attention. He took stock of what was stored within. Inside was a rusted pram, several old books, a china doll with a broken face, and a wicker basket, the type you use for shopping. Tom grinned. He pulled out the basket, blowing the dust from it, and waved it triumphantly at Tike.

"I hate to be the bearer of bad tidings, Thomas, but that is a shopping basket," said Mildred, as she wandered over to join the ghost-enforced barricade. The chest of drawers leaped forward another few centimeters, and it took Monty, Tike, Arthur, and Mildred's combined effort to push it back in place.

"*Come and give us a hand getting this door open!*" came a shout from outside. Grey Arthur looked imploringly at Tom, who, instead of working out what to do, had rather randomly decided to take off his shoes.

Tike rolled his eyes. "Great. Arthur, your human has finally lost it," he cried, as he strained to hold the chest of drawers where it was. Tom ignored him. Carefully, he pulled off his socks, and with great finesse, flung them into the shopping basket.

"Now," he said dramatically, "it's a laundry basket."

"You're a loon, you know that, don't you?" asked

Tike, as he shouldered yet another barge at the door. Tom nodded enthusiastically.

"Just give it a go. What have we got to lose?"

Another thump at the door, and this time the door opened a crack, and no amount of pushing would force it shut again.

Tike shook his head, disbelief clear on his face. "It won't work."

"TRY!" begged Tom.

Tike sighed, that sigh that says I'll-Indulge-You, the sigh that says Here-Goes-Nothing, the sigh that screams But-It-Won't-Help-at-All, and with a huge leap, dove into the shopping basket—and tumbled out of sight.

Tom could have danced with joy, if he wasn't in the presence of the Eldritch, and if he wasn't about to get caught on national television. Instead, he gestured for the world's first Screamer to follow Tike. The Eldritch hissed apprehensively, but with a little persuasion from Harry (Tom assumed the growls and moans Harry was making were persuasive, at any rate), he jumped into the basket, long claws trailing behind him, and was gone.

"Go, Tom," hissed Arthur, as he strained to keep the door from opening. Montague and Mildred were pushing as hard as they could, but the door opened farther still. A hand slipped inside, feeling around, trying to see what was blocking the way. Outstretched fingers brushed through Monty's ghostly body, and immediately recoiled, shaking to chase away the tingly feeling of cold. Grey Arthur nodded his head frantically toward the basket, eyes wide. "We'll catch up. Go!"

Tom nodded a good-bye, scooped up his abandoned shoes, and with a grin, jumped into the Laundry Run.

A Veritable Grotto

IT WAS AN UGLY HOUR IN THE MORNING WHEN THE Invisible Friends, Tom, and the Eldritch spilled out of Mrs. Scruffles's laundry basket and into her house. Mrs. Scruffles rushed to greet them, and while her nicely lit home offered some refuge from the worst of the Eldritch's horror, it wasn't nearly enough. Her carefully hoovered landing became threaded with shadows, her floral curtains appeared tatty and stained, and the many cats that milled around began to arch their backs, hairs on end, and hiss uncontrollably. Mrs. Scruffles, however, remained unflustered. She smiled at the Eldritch, that smile of caramels and marshmallows, warm tea on a cold day, that comforting smile of hers, and led him to the room at the far end of the landing. Mrs. Scruffles threw open the door and gestured for the Eldritch to enter.

The spare room was lit up like the best Santa's

grotto in the universe. Masses of fairy lights sprawled across the floor, and the shelves were lined with lava lamps bubbling, torchieres glowing, candles burning, bedside lamps gleaming, and flashlights scattered across the floor like chunky, bright confetti. Her next electricity bill was bound to be something ruinous, but for the time being, that didn't matter. It took a little coercion to get the Eldritch inside, he and Harry having what one could only assume was a conversation, consisting of wails, clicking noises, and muted screams, but eventually he threw his clawed hands into the air in defeat, and slunk into the far corner, safely cocooned in a halo of light. A few shadows still managed to seep out under the door, a few disturbing noises escaped through the house, but nothing that really mattered. The cats finally calmed down, the chorus of hissing returning to the background noise of meows and purring, and Mrs. Scruffles's house was returned to its familiar, welcoming self.

"Now," she said, looking proudly at Tom and the Invisible Friends, "something tells me you could all do with a nice cup of tea."

You've never heard a murmur of agreement quite like it.

Tom and the Invisible Friends wandered down the stairs, exhausted, relieved, victorious, with cats lining the path like a furry welcoming committee, meowed calls of congratulation following them as they walked. Tom and Arthur grinned at each other. They'd done it.

They weren't sure entirely how, but they'd done it.

The answer to the question of how was discovered when Tom, Arthur, Mildred, Monty, and Tike staggered wearily into the kitchen, in desperate need of refreshment, and found Essay Dave, resplendent in his paperwork suit, drinking a cup of coffee with Eliza Nimble, John Method, and Claudia Sage. The table had expanded to enormous dimensions in order to accommodate so many guests—ten ghosts and one human in total. Agatha Tibbles was perched on Essay Dave's lap, heavy paws padding, and Dave's suit crumpling under her weight.

"I should have guessed." Arthur grinned as he waved cheerily at his friend. Essay Dave nodded.

"Mrs. Scruffles told me what you were doing, and I thought the least I could do was lend a helping hand. It was all her idea, I just pulled a few strings."

Mrs. Scruffles floated into the kitchen and made a beeline for the kettle. "Actually, it was something Eliza had said, about villagers with—"

"Burning torches, and how the Eldritch was more powerful at night," said Monty, finishing off her sentence for her. "Tom had already worked that part out."

Tom smiled proudly as Essay Dave, Claudia Sage, John Method, Eliza Nimble, and Mrs. Scruffles looked impressed.

"Except he just had a few measly handheld flashlights," moaned Tike. "Which were next to useless."

"I was on the right track, though!" said Tom

defensively. "It's not my fault that I don't know how to summon electricity."

"Well, luckily for you, dealing with red tape is something of a speciality of mine. All it took was a little tampering with a few forms, a hint of misdirection, and there you go," explained Essay Dave. "Power restored to an abandoned building. All that with just a few hours' notice. You should see what I can achieve in a week."

"Thank you," said Mildred, as she took her seat at the table.

Essay Dave shook his head, chuckling. "Don't thank me, it was absolutely nothing. The poor Red Rascal got the rough end of the stick."

"The Red Rascal?" asked Tike excitedly. "Is he here?"

"Nope," said Eliza, her mouth twitching as she tried not to laugh. "He's at the . . . oh, what do you call it again?"

"Zoo," explained Claudia Sage, a tinge of amusement infecting her normally haughty tones. "He's at the zoo."

The Harrowing Screamer made a quizzical moan.

"Collecting panther droppings," Eliza told him, a snort of laughter escaping her. "Mrs. Scruffles asked the obsessively tidy Poltergeist to do it first, but she had a complete fit at the idea, and point-blank refused. Something to do with germs, whatever they are. So the Red Rascal got roped in."

"This might be a stupid question . . . ," Grey Arthur said slowly, "but why is he collecting poo?"

"We need people to believe there really was a panther loose in the woods. Short of stealing a real one, and teaching it to walk on its hind legs, this was the best alternative. They'll go searching for it in the morning, find the droppings, which will prove a big cat was there, and just think it must have escaped before they set up the barricades," Essay Dave replied. "Hopefully, it'll be enough to convince the children who saw the Eldritch that they were mistaken too."

Tom slumped tiredly into the kitchen chair and scooped up Carrot Cake for a hug. The old ginger cat purred loudly, and Tom smiled, albeit a little half-heartedly. The image of the Red Rascal dashing around the forest, scattering giant cat poo in his wake, tickled him, there was no denying it, but hearing the ghosts talk, it occurred to him that this wasn't quite the perfect happy ending. He rubbed his eyes tiredly and frowned.

"We still haven't worked out how to de-visibilize you though," he said to Eliza. "So what's going to happen now? According to our agreement, haven't we run out of time?"

"Well, about that . . . ," said Eliza, grinning. She threw her chunky red dreadlocks over her shoulder and leaned her elbows onto the table. "We've been talking with Claudia here, and we reckon we might have come up with a solution."

"A cure?" asked Grey Arthur hopefully.

"Not a cure, as such," replied John Method, in

that bland, expressionless voice of his. "More of a compromise."

"Something that will keep all of the Terrible Trio happy, and the humans quite oblivious," elaborated Mrs. Scruffles, as she poured out eleven cups of tea. "And we've got Claudia to thank for it."

"Actually, the inspiration came from Tom's parents," corrected Claudia, tapping the table with her finger. "So, I can't take all the credit, much as I'd like to."

"It did?" said Tom, shocked. "What is it?"

"Well, that would ruin the surprise," chuckled Eliza. "You'll have to wait till next weekend to find out. . . ."

One Hundred and Twenty-Eight Hours Later, Give or Take

IT WAS A LONG WEEK, ESPECIALLY WITH A SECRET LODGED at the center of it. Tom and Grey Arthur asked, and quizzed, begged, and bribed, demanded, and stamped their feet, but nobody would reveal the big secret. All anyone would say, with a wry smile, was "Wait and see." So the week dragged on, Mrs. Scruffles's house glowed brightly day and night, the writing on Tom's head slowly faded, the TV crew came to terms with the fact that the "escaped circus panther" had escaped once more, and the weather edged just a little bit closer to spring. The Invisible Friends spent their time looking after their humans, Tom spent his time going to classes, daydreaming in Science lessons, and the human world went around ignoring the Ghost World, as it had done for the longest time. All in all, it was a bit of a dull week, with one notable exception.

Saturday was the grand opening of Thorbleton's first theme park.

Impatient with waiting for the ghosts' grand plan to be revealed, Tom, Grey Arthur, and the Invisible Friends had decided to take their minds off it all with a day trip out. Mrs. Scruffles had arranged it all with Tom's parents, and despite their protests against the place when it was under construction, they gave their blessing for Tom to go. Not that they had much choice—Tom was bouncing around the lounge like a maniac, singing a hastily constructed song that went something along the lines of "I'm going to a theme park, it's going to be grrrr-eat, la la la la!" and it's a brave parent that says no to that.

That Saturday morning was one time when Tom didn't need persuading to get out of bed—he was up, bright and early, and off out of the door before you could say "Scary rides and candy floss," practically skipping down the road (as much as boys do skip) with unbridled excitement. Grey Arthur, Tike, Monty, Mildred, Harry, and Mrs. Scruffles had to struggle to keep up, and the concealed plans of Terrible Trio appeasement were very much forgotten. It was quite a walk, but passed quickly in a haze of excited chatter. The ghosts had never been to a theme park before, and were looking forward to it every bit as much as Tom. Mrs. Scruffles escorted them, feeling very much like a schoolteacher leading a very unusual school trip.

Eventually, after the longest queue in the history of mankind (or so it felt), Tom dashed through the entrance, Invisible Friends at his side, into the world of flashing lights, swirling rides, helium balloons, bumper cars, toffee apples, spinning teacups, big wheels, burger vans, runaway trains, helter skelters, sugar dummies, ghost trains . . . and Claudia Sage.

"What are you doing here?" asked Tom, stunned. "I didn't think this would be your cup of tea at all."

Claudia was standing outside the ghost train, looking exceptionally out of place. Happy, giggling, sugar-crazed children dashed all around, balloons shaped like Mr. Space Pirate bobbed past her face as she tried to elegantly swat them away, and the distinct jingling tunes of disco mania pounded in the background. It was hard to retain a dignified poise when a huddle of kids are laughing so hard that lemonade is pouring out of their noses right next to you. Claudia tried her best, though. She stood, a vision of seriousness dressed in stern colors, against a backdrop of colors and noise.

"Good morning, Tom, and Invisible Friends. You're just in time," she said. One of the children next to Claudia burped loudly, and she gave them a withering look. They rapidly relocated to a different area. "The first group should be coming out any second now."

"What?" asked Tike, confused. "Group of what now? What's this to do with?"

"It's to do with solving a problem. Look behind me," she said cryptically. Grey Arthur and Tom shared a bemused shrug, then tilted their heads to see what Claudia was referring to. Tike, Monty, Mildred, and Harry did the same. Only Mrs. Scruffles remained as she was, a knowing smile on her rosy-cheeked face.

Just a short distance away was the ghost train. Not just any ghost train, though. A large banner next to it proudly proclaimed EXCEEDINGLY HAUNTED HOMES' GHOST TRAIN. The outside was decorated with pictures of chain-rattling spooks, a moss-covered gravestone, a skeleton with red eyes, and a very good likeness of Claudia Sage, staring haughtily out at all the people queuing up, her face plastered at least ten feet tall along the main doors.

"I had to pull in quite a few favors, but it's amazing what being on television will allow you to get away with. Apparently, they thought it would be good publicity having our program associated with them, and were very accommodating of all the changes I demanded."

"Changes?" asked Monty, a curious smile twitching beneath his mustache.

"I'm a very demanding woman, Montague. If I'm going to be associated with a ghost train, then I absolutely must have the best possible *actors* involved."

She raised a finger in the air, signaling for everyone to wait. "Here it comes . . ."

The most ear-piercing chorus of shrieks erupted from within the ghost train, the sound of numerous children and their accompanying parents screaming in unison. The noise was so loud that it actually made Tom jump. There was a nervous silence as they waited to see what would happen next.

The exit doors burst open, and the train rolled out into daylight, its stunned occupants still sitting down, openmouthed, pale. Tom watched anxiously. The humans looked absolutely terrified—white knuckles gripped tightly around the safety bar, eyes wide, unblinking, fear clearly etched on every inch of their faces. Tom swallowed dryly.

"Wait for it . . . ," whispered Claudia.

It was just as if somebody had thrown a switch. Suddenly, everyone's face in the ghost train lit up—some people laughed, some shook their heads, amazed, but each and every one looked like they had had the time of their lives—and they bounced out of the seat, allowing the next lot of passengers on board, and straight back into the queue. All apart from two. Pete, who was once known as Pick-Nose Pete, spotted Tom standing nearby and raced over to see him, his slightly pale (but wildly grinning) dad being dragged behind.

"Tom, you have to go on this ride!" he screeched excitedly. "It's amazing! First off, you don't even hand over the money—you have to hide it on you, and it just magically disappears after this weird dreadlocked woman walks past. Secondly, there's this ghost in there who is just The Coolest knight in the world, with his sword all *swoosh*, and you drive *right through him*, which is just awesome, but wait, that's not the best—the best bit comes just at the end, when you think it's all done, because the lights start to come up, and then the most scary ghost—I mean, I don't want to spoil it for you, 'cause you'll see for yourself—but the scariest ghost in the world leaps out at you, all claws waving and teeth, and everyone starts screaming and I was screaming and Dad was screaming and then, bam, you're outside." Pete stopped to catch his breath, and then shook his head disbelievingly. "Dad reckons they use smoke and mirrors to do it, don't you, Dad?"

Pete's dad nodded, still visibly shocked, unable to lose his mad grin.

"But I reckon it's holograms. Or lasers. Whatever it is, it's well cool. Best ghost train in the world, easily. We're going to have another go, aren't we, Dad?" gushed Pete, and, without giving his poor stunned dad a chance to respond, grabbed hold of him and dragged him back into the line, waving cheerily to Tom as he did so. He was so excited he didn't even notice Claudia Sage stood close by, which was probably just as well, as it would have prompted more questions than Tom would have liked.

"That's very clever," said Monty approvingly,

watching as the train set off once more inside, packed full with eager humans.

"That's genius!" roared Tike, laughing.

"Well, we had to think of some way to keep the ghosts doing what they loved, without risking the human/ghost balance. And, after all, sometimes the best place to hide is in plain sight," said Mrs. Scruffles with a smile. "Sorry we didn't let you know sooner, but we just thought it was much more fun this way."

Tom and Grey Arthur couldn't stop laughing. It was inspired.

"So this is here to stay?" asked Tom.

"The ley-line magic might wear off in time, like the writing on your forehead has, Tom," Mrs. Scruffles said. "If it does, this will just convert back to a normal, plain old-fashioned ghost train, with puppets, and actors, smoke and mirrors, and the Terrible Trio can wander off and be normal ghosts like the rest of us."

"Until then," Claudia added, "they're more than happy with the setup. Eliza gets to steal, John gets to act, and the Eldritch gets to scare, and best of all, humans love them for it." Claudia smiled, and for once, it wasn't that synthetic presenter smile, but a genuine one.

"Can we . . . ?" asked Tom, looking eagerly over at the ever growing queue.

"Of course you can." Mrs. Scruffles chuckled. "I think they'll be delighted to see you all."

By the time she'd finished that sentence, Tom was

already halfway to the ghost train, and Harry, Mildred, Tike, Monty, and Grey Arthur weren't far behind. Claudia and Mrs. Scruffles watched them go.

"Isn't it nice," said Mrs. Scruffles, "to know that every cloud really does have a silver lining?"

To Forgotten Foes

FOR EVERY CLOUD THAT HAS A SILVER LINING, THERE IS another waiting to soak you to your skin, or throw down hailstones. That's simply the way life works. So while Tom, Grey Arthur, Mildred, Montague, Tike, the Harrowing Screamer, Claudia Sage, and Mrs. Scruffles wandered around Thorbleton's first ever amusement park, chewing candy floss, going on the magic teacups, giggling at the shocked faces of people staggering from the ghost train, elsewhere darker events were unfolding.

There was one person in England who had slipped under the radar. One person who hadn't had the existence of ghosts proven to him by an old-fashioned Thesper, a light-fingered Poltergeist, or the legendary Eldritch.

One man who had found his faith in a flurry of stampeding Screamers.

Dr. Brown.

Somewhere in England, trapped in a bleak grey cell, Dr. Brown lay back on a thin, grimy mattress, staring at the ceiling. When all this had begun, he hadn't really *believed*. It had just been a means to an end, a hare-brained scheme, something he'd started on a whim. Before that, he'd been working on turning lead into gold, before that, chasing across Britain's countryside in a stolen jeep, trying to see if there was really a pot of gold at the end of rainbows. Before that . . . well, that didn't matter anymore. Everything had changed when he met Tom Golden, but even then, even when he'd kidnapped him, doubts had remained, small flickering doubts that had danced across his mind from time to time. He'd never been 100 percent sure if a mystical Invisible Friend was really behind all these strange events, or if somehow Tom Golden was responsible. Tom believed it, that much was certain, but that didn't mean it was true. All that had mattered was whether or not it would work. His faith didn't need to be there, as long as the results were.

Perhaps he shouldn't have been so blasé.

Dr. Brown winced as he remembered that night, the darkness in the woods crashing down on him, the fear that crawled through him, and Tom Golden vanishing, along with his hut, into the thinnest of air.

Something like that can thrust a belief on even the hardest skeptic.

For ages, the doctors at the prison had tried to convince Dr. Brown that he was crazy. They didn't use those words, of course, they dressed it up with descriptions such as delusions, paranoia, hallucinations, but the meaning was all the same. Again and again they would tell him that it couldn't have happened, that it was his own guilt playing tricks on him, his own mind turning against him. It had almost worked, too. Dr. Brown shook his head, trying to chase them from his thoughts, and slowly sat up. Stretching the kinks from his back he stood up, strode over to the barred window, and looked down into the courtyard below. A dark smile twitched on his lips.

It had almost worked, until a Screamer had moved into the courtyard.

Dr. Brown waved at the creature, who hissed back, talons sweeping the air. It clung to the shadows of the wall, never straying into the light.

It had terrified him, the first time he saw it. He'd refused to leave his cell, and he whimpered when the order came for lights out. The noisy night, already filled with the sound of cell doors being slammed, insults being thrown, keys jangling, footsteps echoing, was overlaid with a constant stream of howling, screaming, unnatural wailing. During what little sleep Dr. Brown had managed to snatch, the screams would sink in there with him and chase him through nightmares.

But you can only stay scared for so long.

Dr. Brown stared down at the ghost, and it took an almost inhuman effort not to laugh. He rubbed his arms, trying to force away the goose bumps, and bared his teeth at the ghost. It tilted its head slowly, studying him back.

A moment of recognition flashed between the two, and then was lost as a guard marched into the court-yard. The Screamer retreated farther into the shade and howled. At first, that sound had nearly brought Dr. Brown to his knees, but in that precise moment, listening, it sounded quite amazing.

That was the sound of everything changing.

Now Dr. Brown just needed to work out how to make this work for him.

It might take a while, but when you're in jail, time is the one thing that you have plenty of.

The Ghostly Glossary

Agatha Tibbles: One of Mrs. Scruffles's cats. A mighty Persian, built like a rugby player, with a deep chocolate MOW instead of a meow.

Ballpoint Bill: A rather unambitious Poltergeist who steals pen lids, ink cartridges, and stationery from Thorbleton School.

The Calming Whisperer a.k.a. "Carl": A Contrary Screamer who is a bit of a hippie. A reassuring presence who is more dusty grey than shadow black.

Carrot Cake: One of Mrs. Scruffles's cats. An elderly ginger gentleman now, Carrot Cake is more sprightly than his skinny frame would lead you to believe.

Claudia Sage: TV psychic with *Exceedingly Haunted Homes* who hides a supernatural secret.

Contrary Ghost Association: An organization for the misfits of the Ghost World, spirits who do the opposite of their expected roles. Run by Lost and Found Freddie, current English contraries include Miss Lilly, the sweet-scented Snorgle, and Carl, a reassuringly placid Screamer.

Dr. Brown a.k.a. Gavin Snark: A prolific criminal who masqueraded as a child psychologist in order to befriend Tom Golden and his family. Kidnapped Tom to force Grey Arthur to help him rig the lottery. Currently in jail.

Essay Dave: The world's leading paperwork Poltergeist. If you've ever mislaid a phone number on a scrap of paper, your homework, an important document, chances are you've been paid a visit by Essay Dave.

Grey Arthur: The original Invisible Friend. A grey-colored ghost with lopsided ears, and hair that looks as if it was made for someone with a different-shaped head. Invisible Friend to Tom Golden.

The Harrowing Screamer a.k.a. "Harry": A Screamer who turned up in Tom's bedroom one night, presumably to become an Invisible Friend. He currently lives in Tom's shed.

Janet: A Faintly Real Ghost who works with Tom's mum at the castle.

Laundry Run: A favorite occupation of Poltergeists, traveling from laundry basket to laundry basket, stealing socks, putting red clothing in the pockets of white clothes, smearing stains on treasured tops . . .

L. F. Freddie: Lost and Found Freddie, a Contrary Poltergiest who likes to reunite people with lost items. Freddie is the Chairman of the Contraries. He lives in the Lost and Found Department at London's Victoria Train Station.

Mildred Rattledust: Once a Faintly Real who didn't look very real at all, Mildred is now an Invisible Friend. With her stern, straight-cut fringe, her pale skin, mismatched eyes, and predisposition to wearing black, Mildred looks a somber figure, but she cares deeply about her work. Invisible Friend to Holly Mayer.

The Mischief Twins: Mike and Miranda, two young Poltergeists who spend much of their time on the Laundry Run.

Miss Lilly: A Contrary Snorgle, who is a delicate shade of lilac, and smells of the type of perfume mums wear for a special night out. Almost unbearably adorable.

Montague Equador Scullion the Third a.k.a. "Monty": The legendary Thesper, a ghost celebrity, who turned up in Tom Golden's house in search of a new challenge. Monty has now, for the most part, turned his back on ghostly theatrics, and instead relishes the drama of his latest role. Invisible Friend to Mrs. Wilson.

Mr. Hammond: Tom's favorite teacher—a friendly bearded fellow who teaches History.

Mrs. Scruffles: A Faintly Real who lives in an abandoned house just round the corner from Thorbleton School, and walking distance from Tom's house in Aubergine Road. A friendly, warmhearted ghost who looks like a grey-haired aunt, Mrs. Scruffles adores baking cakes, making cups of tea, and taking in stray cats.

The Red Rascal: England's most famous Poltergeist. A larger than life character who is legendary for once stealing an entire building.

Sorrow Jane: Believed to be one of the oldest ghosts still in existence. A Sadness Summoner of great power. Lives in Thorblefort Castle, usually found on the grounds of the graveyard.

Tike: A scruffy urchin of a Poltergeist now turned Invisible Friend. A compulsive thief and a bit of a rogue, but deep down he has a heart of gold. Invisible Friend to Frank Longfield.

Tom Golden: He-Who-Can-See-Ghosts. An eleven-year-old boy, the youngest in his year. A boy who moved to a new school and struggled to fit in. A boy who somehow managed to get the nickname "Freak Boy," despite there being nothing particularly freaky about him. Tom Golden is the reason Grey Arthur decided to become an Invisible Friend. Tom was oblivious to his ghostly companion until a car crash seemed to trigger an ability to see the Ghost World.

Tom's mum: Works in Ye Olde Tea Shoppe at Thorblefort Castle.

Tom's dad: Designer of socks with the company Svelte Socks™ (The Socks That Say Style with a Smile!). Inventor of the Anti-Static-Shock-Sock.

Woeful William: One of Grey Arthur's oldest friends. A melodramatic Sadness Summoner.